T0369544

Purification

The Indivisible Light Trilogy
Book III

David Pedri

Inspiring Voices®

Inspiring Voices books may be ordered through booksellers or by contacting:

Inspiring Voices
1663 Liberty Drive
Bloomington, IN 47403
www.inspiringvoices.com
844-686-9605

All Scripture quotations are taken from the Douay Rheims Version.

ISBN: 978-1-4624-1342-3 (sc)
ISBN: 978-1-4624-1341-6 (e)

Library of Congress Control Number: 2023906504

Print information available on the last page.

Inspiring Voices rev. date: 04/09/2024

Contents

Preface

Scripture cautions us to be ready for *the Day of the Lord.* Jesus warned the Apostles with Him at the Garden of Gethsemane to 'watch and pray': that they might avoid the temptation to be scandalized by the death of the God-Man and the apparent failure of their divine Savior's promises and works. This grace to overcome that temptation to *despair* (to lose faith in God) was rejected in some measure by Peter and those who ran away at the time of Jesus' arrest; yet they were the Twelve Chosen ones of the God-Man, Jesus Christ. The twelve Apostles represented their archetype, the Twelve Tribes of Israel. Both rejected their Messiah, Jesus, in the face of the despotic power at that time, Rome. Even though the Apostles, the first of the elect, would not be denied eternal life or the joy of Jesus' victorious Resurrection, the question remained, did these joys and promises teach them that *Jesus* is worth one's *life*, Himself the Source of Eternal Life, the Source of all help. No, that lesson was learned by their *own acts of Faith*, where they risked their lives, their livelihood, their social position, and reputation. Above all, this lesson is not learned when there is *presumption* due to the privileges and promises one has been given. Such gifts are to be used *to prepare for battle,* when and where the spiritual warfare rages by which every person will decide their eternal destiny.

In warning the Apostles, Jesus was warning their posterity, Christians: '*do not to be complacent regarding* My Coming, where everyone will have to render an account of their life.' Catholics call the accounting, rendered immediately after death, the "Particular Judgment". Jesus also warned us *not to be afraid* when Satan *appears* to triumph, because he never can;

he is a trickster, playing with appearances. If the Apostles, even their Chief, Peter, had feet of clay, our fate is all the more certainly in *God's Hands*, both in time and eternity. Do *not* presume on the mighty gifts God gives, even His Real Presence given through the Mass and Holy Communion. Despair and presumption are the two final, grievous sins that lead to perdition.

Jesus requires gratitude for all we have, which comes from His Bounty. He warns Christians, His chosen people: '*Maintain your Faith in Me <u>until the end</u>*! Do *not* be complacent in your Faith because, like everything else you possess, Faith is unearned, a free gift from Me, which should elicit *gratitude*, not pride.' Jesus said, "*I am the Way, the Truth and the Life.*" (John 14:6) Arrogating to oneself eternal Salvation, a free *gift* of God's election and Mercy, which no one merits, is a most audacious presumption. It is the essence of all *protest* against the Word that the true Church protects and preserves. Therefore, says the Lord and His Saints, since your will is formed definitively only in time, you must *habitually* pray for, depend on and trust in My promises, My help. In this, you prepare your soul in *readiness* for My Coming. Because you are weak by nature, Jesus teaches, ask for the grace of *final perseverance*, and you shall receive it, because I have promised: "*Ask and it shall be given you …*" (Matthew 7:7)

Jesus warned us that while true *Faith* is alive, *complacency* is like an addictive drug or the venom of a poisonous cobra, causing a deadly spiritual *sleep* from which we may never awake. It will *fail to recognize* the time of the Master's Coming, whether in one's Particular Judgement at death or in the mini-judgment that is close upon us, which we call the *Day of the Lord*, that precedes the General Judgement. *Presumption* is (by analogy) the 'sleep' that overcame the virgins awaiting the Bridegroom in Jesus' parable. In our sensual, selfish impatience, we tend to become bored, thinking Our Lord is *too long in coming* to suit our private timetable. In this we forget that God knows all and can, therefore, choose the perfect time. We have so often heard the admonition: 'watch and pray' that the urgency no longer pricks us from our tendency to the lethargy (laziness) that leads to a slumbering conscience, which is the road to the death of the soul.

Yes, Book III is fiction, but my research backs it up, literally, with references from Holy Scripture, the Magisterial teaching of the Roman Catholic Church and its Traditions, as well as with the testament of God's Saints (proven Saints by miracles) and the "private" revelations from Heaven given to us for our times, "revelations" which the wise (wakeful) Christian examines closely. St. Paul says, *"Despise not prophecy. But prove all things; hold fast that which is good."* (1 Thessalonians 5:20-21) But even more important are the multitude of references in my mind, of which I cannot recall the literal sources which have become one with my thinking. I have attempted to trace a path of End-Times events based on all these sources, tied together by a plausible, though sometimes fanciful fiction. My own informed speculation is also a part of the narrative fabric. The final scenes of Book III are meant to dramatize the forces of evil at play in the world near the "end of time as we know it".

I could have said much more in Book III, but I think the reader will agree that I have said enough. Book III, *The Purification*, is not meant to be a catechetical encyclopedia nor a complete history of End Time events. It is fiction which can carry only so much didactic dialogue gracefully, and I realize those limits have been pushed. For this author, the message is more important than the story groaning under its weight. I am quite aware that I have sacrificed popularity and easy reading for what I consider vital Apostolic content. Yet, I have tried valiantly to make all I have to say understandable, probable and palatable. My motives? I have felt compelled to share the contents of this three year trilogy out of charity, knowing that the fate of certain souls and the betterment of all could hang in the balance. Please help me broadcast the truth, if you recognize it. My audience is *Everyman.*

I seek to give my audience enough reason to embrace *for themselves* what divine Faith teaches. Faith is an infallible gift of Truth, that will recognize itself in the Person of Jesus Christ (John 14:6). Faith is a gift born on the 'wings' of Divine Love, sent to us directly from the Sacred Heart of Jesus. True Faith is authorized by Him, and it is eternally rewarding for those souls with the courage to be its witness. Faith provides the final reason for being, acting and having.

In *Purification,* to the best of my ability, I have unintentionally bottled for sale the *living water* which Jesus promised to give the woman at the well in John 4:10. Yet I do not presume to have the gift of preaching bestowed on the clergy of Christ's Church by Jesus Himself. Therefore, I submit all my opinions in this trilogy to the judgement of the Institution actually guarding and preserving the Deposit of Faith, traditionally guarded by Christ's One, Holy, Catholic and Apostolic Church. In *Purification*, I attempt to draw a rough road map of future End-times events on the back of a fictional vehicle; this "map" is not intended to be complete, detailed or correct in every respect. I have been a student of the matters discussed herein for the last forty years, so this book for me is something like an informal "term paper". But I make no claims for this work of fiction other than it is my best effort to witness to the Lord, whom I desire to love and serve.

We see evil in our world, yet believe in an omnipotent, loving God. If that is not enough of an apparent contradiction, add the *apparent* impotence of confident prayer to that same God while enduring the evil He permitted. Book III presumes the following explanation for these apparent contradictions: for evil to exist in a world created and controlled by a loving God, He must permit evil, because an Omnipotent God is not powerless to stop it, and if indeed He is good, there must be a good reason for that permission. Yes, I admit that the loving and omnipotent God *permits* evil, but He does not *ordain* it. That would be a Divine defect, which is philosophically and theologically absurd. Therefore, it seems clear that God must permit evil out of His immense Love to save souls from eternal damnation and, conversely, for their eternal happiness. How can these opposites be compatible?

God allows evil as the natural consequence of man's sinful exercise of his created free will, i.e., in choosing evil over good, chaos over order. Unrepentant sin is the only act that damns a soul to eternal punishment, while the repentance and rejection of sin followed by doing good, gains eternal happiness. Only a cruel god would hide the consequences of sin, short term or long term, while a loving God, not willing to mutilate His creation by removing man's free will, permits evil and its consequences as a lesson to the sinner: that sin is evil and involves a decision in time to defy the Eternal God, and His Commandments, His Creation and reality itself. Only the Devil and his diabolical assistants blame and demean God for allowing evil; they pretend to be mankind's savior, proposing a utopian world where their technology supposedly erases all trace of pain (evil), which they consider the ultimate thus "saving" man (for hell). The assistants of Satan are like smiling friends, bearing bribes, yet holding daggers behind their backs. On the contrary, God holds out an eternal gift for those who freely repent of the evil they freely willed, while God Himself repays their eternal debt for their sins, a debt no one but God can repay.

Man's repentance assures God that man sincerely desires the good he is asking for: forgiveness of his sins, salvation, reparation for the damage his sins have caused and help in resisting future temptations. The unbeliever never stops asking: why do the innocent suffer for the wicked acts of others? The victims of a terrorist bombing provide enough examples: little children cut down by shrapnel, draped over their own mothers' corpses, blood still running from their little bodies as the medics arrive and frantically administer all the life-saving techniques at their disposal, to no avail. Soon the victim's relatives arrive, tears flowing copiously, while a whole world of viewers weeps for the victims of the senseless murders. And God is silent; we all ask: Why? History is not silent on this point as we view with horror Herod's Slaughter of the Innocent children at Bethlehem, seeking to kill Jesus, King of the Universe, as a baby. Imagine the grief, the weeping that does *not* follow abortion, the slaughter of millions yet these are the sacrifice of innocents acceptable to God for the sins of generations. But Jesus' Crucifixion is the prime example of God accepting the sacrifice of Innocence Itself in order to save helpless sinners from eternal damnation. The redemption of sinners by the sacrifice of innocents all resemble and participate in Jesus' Sacrifice. This sacrifice is the *life* of Christianity, the life that appears to resemble earthly death, a life unappealing to those who fill the pews of Catholic churches today. These poor wannabees have been deceived by Freemasonic infiltrators since Vatican II into being non-Catholics. Therefore, this book is addressed to them as well as every other non-Catholic; for Jesus established only *one* Church; for certainly God would not do otherwise, deceiving and confusing us with multiple creeds and various pretended forms of worship.

In the wonderful secret of sacrificial Love is the passionate reason for Christianity and its two thousand years of martyrs who were "guilty" of witnessing to God's Love for us, a love *hidden* from the "blind": selfish unrepentant sinners.

I invite you, my readers, to rejoice with me: a sinner redeemed by the Sacrifice of Divine Innocence, in my behalf (and yours). This is why Holy Mass is the center of Catholic worship. *Personal repentance* is the one and only human contribution that opens the door to infinite bliss through God's Mercy. Our confession of truth about our life (of sin) before the Judgement Seat of God, draws God to us. God, by nature is merciful, since He sent Himself in the Person of His Son, Jesus, to rescue us by bearing the punishment of death deserved only by sinners. This is the *good news* of the Gospel. This is reason for all to *rejoice*, and it is the story I wish to tell, the seed I wish to sow. However, the harvest is only possible if we believe sin is the greatest evil, not death.

A bold enterprise, YES!! So much so, that in all honesty, I must dedicate the entire trilogy *to you*, my readers, because the love I have been given seeks to do good, first to God, Who in turn desires the salvation of all souls, for the submission in asking.

David Pedri

Chapter 1

WARFARE'S NEW RULES OF ENGAGEMENT

"We have some really bad news that just may be their Plan B," said Andrew, David's chief intel officer. He stood, hands clasped, in front of David, who just stared at him. Andrew muddled on, head hanging like a ripe pumpkin. "That's dirt from the source of a source that has its source deeply embedded in the muck of a pig's sty."

"Sounds slimy; get to the point," David said, noting that Angela was still listening from the doorway. David held up his hand for a pause. "Angela, please, sweetheart, come in and sit down. Sooner or later, you will hear what I suspect may be coming from Andrew and his research. I know you are a prayer warrior, truly at my side in every conflict, and I want you to know the enemy we are both up against."

Angela walked silently into the room in sock feet, the men stepping aside with a sense of chivalry for the woman they admired and honored. She came up quietly to David, leaning against his arm, sad but not fearful; for she truly was a woman of courage in her own right, not afraid of the stark truth but finding strength in the virtuous humility of a godly man, whom she believed to have been a gift to her from God, a loving companion and dependable soulmate.

"The bad news, sir," said Andrew, stiffly, "is that we strongly believe, on good evidence, that there is a hit squad out for your life and probably Major Michael's life as well. This notorious squad has a reputation for being inhumanely monstrous, savage, and seven in number."

"Suspected of having preternatural powers by intellectuals of Faith?" David asked calmly.

There was a long pause, then Andrew said, "Right. At least some speculate the demonic is involved."

Angela gasped upon first hearing Andrew's news, her eyes widening. She turned toward her husband and slumped against him, eyelids fluttering. Knowing she was prone to fainting, David caught her about the waist and excusing themselves, he helped her into the bedroom. Charlene followed, quietly weeping. As David lay Angela down, Charlene began a low mournful wailing. Alarmed, Michael came in to comfort his wife. David returned with smelling salts. Angela revived and David left her with Charlene who was better composed, wondering if he was foolish in ever having them listen in when they had recently been under such stress concerning the safety of their husbands in the Pacific.

David returned. "What is meant by preternatural powers?" asked Michael, knowing that Charlene would also have to be considered a collateral target, since he and David would be under pressure if their wives were threatened.

"Okay," said David, "time for an explanation of what I suspect is going to be a new phase of warfare, one which we may have pushed the evil ones into by winning the big battle at sea against their surrogate, the Red Chinese Army. We are going to be fighting the same filthy demonic beasts, but since their attempt at a conventional, proxy war by their human accomplices and dupes (useful idiots) was foiled, stopped cold at God's Providential Command, I believe they must now, as a price of their defeat, be stripped of their invisible disguise, dispensed of human instruments and come at us as *they really are*, diabolical spirits, usually inhabiting human bodies. God has 'called them out'. Now it will be a different kind of war, a war of the spirits, good versus evil, nakedly evil spirits. Good angels may also appear to us in visible form. By this mankind can see how wicked the enemy is that he has been fighting for his eternal soul and that of others, as well as for their happiness on earth. He would also be shown the angelic warriors on our side, ready for our calls for help. Our combat will have different rules of engagement, different weapons."

"Different weapons?" Michael asked incredulously.

"Can you kill a spirit with an AR-15, Michael?"

"I don't think so. But I wouldn't know what else to use, either."

"As you know, Michael," explained David, "Satan is not stupid; he will not attack God, who defeated and punished him, nor will he attack what is truly holy, set aside for God and imbued with His Holy Spirit. Therefore, Satan fears holy people and blessed objects, according to the degree of their sanctity. Satan cannot harm a person or even touch them without God's inscrutable permission. Those in the state of mortal sin, the devil can possess or molest with more freedom, but still only as God allows for the salvation of souls."

"And those Satan fears, would they be the members of the Church?" asked Angela, her arm around Charlene, whose face was blanched white. With grim determination, Angela and Charlene had rejoined the conversation. They leaned against each other for support. David looked at them with love and admiration, but also with deep concern.

"Yes, it is our spiritual mother, the Church, that Satan hates and fears most," said David, "but he especially hates, harasses and persecutes its *Faithful* members who stand against him in the Church as one body, which is much more effective in prayer than one person, as Scripture tells us.[1] Satan's hatred is fearful, if not deflected by Faith; it towers like a giant tsunami coming ashore, crushing and grinding up anyone so unfortunate as to be sucked into its fearful maw."

"Does Faith shield us from fear, David?" asked Charlene.

"Perfect Faith puts us in contact with perfect love, which 'casts out all fear'[2]. The servile fear we are dealing with now is fueled by despair, a sense of *overpowering* doom," explained David. "Faith does not acknowledge despair because it places all hope in God alone, Who cannot fail. Faith does not live in these waters of doom. Faith believes in God's promises and conceives by God's grace Hope of Salvation, which destroys gloom and makes room for courage, which is founded on hope of future victory over evil and the possession of everlasting good – all by the theological virtue of Hope."

---

[1] St. Matthew 18:19-20

[2] 1 John 4:18

"Just what evil beings are we looking at here, boss?" asked Michael. "I can't grasp these vague images."

"We are looking at *ogres*, evil spirits inhabiting dead bodies," David finally said, with blunt force.

"Ahhgg," said Michael. Angela's grip dug into David's arm. "And how do we fight this kind of thing, boss?"

"We chase the evil spirits off by being in the state of sanctifying grace ourselves and by wielding holy weapons, like holy water and other sacramentals. When fired upon and hit by our holy weapons, the dead body which the demon had possessed is abandoned and drops dead again, because the evil spirit no longer animates the body in order to make it appear alive."

"The body was already dead, but the evil spirit made it appear alive?" Michael asked, grimacing, grasping for a fix on the concrete.

"Correct," answered David. "An evil spirit hates, fears and envies a good spirit, beyond our imagination. For one thing, a godly soul or angelic spirit reminds the demon of all the good it has *forever lost,* and this, perhaps, is the greatest of its eternal punishments. Also, good has absolute and final power over evil, because *evil*, by definition, is nothing but the *absence of good*. Evil is not even a real thing in itself. All reality is good because it was created by God with an end, a purpose. Evil spirits have lost all that is good by their own willful, eternal choice."

"But didn't Jesus conquer evil?" asked Angela.

Above all, David wanted to give them hope, without denying the truth. A non-fictional story was the best way, thought David. Fiction would fall apart in the heat of battle. "Jesus, Who is Infinite Goodness, cancelled or defeated all evil, but in time, our sins invited evil back; so we have to confess our sins to Him and beg for His mercy and help for the salvation of others. By the Mercy of God, our repentance overcomes the infernal enemy. And we are now being inundated by evil spirits because too few people are repentant, despite all God's actual graces."

"Okay, I understand that good and evil cannot tolerate each other's presence," said Michael. "Now, tell me again how we *fight* these ogres?"

"Well, first of all, as I said, we must be united to God by His mercy and our repentance. Then, being good ourselves," said David, "we are in the state of sanctifying grace. So, we will confess to God's priest and receive absolution of our sins, thus putting on our suit of armor. Then we will receive our God, Jesus, in Holy Communion which will be our Sword, our main weapon. But in order to fight, we should first receive the Sacrament of Confirmation, where we receive the grace in general to become *soldiers* of Christ."

"And I have received that Sacrament?" asked Michael.

"Yes," said David. A broad smile of satisfaction slowly filled Michael's face. David held Angela's hand in both of his; she looked up to him as her guide and guardian with love and trust. Charlene missed nothing. She copied her friend, looking at Michael in a new way, in the same light as Angela saw David. Charlene took Michael's arm, laying her head against his shoulder. He responded by looking down on her with loving protection.

"Even naked spirits, Michael, must have a physical medium to be present upon earth," said David, looking at his friend. "Satan can work through an unrepentant sinner. He can possess him or anyone not in the state of grace because mortal sin takes that soul from God's protection and makes him Satan's conquest. These souls are like him in spirit, and he owns them in that sense. Satan can work through anything or anyone that is intentionally or unintentionally '*consecrated*' to him, through mediums like rock music, tarot cards and other satanic symbols and objects. Persons using satanic symbols, like the peace sign, may be influenced by Satan to a degree depending on their intention. Satan has 'sign language' that 'speaks' for him. The body of a person in the grave whose soul is in Hell, can be animated by an evil spirit. A material object or body of some kind, dead or alive, even animals, can be a medium for the evil spirit's operation. UFO's are demonic transports. But God's grace also inheres in matter. For example, Jesus knew when the woman in the crowd touched His cloak because grace flowed through it to heal her. Therefore, the relics of Saints, pieces of their bone, for example, can be mediums of Christ's grace which effects healing or protection or some other good. Holy relics or objects like blessed water, candles, beads of prayer (the Rosary) become conduits of grace to the virtuous, the power of God against evil spirits. And ..."

"And these are called sacramentals," interjected Angela. "The crucifix, the Brown Scapular and the St. Benedict medal are other important sacramentals that David did not mention." She cast a brief look David's way. He smiled at her with love, gratitude and admiration which he could not conceal or hold back, despite the company of others.

"These sacramentals are your greatest armor and your weapons against evil spirits," David concluded, looking directly at Michael. "With your full consent, we can now clothe you for battle."

"Do it. I'm ready," declared Michael, standing up, stiff, like the soldier he was.

"Prayers, like the St. Michael Exorcism, are powerful weapons, just like the Rosary," said Angela. "Remember, this is a spiritual battle. I think you should learn to say the Exorcism and the Rosary if you are going to do battle. We say the short St. Michael exorcism after each decade of the Rosary. But the Brown Scapular of Mount Carmel is the most powerful protection of all. Right, my Love?"

"The Scapular is like the chain-mail shirt worn by the knights of old under their heavy battle armor; it is an invisible armor," said David, "like the spiritual habit of virtue and holiness that clothed Mary, the Mother of God. The Brown Scapular represents our imitation of this habitual holiness of Mary. She promises that those wearing her scapular at death will not suffer Hellfire.[3] Mary was the one God designated in Genesis to 'crush the head of Satan[4]. In wearing this scapular, she becomes your continual intercessor, companion, protector and leader in battle."

"Then I definitely want one," said Michael.

"And who could better intercede with God for man than His own human mother and ours? Isn't that right?" Angela said, glancing at David for confirmation, knowing that as a new convert, she was still under his tutelage.

"But, you might ask, isn't she too shy to be a warrior who will defeat such a fearsome adversary?" David said.

"My thoughts, exactly," said Michael.

"For an example from history that answers your question, read up on St. Joan of Arc. But the general answer is this: Satan's greatest weapon of war is pride," said David. "With it, Satan rejected God's goodness

---

[3] https://www.ourladyspromise.org/scapular.php

[4] Genesis 3:15

and then recruited like-minded souls, proud of their possessions, accomplishments, and worldly status, which distains good out of pride in order to fight alongside him. But Satan is vanquished by pride's opposite virtue, humility, shining perfectly in the person of Mary, whom God created to be the human mother of Jesus, the Christ, and therefore, the Mother of God. Satan knows how lethal pride is, using it as his principal tool of temptation and rule over his followers. Pride, with its many daughters is Satan's major vice by which he lures souls to imitate him and unwillingly earn his reward: eternity in Hell. We know that St. Michael, the Archangel, challenged Satan and rallied his troops by the immortal words: '*Who is like God?*[5] But the Virgin Mary is the supreme model of humility and therefore the most powerful warrior against Satan's fallen nature. In his proud nature Satan *so* admired his own excellence and status as God's most beautiful and most perfect creature that he challenged God's Authority and was cast out of Heaven into Hell."

"So, here's how it works, Michael. By *not* overestimating our own excellence and independence, as our fallen nature's *pride of life* tempts us to do, we must depend *entirely on God*, our Creator, Who is infinitely more perfect than His creatures. Jesus' Mother and her spiritual children help us to imitate her in emptying herself of the pride which depends on human nature; instead, she depends totally on her Divine Son as the Source of all power and goodness. This is why she will crush the head (pride) of Satan. By sharing in this submission of our spiritual mother to God, we also receive her Son's power and grace. Does this make sense? By the humility which makes us channels of Almighty power through the sacrifice of our 'own' God-given nature, we do what Satan did not do. By her humility, Mary overpowers the highest angel God ever made, Lucifer. Only the elect can grasp her total Sacrifice, in which she imitated the Sacrifice of Jesus' divine nature: being born man, taking on man's sins, and dying on the cross to redeem us. Mary's virtue actually draws Christians to her Son by showing them how to obey His words, 'follow Me,'[6] because she imitates *His supreme self-sacrifice* as much as humanly possible."

---

5 https://www.catholic.com/encyclopedia/michael-the-archangel-saint

6 St. Matthew 16:24, St. Matthew 19:21, St. Mark 8:34,

David looked at Michael whose heart was visibly moved, though it seemed his head was somewhat befogged. "I really like that," Michael said. "I think I even understand what you said a little."

"Michael and Charlene should both be invested in this scapular by Fr. Keogh as soon as possible," said David, touching Angela's hand.

"The Brown Scapular must be made of 100% brown wool," said Angela. She left briefly and returned with one scapular for Michael and one for his wife. "It consists of two squares of brown wool connected by a cord, one square laying on the chest, the other on the back. You can wear them now, before your investiture."

"These sacramentals are not do-it-yourself trinkets," said David seriously. "They are gifts from Heaven, empowered through the infinite merits of Christ after the investiture prayers of a priest (in the past of the Carmelite order) who is given the necessary authority and powers. As Catholics we believe this scapular was given by Mary herself for all mankind in 1251 AD to the Carmelite, St. Simon Stock."

"Did we forget to mention the special promise of the Brown Scapular, that those who die wearing this scapular *will not suffer eternal death*[7]?" asked Angela.

"Yes, Sweetheart. Michael, *sacramentals* like this one, are usually given to us by God through His Saints," said David, "then the Church adopts them for use by the faithful. A warning though: never treat a sacramental with disrespect. That would be a sacrilege, a very serious sin."

"Like we don't give guns to kids," joked Michael.

"Serious up, Michael; that borders on disrespect. These are not your personal weaponized toys. They are gifts you are privileged to have, and their efficacy depends on your conformity to what they mean. You don't live on easy-agnostic street anymore, you know." Michael bowed his head slightly at this rebuke.

"David, the angels. Tell them," said Angela.

"Thanks for the reminder. Okay, God has given every human being a guardian angel for life. We can have them do good deeds for us. They can greatly help us in fighting the evil one, Michael, in case you don't feel you are packing enough firepower yet."

---

7 https://stswithuns.org.uk/brown-scapular

"I've heard that we can ask our guardian angel to pray the Rosary for us when we can't do so ourselves for some good reason," said Angela. "We can also pray to him for help in overcoming a temptation or ask his protection from mishaps or creepy, diabolical things," she added. "He's always there to help. There is this prayer to the angels," said Angela, who had an excellent memory: *Angel of God, my guardian dear, to whom His love entrusts me here. Ever this day be at my side, to light and guard, to rule and guide. Amen.*"[8]

David said, "We honor God by asking his Saints for help. Aren't we honored when others ask us to help them? Remember that, Michael, my friend. It is your choice: ignore Him and tarnish His friendship or beg for what only He has to give, then His treasures are at your disposal."

"We are made in the image and likeness of God, which is our intellect and our free will," said Angela. David's assistant was visibly overflowing with the happiness that comes with love well directed.

"The faculty of rational free will is why we can please God, love God, love ourselves or love anyone," said David. "If someone 'loves' you out of fear and not freely, it is not considered genuine love. So, if God were to suspend that free will to choose and give us a free ride to Heaven for fence-sitting that would be to annihilate us as we are created. But God does not create us with free will and then change His mind. This means we have a great responsibility."

"So, we always have the obligation to respond to His gifts?" Michael asked, struggling to summarize, "at least with gratitude."

"Yes, gratitude is primary in what it means to take responsibility," said David.

"So, we can go to Heaven or Hell but only by our free choice?" asked Michael.

His attitude is much improved, David noticed with relief. "The *consequence* of mortal sin is Hell," he continued, "but we cannot choose evil as such, because the will is made by God so that it chooses only good or an apparent good. What is sinful may *appear good*, but that is a deception. For example, adultery is evil but the sexual pleasure that

[8] https://aleteia.org/2017/10/02/who-composed-the-angel-of-god-prayer/

accompanies it is a good, in and of itself." David saw that this went over Michael's head, but he gave him an approving glance anyway.

"Michael, listen," said David, leaning towards him to better garner his attention. "There is an angel assigned to each nation, to the earth, to each planet, to each star, to each galaxy, to each state, each city and to each individual, because all things must be guided and moved by a higher spirit or chaos would prevail. But man must willingly choose to be ruled. That is even confirmed by the second law of thermodynamics," said Professor David, "which says that only a higher energy source prevents an inferior being from decaying. But in the case of human beings, proud self-interest can prevent the rule of God's nine choirs of angels."

"Now maybe David will return to our original investigation," prodded Angela. "Michael should know that God controls the evil spirits."

"Right. They can do nothing God does not allow them to do in order to accomplish His inscrutable designs for our salvation," said David.

"What do you mean?" asked Michael, his brows arching, forehead wrinkling.

"For example, even the demons might serve God's Providence without any good will on their part," said David carefully. "God might use them to administer His corrective punishments or to test our fidelity by temptations, just like Adam and Eve were tempted in order to test their love and their obedience to God."

"So, God loves us, but He shows this by disciplining us like good parents discipline the child they love," said Angela. "In recognizing this, a Christian can endure the evil of suffering with equanimity."

"Do you not notice that the spirit that exists in you at the time of combat is crucial to how you perform?" David asked Michael.

"Yes," said Michael. "Having a slovenly, depressed or cowardly spirit is like being weighed down by shifting sandbags. But with a confident, courageous spirit, I am sure, swift, accurate, confident and *deadly*. So, can we shoot an ogre?" asked Michael, always returning to the practical.

"Sure, but I would sooner trust holy water than a bullet. Actually, I was thinking of consulting Fr. Keogh on these matters or maybe the exorcist I know in the capitol. Okay," said David, standing up, "enough rambling. I want a ten-man guard stationed around wherever we live from now on, all armed with M-16s, the Brown Scapular and the St. Benedict medal."

David continued, turning to Michael. "So, to summarize our new rules of engagement and identify our leader in battle, we fight primarily with *Faith* in God through which He gives us knowledge of the Truth about all things. We also fight with *Hope* which encourages us and overcomes fear, the primary *screwdriver* in Satan's toolbox. And we fight with *love* for God and His salvation of souls. Satan is vanquished by our offering of true Faith, Hope and Charity, which, through the humble mediation of the Virgin Mother of God and Man, engages Divine Power, which alone is *invincible*. In Mary, our human race is represented at its best, as pure, perfect and holy, as it was before the Fall. Note that the Church pronounced Mary in the 19th century as the Immaculate Conception: meaning that she was conceived without Original Sin so she could be our Immaculate Mother and our perfect intercessor.[9] Our Heavenly Mother, who at Jesus's command from His Cross was made our Mother, made possible our adoption as *sons of God*. By trusting God through Mary's intercession, God acts in us by His power and grace, not out of necessity but by His wisdom and by the love of His Mother. With her intercession, we are able to conquer our enemy, Satan, who by nature is far more intelligent and powerful than the entire human race."

"Could you repeat why we should go through Mary, again, Boss? I'm slow." Michael asked this sincerely.

"Pride, in protesting the intercession of Mary, motivates many to think they can go to God directly without going through the Mediatrix[10] He has designated out of His Love for us. Tradition holds this is the same sin Lucifer committed. This pride greatly offends God's Love for Man. Pride of place and competition for the highest place in Heaven was Satan's problem with God, but we know that a King is approached through his *appointed* ministers. What most pleases God, *the King*, is the virtue of humility. This virtue was expressed in Mary's obedience to God's will. Humility led to Mary's *station* as God's Mother. We are

---

9 https://udayton.edu/imri/mary/_resources/docs-pdfs/i/immaculate-conception-ineffabilis-deus.pdf

10 https://en.wikipedia.org/wiki/Mediatrix_of_all_graces

not able to duplicate these virtues of Mary. But God expects us to follow Mary's example of humility as best we can in obeying His commands. In consecrating ourselves to the Immaculate Heart of Mary, men and women are sure to be saved by her Son, Jesus Christ."

"It would seem foolish and arrogant not to approach God through the mediation of His own Mother," said Angela, firmly.

"So, we really have no chance for victory without seeking God's power through Mary?" asked Michael.

"That's right, not if victory is found in humility and Mary is ordained by God to be mankind's 'Mediatrix'. On our part, we show humility in asking for her intercession. Her request on our behalf then draws down God's favor and power," said David. "To be a man of Mary, spiritually, is to be a man formed by the same human soul by whom, Jesus Christ, was conceived and formed."

* * *

The next morning, David and Michael spoke to 'Ricky Recon', the intelligence officer who worked with Andrew. His statement read ominously: '*Seven ogres will pursue you until you are killed.*'

"They are known to carry all manner of weapons," said Ricky, a very thin man, quivering slightly as he stood wide eyed before them. "And they send their personal declaration of war against you two and those who choose to stand with you. Their message was sent to the *Patriot News* this morning."

"Sounds like they have our number," Michael said, looking more worried than David had ever seen him. "I wish I could see them."

"That is the chief disguise of Satan and his minions, camouflage to the point of near-invisibility except to Christians alerted by their signs. Disbelief in their reality is their greatest disguise. Is not camouflage a major weapon of an enemy in your experience?" asked David, looking at Michael intensely. Michael nodded his assent.

"Let me continue explaining the ogre-phenomena, Michael. Only understanding will help you grapple with it because it is outside our normal human experience. Let's start with the case of artificially conceived children, 'test tube babies,' as they are called. These 'babies' are human in body, but they do not have a soul created by God, because they were not conceived by His design, through sexual intercourse between a man and a woman. By that act the man and woman *cooperate with God* in order to conceive a human being. Man can conceive a baby 'artificially' using human sperm and eggs, but the Church teaches us that it is *God* who chooses to instill the soul at conception. Like the ogres we will battle, these artificially conceived babies are animated and made to seem normal by a demon or demons. These babies are not *fully* human beings, even though they seem to possess all the physical characteristics of a human person, which the demon can easily mimic. This is one way we are allowing Satan to enter this world. Many mass murders are claimed to be committed by the possessed. The demons could have left soulless bodies at the moment of suicide, when their murdering had ended. In this way, they conceal their diabolical presence."

"Gad! This gets heavy," said Michael, holding his head in his hands. "I hope I don't have to sell this story to others."

"Fr. Keogh did say that Satan can possess any soul in the state of mortal sin," Angela added.

"Yes, he can possess any soul in mortal sin, but he doesn't necessarily," said David. "Possession is allowed selectively by God to spiritually dead souls not in the state of grace for reasons we are not given to know. I presume because we don't need to know."

"So, God's Will decides, yes or no, whether test tube babies have immortal souls?" asked Michael.

"Yes," said David.

"So, let's please boil this down to the practical as much as possible," said Michael. "Is it true then that we could kill with a bullet through the heart, a living person who became possessed by an evil spirit, but we could *not* do so to a body dragged out of its grave and enlivened by an evil spirit?"

"Right," said David, "and in the last case, that thing could not do anything rational, good or essentially human, because it is totally evil due to the diabolical spirit that moves it. And that is the *ogre* we are talking about."

"So, how do we tell the difference between an ogre and a possessed person?" asked Michael.

"I'd say, shoot first and ask questions later," David said with a wry grin.

Michael laughed, "This is no time for humor, boss. Give me a break."

David smiled, then said, "In my opinion, the best way to kill an ogre is to separate the demonic 'soul' from the dead body it is using by putting a sacramental on that body so that the demon would have to flee. The dead body would then collapse. The possessed, living person, who can also benefit by sacramentals, is subject to death by the same means you or I would be, because the demon can only possess his body, not pretend to replace his soul by animating a dead body. So, the human soul and body can still be separated in the possessed person by death."

"You said a demon inhabiting the dead body cannot stand holy things, right?" asked Michael.

"Right. And at the same time," said David, "we should always wear these same sacramentals for our personal protection. We can also carry other items blessed by the Church, like this crucifix I wear," he said, pointing to a wooden cross with a metal corpus, which hung on a chain around his neck. "We should put crucifixes above each entryway to our homes as well," he added.

"Defenses are good but I prefer weapons," Michael said, zeroing in on combat essentials.

"Padre Pio said the Rosary was his weapon against demons and other evils," Angela said. "I wear mine around my neck, a strong one made of nylon cord, but some men I know keep one in their pants' pocket."

David looked at her and nodded. Then he chided her playfully, "Where did you get all this knowledge? You've been a Catholic for less than a year," said David.

"Mom and I cheated; she taught me a lot, ever since I was young."

"So maybe you were on the lookout for a Catholic guy?" David asked.

"Maybe unconsciously I was," Angela admitted. "I sure am glad I fished deep and caught the big one I did. Maybe God baited my hook," she said with a teasing grin. "I didn't catch a guppy, I can tell you that! It was a fine game fish. Jealous?"

"Oh, yeah!!" exclaimed David.

"Hey, guys, I hate to interrupt, but we were having this really serious conversation," said Michael. Charlene approved his complaint with arched brows, which poorly hid her humorous appreciation.

"We will not flirt anymore but be good from now on," said Angela.

"I don't presume to know all the answers," said David, looking at Michael with concern. "It would be nice to question an exorcist, but even then, he might have to reason from general principles, and we are left with his limited experience to answer these questions. Let's try a different approach. What destroys darkness, my friend?" asked David.

"Light?" said Michael.

"Okay. A physical light is divided by what it strikes, so that it breaks into divided shafts of light, and when it strikes an object, it casts shadows."

"Okay," said Michael.

"But Divine Light would be an *indivisible light* and it would pass *through* any object or spirit, so that there was no shadow. Of course, in this analogy light is good; darkness or shadow is evil," said David. "A spiritual shadow would be caused by a soul that in its unrepentance, freely wills to refuse God's Light."

"Okay, Boss, I can handle this so far, but go slow."

"Well, the source of this Indivisible Light is certainly not human, so what is it?" asked David playing 'Socrates' while looking at his student, Michael.

"That would be God."

"Then here is a question for you: Since evil is the *absence* of God's light, if we shine the Light of God on diabolical Darkness or pure evil it …?"

"Disappears! It runs like Hell," said Michael, chuckling at his fortuitous pun.

"Actually, Hell would be much more tolerable to a damned angel or soul than the Light of Christ, because they cannot tolerate that Divine Light, i.e., the Goodness, the Truth and Mercy they rejected and can never have, even potentially. They can never again choose to be good; they are locked into evil, their wills frozen in malice. Their time for choosing between good and evil is forever gone."

"So, in other words," said Michael, "light fries them; light burns …"

David continued, "…burns like Hell; nicely put, Michael. Divine Light illuminates what they have become through their own fault which leads to their eternal loss. This sense of loss may be the most painful aspect of damnation, yet their will constantly chooses it. So, you can see where being in the state of grace is like being a clear diamond in comparison. Remember that souls in the state of grace are like magnifying glasses that focus Divine Light while evil is opaque and blinding. In this new kind of warfare, being in the state of grace is our greatest weapon and shield against the demonic. So, I pose a final question for you three, then class is over. What *is* our greatest magnifying glass or 'spiritual laser gun', the greatest Light source we can use to drive Satan or his assisting demons away, including their evil works and temptations, their evil use of persons, places or things?"

Angela spoke first. "This Indivisible Light must be Christ in the Holy Eucharist."

"A Consecrated Host. That is correct because that is the *Real Presence of Jesus*," said David. "Reception of Holy Communion even absolves one from venial sin."

"So, if Christ is Light," Angela continued seriously, "darkness is the absence of Christ, and that would be the Antichrist?"

"Good observation. But Antichrist or his shadows are not just rendered absent. The light of Christ destroys his *pretense* of being a Christ or a Messiah himself because the Antichrist can only *pretend* to be good. I think we understand that there have been earlier antichrists. Nero, for example, was an antichrist figure but not *the Antichrist*. Of course, as a people, the Antichrist would be like those who killed the Savior, Jesus Christ, historically. In fact, the Fathers of the Church say that *the* Antichrist will come from this people."

Michael raised his hand, David nodded. "So, the evil spirit animating an ogre would have to leave the dead body it inhabits, if exposed to this spiritual laser gun, the Eucharist. It always seems to boil down to a war between pure good and pure evil," said Michael, thoughtfully.

"At this time, it is an undisguised battle between the spirits of good and evil, which is one sign of the end times," said David. "Now they are allowed to approach us as naked, undisguised evil, and so those of us in the know resort to naked good as our weapon of choice, the laser gun of what I call the Indivisible Light itself."

"This theological boot camp stuff might be worse than the war itself," Michael, the Grouch, complained, in his best rendition of the too-tough-to-care, grumpy guy.

David chuckled. "We are just training for an enemy we cannot see coming with our eyes, Michael, and God is helping us in that. He is teaching us to fight for Him. How could it be otherwise," said David. "Do you realize that the combat we are about to enter into is analogous to that between David and Goliath, where the contestants are of unequal strength, but they win or lose for the whole army, which is protecting the entire people they fight for? Therefore, it is a great honor to fight the personification of evil for our Lord and His Chosen people, true Christians: Roman Catholics. Their divine gift of Faith penetrates 'stone', that is, the hardest of hearts, because this 'Sword' is drawn from the Rock of His Real Presence. Wielding this Sword of divine Faith is a great responsibility. I think this is a good time to warn you of the heresy of dispensationalism[11] which mistakes the chosen people with the Zionists who have taken over the modern state of Israel pretending to have the right to inherit that land based on the promise of God in the Old Testament."

"First of all," David continued, "99% of the 'Jews' in the world are not even Semites, but Caucasian. Zionists are political atheists, secularists of the worst kind. They are not even religious. Judaism is not their religion. That is their pretense, perhaps, but they have no use for true believers or heretics. Therefore, Christians who support them are misled. They should know better. Jesus Christ is the fulfillment of the Law. Therefore, Christianity is the spiritual 'Israel'. Believers in Jesus Christ are now the 'chosen people' of God. Since rumor has it that a Zionist bailed Trump out of debt and financed his campaign, there is reason to suspect Trump's honesty, since atheism is a hallmark of the radical Left (Communism), not the right. Was Trump paid/bribed to lure patriots into the open for identification by the Left so they can be 'managed' as terrorists? This scenario becomes more plausible when the head of the military (Trump) does not order them to arrest the traitors that betrayed the people (74 million patriotic votes). Are Trump-supporting podcasters leading their hopeful audience on to hope Trump put the military in charge when, in fact, he did not? Such a Trump gambit is possible, but it is risky to arouse the 74 million armed patriots, if you want to subject the USA to tyranny. But, if Satan's time is short, he might be so bold."

[11] https://testallthings.com/2007/03/20/the-heresy-of-dispensationalism/

"Do you know who your patron saint is?" asked Angela, staring at Michael with respect and admiration.

"Michael the Archangel who cast Lucifer into Hell at the beginning of time," said Michael.

"You do impress me, Michael!" said David. Charlene's emerald eyes turned gratefully toward David.

Michael too smiled at the compliment, a rare event for him. "I have a good teacher, Boss," he said finally. "He's demanding, though, cracking the whip over a guy like Charlene does." Michael looked affectionately at his new bride, who seemed perfectly ready to soak up all the oblique compliments he had to offer since she considered them as 'sunshine'.

"Remain humble, Michael, and believe in your Christian identity more and more. As a Christian, Christ gives you a new identity and a new name, even though you retain your baptismal name of Michael and your confirmation name, which is?" asked David.

"James."

"How fitting," said David. "James was a courageous man; one of the two 'Sons of Thunder', so-called because their father was known by the name of 'Thunder' in his day. St. John the Evangelist was James' brother. Michael, *pray* often to your two namesakes, St. Michael and St. James, plus your own guardian angel, because they have been specially commissioned by God Himself to instruct, guide and protect *you*. They have special powers and privileges *designed* to help you." Then David gave him an order, military style. "As my right-hand military man, form a *solid habit* of placing yourself under the care and protection of these two Saints. It could mean the difference in saving or losing your life, winning or losing a battle."

"Okay, Boss, will do," said Michael soberly.

"My confirmation saint, by the way," said David, "is St. George, the dragon slayer, according to legend."

* * *

Ricky Recon showed up again the next day. "More bad news," he said. "The ogres, as you call them, look like normal humans. Each one is the commander of his own personal squad of evil creeps: hard core assassins, some of whom are programmed robots, as in micro-chipped human robots." Ricky spoke softly, making sure Angela didn't hear.

"Good," said Michael. "Those we can kill the old-fashioned way."

"So," said David, pulling out pen and paper for help visualizing what had become complex. "1) We have ogres, demons in dead bodies; 2) We have live humans possessed by demons; 3) We have normal human beings, evil or, possibly good but who are in error, serving the devil as Lenin's 'useful idiots'; and finally, 4) We have live humans who have been programmed by the enemy for their evil uses through the implantation of microchips in their brain or central nervous system. Mind control technology uses microchips and drugs, like Prozac, probably both."

"Pro-chips!" laughed Michael.

"Your humor assassinates me," said David with a chuckle.

"This is what we get for defeating a million-man army?" Michael asked dryly.

"We defeated them by arranging the manner of their death," said David, "a death that their controllers exposed them to in an unjust, sneak attack war without provocation upon the orders of the New World Order. Satan provoked their attack, but God heard our plea to be spared to remain a Nation free to worship Him. Essentially, God defeated them. God used their criminal (sinful) arrogance and dishonesty to lure them into a battle where they could be destroyed."

"I like that version," Angela said, startling them both, with a jolt. She had been listening near the doorway again. "Well, I'm sorry I can't hang out with ya'll. You see, I've got something to do, like serve up the hamburgers that are *ready* on the grill, *when* you decide to take a break, by which I mean *now*!" David knew Angela was just having fun with her sassy tone. She came into the room and without warning bumped David with her hip as she moved past him towards the door.

"Commander Severe has given us an order, Michael. We better get another brew. We'll need to loosen up for the *really* juicy stuff coming up that we still have to talk about." David said this before Angela exited the room. Michael really did look a little dazed after Recon's news David thought, as he took two cans of Coors out of the fridge, handing one to his friend.

Entering the kitchen, Angela stared mock daggers at David, pointing a very straight index finger at him, "I need to see you later, Buster."

"Right. I hit the sack around 11:30." That drew chuckles from all but Angela, who couldn't, however, resist lowered lids and the beginnings of a smile, afterwards correcting her indulgence with an angry flash of her attractive eyes.

'My very own beautiful, provocative eyes,' thought David, as he followed Angela to the Delft blue Formica countertop that complimented the faux marble kitchen tile above the sink, then across the deep-pile wine colored carpet of their formal dining room.

"Hurry! She might change her mind on those hamburgers, since ya'll have been so *smart mouthed*," David said, whip-snapping the last two words. Soon after this, sitting at the counter, he felt his recompense, a somewhat unpleasant, accidentally-on-purpose elbow to his ribs, perhaps from the one he was ribbing. Charlene joined them at the kitchen bar, reluctantly leaving the comfort of the black leather recliner in the living room where she had been reading Genesis in their leather-bound *Douay Rheims Bible*.

After the meal and a little more humorous banter, the two couples sat down to discuss Ricky Recon's news and how to handle the approaching situation. The discussion started with David's low-voiced statement, "We will need to return to the cave." All groaned. "I can keep us here one more day, with a ten-man security detail. I think we may have been personally targeted because of all this gratuitous publicity about the possibility of my running for President," David said, with a questioning look at Ricky, who had been invited to join them by Angela and David.

"I would probably have to agree," said Ricky. "At least that was part of it. But as soon as they identified you as the top patriot leader, they were generating assassination attempts, as proved by your honeymoon experience at Many Glacier."

"We are no longer surrounded by an army," said David. "We have about twenty men who have stuck around at considerable personal sacrifice, most of them from our original fourteen. We need to bring them up to speed, asap," said David, looking at Michael. "We are going to need the help of every one of them. Michael, tell them I am putting all of them on salary and then negotiate a pay scale based on rank and what they need. Promote them all. Also, reward them by a bonus pay system based on their length of service and combat experience. Like I said, all of them who volunteer to stay with us for more than six months are to be promoted. I would like to see two captains, seven lieutenants, and the rest sergeants. And we need to be looking for as many as three other caves, two of them small, but at least one half the size of the present one. We must assume they will come to know of our present cave's location. When we do abandon it, let's have it monitored by trail cams, Rick. We need you more than ever now, Captain," said David, laying a hand on the young officer's shoulder.

When the girls returned to the kitchen to clean up after the meal, their excited conversation clearly showed they were concerned about all the details of their upcoming lifestyle change in the cave. They all ended their last enjoyable evening playing with the twins and, after they were put to bed, playing a game of Canasta.

That evening, Angela sat with drooping shoulders on the edge of the bed. The crushing weight of worry had come over her again, despite her efforts to be a "big girl", as her mother used to say. As she saw it, powerful forces were planning to annihilate her little family, so they had to crawl into a hole and live in darkness, fearing to leave. David stood looking at her, helpless, sad and worried himself behind his military mask. This new turn of events was more personal than war. He knew that from now on, he had to let Faith take him to a higher level of trust and confidence in God than ever before.

The next morning, as he was sitting down to breakfast, a knock on the door sent him scrambling for a sidearm. After looking out windows and through the front door's peephole, he cautiously opened the door a crack to see a well-groomed, middle-aged woman in a dark, pinstriped, blue-gray business suit, short dark hair and foxy, half-tinted spectacles.

"Mr. Peterson, I am Betty Smith with the diocese. The bishop sends his greetings, along with a special invitation. May I step in? I am alone. I just need a couple minutes of your time." Stepping into the small entryway, the woman explained that the bishop was requesting David's attendance at a meeting in the capitol with other important persons like himself. A meeting at which the representative of a giant corporation wanted to make a proposal to every U.S. diocese, through its bishop, concerning a plan to fund a vast expansion of certain time-tested humanitarian projects, if the laity decided it wanted to back the bishop's decision. Before David could ask, she said, "The important twist is that the funding corporation would have advertising rights in parish bulletins, diocesan newspapers, etc., and of course, they would be given credit for the major donation they would be making to the Church's overall humanitarian effort in the U.S. The bishop wants to consult Catholic leaders in the Wyoming community," Betty said. "All details," she went on, "will be presented at this meeting and hopefully a discussion will follow. The bishop thinks the proposal is 'entertaining', but all questions or comments, favorable or not, will be welcome."

David was told by the woman that he was one of eighteen influential members of the diocese, representing various "points of view" (the bishop's words), who were being asked to personally evaluate the proposal and advise the bishop of their opinion in writing within the next two weeks.

David left the woman in their small foyer to speak with Angela in the kitchen. She had not been invited to this event. He returned, somewhat reluctantly agreeing to attend. It appeared to him an opportunity to cooperate with the diocese for a change, which could prove beneficial later. Maybe some good changes were afoot. 'Miracles will never cease,' thought David. The woman left him a card with the residential address for the meeting at 7 PM the next day.

David made sure a trusted ten-man team guarded Angela the next evening. Charlene and Michael were asked to stay overnight with Angela while David attended the estimated two to three-hour affair, in addition to five hours driving time there and back. David left the next day, feeling a little uneasy. He finally arrived at the white, two-story stucco mansion located in a high-end Cheyenne neighborhood. A valet took his car and a doorman welcomed him, holding open the white, wrought-iron front screen door. Inside, other greeters received him with an extra warm welcome. Finally, at the coatroom, a very attractive brunette, wearing a nametag that identified her as Melissa, gave him a cordial greeting as she took his raincoat and driving cap.

Scanning the fairly crowded room, David recognized a few V.I.P.s. He commented to the coatroom attendant, who had remained standing near him, that he didn't see the bishop. She replied, "He is not here yet." Then she said somewhat confidentially to him, "You are the last on my list to arrive. Susan there can see to any others, but I believe my duties here are over. May I introduce you to the few people I know?" she asked, a bit vivaciously, he thought.

"Sure, lead on," David said, letting himself unwind a little after the tension caused by his recon team.

After a few introductions, she said, "I don't know that many people at this level of society. You see, I was just employed to be at the door to help the hostess, first at the coatroom and then if anything else came up. In fact, the gentleman hosting this event, my employer, is over there," she pointed to a tall, slim man, "the man with short, graying hair talking to the plump lady in red with his right side to us," Melissa said.

"Okay, I see him," David replied.

"Here are two chairs, the last two available, I believe. Would you save me a seat? I'd like a drink. May I get you one?" Melissa asked.

"Sure, scotch on the Rocks, Cutty Sark, if they have it, please," said David.

David put his sheet listing the order of speakers and events on her chair to show it was taken. The coincidence that he was the last on her list to arrive so that her duties were over and the fact that she ended up sitting with him, seemed a little odd, especially as he now saw others arriving. He figured it was probably his heightened sense of caution and nothing to get alarmed over. Maybe she was a little attracted to him and just wanted to flirt. She was an attractive woman who had no partner.

The bishop was calling on them for counsel. Then why wasn't the bishop at the meeting he called? David wondered if he was developing a case of paranoia due to the recent assassination threat, which would mean he could not evaluate anything prudently because of undue suspicion. If this became habitual, it could be a crippling problem. He was anxious to establish a sense of what was normal and real.

"I can't drink without getting tipsy," she said, upon returning. "So, I am having a 7-Up, just in case I'm called on." A few sips later it appeared that she had caught the eye of the owner of the house who had employed her. She was motioning for him to come over.

The six-foot, balding, gray-haired man extended his hand to David.

"Hi, I'm Fred Siskin." David noticed that Fred avoided direct eye contact. Was that purposely, he wondered?

"Melissa, would you go upstairs and get the box of brochures we need to pass out when the bishop arrives?" Fred asked politely. "He just called with his apologies for being late and to say he would be here in twenty minutes." Fred glanced at her, "You know, the box we had you and Bill put in that spare bedroom upstairs?"

Melissa got up, started to go, then she turned to Mr. Siskin, "Sir, that box is pretty heavy; that's why I asked Bill to carry it for me."

Siskin looked around the room thoroughly. "I don't see Bill or any of the other guys. I do need to do this now though." Fred glanced at David once, then kept looking around the room anxiously. "The bishop will be here soon," he repeated, with a somewhat edgy voice. Finally, he turned reluctantly to David, saying apologetically, "Sir, I know you are a guest." David was already getting up to help. How could he refuse being a strong young man with nothing else to do?

"With your build it should be easy," Siskin said with a smile of barely disguised flattery. "I have a really bad back," he said, wincing and putting his left hand on his lower back. "It began after my fall on the tennis court last year," he explained.

Melissa led David around the edge of the crowd to the carpeted stairs and started to ascend. At the top, she dropped something. Bending over to pick it up, her skirt rose, exposing her in an eye level view for her assistant. David couldn't help wondering if the incident was really accidental or staged for his benefit. With twenty-twenty hindsight, he realized later some red flags should have popped up at that point, perhaps allowing him to nip trouble in the bud.

Upstairs, she stopped at a wooden door at the end of a dimly lit hallway and entered what appeared to be a bedroom. She flicked on a dim light over the bed and led him to a large closet, pointing out a rather large, heavy box, marked *Pamphlets*. David picked it up and headed for the door.

"Oh, set that box down on that chair for a minute," Melissa said. "There's one more box over here on the other side of this bed that we should get. It's a lot smaller, and I can carry it, if you will be so kind as to get it out of here for me," she asked, giving him a charming, if not enticing smile. "Over there," she pointed. He retrieved the smaller box full of flyers but when he turned back, she was sitting on the foot of the bed. "I've got to get these shoes off for a few seconds. Please, sir."

"Sure, go ahead." She put her ankle on each knee to take a shoe off. He was stunned when she suddenly threw both feet in the air, pulled up her skirt to the waist and spread her legs wide to expose her pink bikini underwear. His habit of strict modesty caused him to instinctively turn his head away, hard to the left. A bright flash from the bedstead behind Melissa helped illuminate two men rushing him from behind out of the darkness. The muscular one, who was closer, wielded a stout six-inch fixed blade in his right hand; the other man had a revolver with a silencer.

Melissa gasped as she saw the man with the huge knife lunging at David, who had jumped up in the air to avoid being tackled. He came down on his assailant with full force, both hands grasping his shoulder-length, black hair to slam his head onto the hardwood floor. David then delivered one quick kick with his heel, caving in the man's skull. He immediately followed this by tumbling into a lightning-fast roll towards the gunman, who had time to fire one wild shot before David hit his legs, knocking him flat on his back. David delivered one lethal blow with his fist to the man's face, driving the nasal bone into the brain, blood splattering everywhere. Grabbing the gun, he tucked it in his waistband and ran to Melissa, watchful of other assailants. He took her by the arm and with a 180-degree discus thrower's spin literally threw her through the upper three-foot square, single-pane, latticed glass of the large dormer window behind the bed.

Before her screams had died out, David stuck his head out the broken window, finding his expected assassins stationed on either side. They were still gawking in confusion, their guns aimed at the form of Melissa, who landed face-down, spread eagle on the cedar wood shingles of the roof below the dormer window she had just been hurled through like a rag doll. David swiftly put a bullet through the temple of each assassin with his newly acquired 357-automatic.

Hearing shouts and multiple running footsteps on the grounds below, David jumped through the broken window onto the roof, tucked Melissa under his left arm like a sack of feed and bounded across the multi-pitched roof to its eastern gable, where he jumped to the ground after tossing Melissa off the roof to land in a large, thick bush below. David did a parachutist's landing, rolling onto back 'n butt, legs bent, heels hitting first in order to roll backwards. He threw a stunned Melissa over his broad shoulders, grabbing both ankles with one hand and running for two blocks before stopping to rest and check their trail for pursuers. Finding none, he let her down.

Regaining his wind, David turned his head to look her sternly in the eye. "I saved you on the hunch you were being used as a decoy and as bait in a murder plot, and now I'm asking. How much were you part of this? How much did you know?"

Still frightened, she gushed, "I was supposed to make it look like you were willingly seduced by me."

"How much did they pay you?"

"One thousand up front and two thousand more after doing the job. I was burglarized two days ago, and I was flat broke. I couldn't ..."

"Of course, you *could* have refused. How long have you been a high-class prostitute?" David asked, playing another hunch.

"About a year and a half."

"Pretty much as I suspected," David said, releasing her from the custody of his gaze. "They probably burglarized you to better get your cooperation, *and* they would surely have murdered you for being a witness to my murder. Did you know they were photographing you and me from behind the bedstead?"

"No! But I did notice a bright flash as I was doing my act, now that you mention it."

"A pre-mounted camera with a flash was tripped by someone with a remote control in that room, probably one of my two assailants. But their photograph would have failed to get my face, as they wished, in a photo of you exposed in the foreground and me staring at you in the background. They failed because I turned my head away the instant you exposed yourself, and that move also allowed me to see my killers in time to defend myself. Thank you, Lord, for helping your poor servant," David prayed aloud, raising his eyes to heaven.

Then, looking again at the girl he said, "I figured it all out when I recalled the remote-controlled camera flash and considered the most likely motives anyone would want with a photograph of me appearing to be seduced. It would make for a sensational front-page cover-story. They wanted to smear my reputation, destroying the image of a patriotic hero by revealing his seamy-side, a less than heroic character in a situation justifying the end of his public acclaim. Only by compromising my virtue somehow could they destroy my whole reputation as an honorable American and a selfless hero. I would be shown unworthy of the respect and emulation needed to be President." This is definitely the work of the enemy that is after us, David thought to himself.

"I owe you my life," said Melissa. "How can I every repay you for that and make up for the wrong I did in putting you in danger?"

"Well, by seducing me you could easily have taken us both to Hell, if only things had turned out differently," David replied.

"I would do anything to repay you," whimpered Melissa, bashfully and weakly, knowing her prosecution was probable.

"I'll tell you how you could repay me," David said thoughtfully.

"How?" she asked eagerly, with a glimmer of hope.

"You work for me. I set the wage, the work, where and how you live, under what discipline, the rules and instructions. We will teach you to value and respect the beauty God blessed you with and thank Him by living as a chaste Christian woman. Your conversion would repay me in full," David said with finality.

"Then I want to do it. Please be patient with me though. I used to be a good girl," she said pitifully, "but I have fallen into a dark hole."

"No one is bullet-proof," David assured her, "especially in regard to mankind's most intense passion which was given to him by God for a goal greater than itself: the conception of immortal souls. You will do exactly as you are told, as best you can, or I will cast you off."

"Yes, sir."

At home David gathered together Angela, Michael and Charlene and told them the whole story while Melissa hung her head before them. Lastly, he explained the deal he had made with Melissa. "She has voluntarily placed herself under my authority in repayment of a great debt: her earthly life and her immortal soul were saved this day, by the grace of God."

"She also set you up to be murdered," said Angela, thinly disguising her jealous anger and horror.

"She did set me up to be murdered, but not knowingly. She only knew that she was to seduce me, which was bad enough, and it shows how easily a lesser evil can contribute to a greater one. All of you are delegated to act for me in regard to the moral discipline her conversion will require," said David, firmly. "She is to be instructed in the Catholic Faith. She is to focus on the virtues of humility and modesty. She is not a slave, because she can do as she wishes, but any disobedience or display of attitude on her part, I want to hear about immediately. Her good will is to be tested and shaped by strict, charitable discipline. Let us all pray now for her complete conversion."

They all prayed. Taking Angela aside, David told her to give Melissa a sleeping bag so she could sleep that night on the deck. He assigned Angela as her chief task master in the future. She was to enter the house only with Angela's permission. "Do not make friends with her yet. She must first prove herself."

That night in bed, Angela turned her back on David and would not be coaxed out of her tiff. Finally, she admitted she was jealous of Melissa, and hated her for almost taking the life of her man. Then she wailed, "And after she exposed herself to you, you bring her into our home like a concubine!" She burst out sobbing. "You did nothing with her?! Did you not even secretly lust for her in your heart a little bit!?" Angela wailed loudly; her suspicion almost tangible.

David was in a state of fear and grief. Choking, he cried, "No, Sweetheart, I did not, not even one tiny little bit, even though I understand that does not seem very believable." David managed to control his emotions and spoke softly, but intensely, feeling her hurt, while he was hurting due to her suspicions.

Angela chose to nurse her rage, turning her face away and screaming into a pillow. David pressed his forehead against her arm in his grief, weeping interiorly. "I guess you really don't trust me," he said after a while, his husky voice drenched in sorrow. "You suspect that I lusted for another woman and am now lying about it to keep her within reach. What's left for you and me then, if I am considered false-hearted and untrustworthy? Nothing much!" David cried out, hoping for Angela's change of heart.

When it did not come, he felt sorry for *himself.* In return for his chastity and fidelity to her, in the presence of temptation, subject to circumstances beyond his control, he was rewarded with an absolute emotional rejection by the only woman he could ever love. He rose from their bed, walked into the bathroom, and took a long, hot shower, subconsciously trying to wash away the stain that offended her and at the same time the hurt and depression eating him up. It didn't work. He knew that nothing but her complete change of heart would heal him.

After shaving, he returned to bed and that is exactly what he got! She wrapped her naked body around him, apologizing in triplicate for her horrible selfishness and repeating with passionate words and kisses that he had her *total* trust and affection *forever.* A tiny tear of relief rolled down from the outside corner of David's eye, as he lay on his side holding Angela. She found the tear and kissed it away.

"You spoke from your wounded feminine emotions, Sweetheart," David said to console the woman he loved, while believing it to be true. She was begging for his forgiveness, waiting with confident anxiety to hear his loving response. Angela's strong conscience was reprehending her with a vengeance.

"Yes, my love, I confess to having that selfish jealousy you saw; I am so ashamed."

"Your error was in consenting to that emotion once you recognized it for the unjust thing it was," said David. "You should have obeyed your right reason. You knew that I was a good man. But finally, you mastered your feelings." David embraced and squeezed her. "In that you have done well, my love," David said.

"I was jealous, David, I admit. I will go to Confession to tell my Lord I *am* sorry I hurt Him and you. It was all about me, not you or what you did, much less about Melissa's welfare. How can I repay you? I will do anything," she giggled, trying to be intimate at the same time.

"Let's get real," David said, with mock severity; grabbing her, they rolled around on the bed, laughing with relief and love at having found each other again.

* * *

Through Angela, David made sure Melissa dressed and acted and worked with a bearable but penitential severity. She was told to study and then recite the catechism repeatedly until memorized. In this way, over time, she gained a solid *knowledge* of the doctrine of faith, which allowed her to have self-esteem and dignity. Eventually, she blossomed into a beautiful Christian woman. Increasingly she sought out counsel from the godly couple who had taken her in, nursing her soul at considerable sacrifice.

Sharing a meal with them two months later, Melissa said, "My downfall started on the day I started acting on the feminism I was getting from almost all sides. It was a phony freedom, founded in complaints and claimed in entitlements. Eventually, I called for a radical independence and *complete*, sexual freedom, including an abortion. This was based on a fundamental hatred for all authority, including traditional religious authority. David showed me that authority was preserved by history. I swallowed hate talk which I had gulped down like a teen downs chocolate milk. The errors of feminism were definitely my downfall," said Melissa. "Those errors initiated my descent into the degradation of sin and then justified it. I disrespected my parents and all the traditional values I was raised with. But I have now embraced those values again, relearning everything much better than before." Melissa said all this with her eyes cast down.

David spoke gently to her, "It sounds to me like it is time for you to go back home and throw yourself into the arms of your parents, confirming their just and wise counsel that you rejected in the past. With heartfelt apologies confess your sins against them and affirm their wise authority and charitable acts of correction, all of which demonstrated their love for you." Melissa looked at him with hope, seeking courage and conviction. "By honoring the 4th Commandment," David continued, "you will justify yourself before God and satisfy your debt to Him by repentance. It was righteous love that your parents lavished on you through their corrections. Now it is time to affirm and comfort them for the painful sacrifices they made for your eternal welfare, while you berated them like the foolish rebel you had become. Leave any faults of theirs for another time. Offer them the affection you cruelly denied them because they loved you enough to correct you."

"Take back all your accusations, *verbatim*," David said emphatically. "Make it simple. Your *apology* should have no ifs, ands or buts. Only in sincerely expressing this repentance, Melissa, can you find closure and rest in the Lord. We can't give you that here," David said with a strong affection for the now beautiful soul before them whom they had helped bring back to life. "You have returned from the grave to a life of sanctifying grace, Melissa. Do not ever return to that grave, for you risk never rising from it again."

"My advice is to lay aside all former resentments against your parents. The debt you owe them is much greater than the one they owe you," David said this to Melissa in parting at the bus depot the next morning. He gave her a one-way bus ticket home. He and Angela gave her a one-armed hug goodbye.

That night David said to Angela, "We allowed ourselves to be God's instruments in Melissa's conversion, just by performing our duty of charity in witnessing to Him faithfully. We must never credit ourselves with more than being dutiful servants, otherwise we do not acknowledge that it is really God Who uses us, rather than us using Him to do good works."

"So, you're saying 'backassward' doesn't work. It is always God who does the good work *through* us. Makes sense, my husband and teacher," said Angela, without levity. "You were so right about Melissa, and I was so wrong." She kissed him solemnly, with the respect, love and tenderness that only a woman was created to give and that a man needs like a drink of cold water in the midst of the desert of his labor.

Chapter 2

SEEKING HOME

On the same day the two couples left their home for the cave, Pope Benedict fled Rome for his life, going into hiding in an undisclosed location. Masonic "Jesuit" assassins sought him in vain. Many believed that God hid him from the wrath of the Red Dragon. For the sake of His Faithful Few (the elect), God preserved the Supreme Pastor of the Church, the Vicar of Christ. The Francis "papacy" was almost universally recognized by that time as zero percent Catholic, but the majority did not distinguish between Benedict resigning the ministry but not the munis. In the end Benedict had not been able to keep silent; something that would eventually cost him his life at the hands of the Jesuit Mafia ruling Rome under Francis. Benedict was deeply disturbed by Francis' grievous doctrinal errors which misled or simply 'turned off' the faithful. Benedict came to see how Francis' initial, at least apparent, substantial errors combined with the human weakness of the laity opened the door to apostasy and schism. Several Catholic prophecies pointed to a pope who would die a cruel death after a short time in exile.

David believed Malachy's prophesized one hundred and eleventh pope, Benedict XVI, the *Glory of the Olive*[12] was truly the last pope. Benedict XVI fled Rome after he denounced the anti-pope who had apparently stolen his office by way of threats, forcing him to 'resign' or lose his life and precipitate the destruction of the Church as well. Italian private revelation showed that Heaven approved of Benedict misleading

[12] https://en.wikipedia.org/wiki/Prophecy_of_the_Popes

the enemy to think he was actually resigning (but not really). David believed the mass deception of the laity that Francis was pope, even in the face of his constant heresies, was due to the prophesied diabolical increase of Satan's power to deceive. God allowed the antipope deception to separate the sheep from the goats, His half-hearted, fickle people who erred out of their sin of human respect. By the time Benedict XVI mustered the courage to publicly demand a correction of Francis's errors, the anti-pope had led a largely complicit laity and clergy deeper into apostasy or schism through the heresies of Humanism and Modernism. Traditionalists had seen these heresies emerging from Vatican II.

Benedict knew that, as the true pope, even in hiding, he could consecrate Russia to the Immaculate Heart of Mary, thus obtaining the salvation of humanity through the promised conversion of Russia, a promise made by Our Lady at Fatima. At the same time, he would purify the clergy, because to accomplish the consecration of Russia in union with all the bishops of the world, as Mary had expressly required in her promise, Benedict would excommunicate every bishop at the moment they *did not comply* with the command to join him at the appointed time in consecrating Russia by the formula he had dictated. This meant that *the only bishops left in the world* were those who retained their office by remaining in communion with the Church and its Supreme Pastor in consummating the command of the Virgin Mary to consecrate Russia to her Immaculate Heart. This consecration, completed within a week of Benedict's fleeing Rome, silently demolished the engine of atheistic Communism which had taken over the entire world. After the Consecration, Communism's separate tactical precincts abandoned the obedient unity that had been their strength, thus losing virility by fighting among themselves, as portrayed in St. John Bosco's vision. The Czar's "Holy Russia" reappeared miraculously to stop Russia's aggressive wars and oppression of peoples, designed to spread extreme socialism or communism.

Near the time of the Pope's flight from Rome, Catholic prophecies said there would be a divine worldwide Warning, which David saw as the watershed event that those still Faithful were hoping would bring about the conversion and peace of the world in conformity to Christ's Church. Only such a conversion could prevent the Great Chastisement, in which much of humanity would perish. Heaven had declared in several "private" revelations, that if the Warning was not effective, two-thirds to three-fourths of mankind would perish in a divinely permitted Chastisement, consisting of a nuclear World War III and the devastating collision of Earth with a giant, divinely guided comet. Physical manifestations would accompany the Warning: the sky would turn white and roll up like a scroll, as described in the Bible's last book, the Apocalypse, where the opening of the Sixth Seal is described.[13]

Days later, in the cave, David felt it was time to call together all those who remained to an informational meeting discussing the diabolical assassins and the Apocalyptic times they were now in. On that occasion, all sat on log benches cut with chain saws from deadfall near a shady mountain glen one hundred yards from the cave. Running through the glen was a tiny stream of clear spring water that could be heard trickling and splashing over its bed of smooth multi-colored rocks. This little stream ended at the edge of the glen, plunging in a forty-foot waterfall. The mist rose up from the falling water, wetting the rocks at the bottom and on the vertical granite wall of the cliff. Giant Ponderosa pines surrounded the shadowed glen.

Small boulders had been rolled together to form a ring to contain a giant fire. A bonfire was built using the deadfall's "slash". Red-yellow flames entertained the group of young people who were gazing into the fire, mesmerized. All had been advised that religious, end times prophecies and events would be discussed by David, consistent with his beliefs, relevant to the times and the coming conflict in which, he believed, they would soon be engaged. Questions and discussion would follow; attendance was advised but strictly voluntary.

David began by telling them of the recon reports of the seven special assassins headed their way. He brought them up to date on the bishop's meeting hoax and the attempt on his life through Melissa's attempted seduction. David told them he thought they should have an understanding of the end-time events that lay ahead for all of them, events they may not have been made aware of. "I feel a duty to, at least

[13] Apocalypse 6:12-14

partially, bring you up to speed, especially since you admittedly brave souls are going to walk the line with me in some degree."

After that brief introduction, he started reading:

"Garabandal is a small village in northwestern Spain. From June 18, 1961 to November 13, 1965, Our Lady (the Mother of Jesus, the Man-God) appeared to four young, simple girls from the poor village of Garabandal. ... These children received messages from the Virgin, who spoke of the *Warning*, the Great *Miracle* and of the *Chastisement*."

"On June 8, 1974, Jacinta Marto, one of the young seers at Fatima, Portugal (1917), said in a locution to another seer: 'It is true that I gave a final message, but I, too, could not give the date -- only to warn the world that a great Warning would come to mankind. It would be a great cataclysm/warning, and then there would be a great miracle. And after that, if nothing changes and man continues to offend the Father, He would have to start this terrible trial, for there will be a great war, and there will be a great, terrible chastisement!"

"On June 12, 1976, Our Lady gave the following instructions to that other seer: "My child, you must pray more, do much penance, for The Warning is coming upon mankind. There will be a tremendous explosion and the sky shall roll back like a scroll. This force shall go within the very core of the human. He will understand his offenses to his God. However, this warning will be of short duration, and man shall continue upon the road to perdition, so hard are the hearts now, My child."

David surveyed his audience, inviting questions or comments; then he continued, "And we can read of this same Divine Warning, I believe, in the last book of the Bible. St. John writes in the Apocalypse, chapter 6, verses 12-17:

> *"And I saw, when he had opened the sixth seal: and behold, there was a great earthquake, and the sun became black as sackcloth of hair: and the whole moon became as blood: And the stars from heaven fell upon the earth, as the fig-tree casteth its green figs when it is shaken by a great wind: And the heaven withdrew as a book rolled up together: and every mountain, and the islands were moved out of their*

> *places. And the kings of the earth, and the princes, and the tribunes, and the rich men, and the strong men, and every bond-man, and every free-man hid themselves in the dens, and in the rocks of the mountains: And they say to the mountains and to the rocks: Fall upon us, and hide us from the face of him that sitteth upon the throne, and from the wrath of the Lamb: For the great day of their wrath is come: and who shall be able to stand?'*

"What is this Warning?" David asked. "It is, according to what all the seers have told us, God's *correction* of every living person's *conscience*, so that they know their sins, that is, how they have offended God and how they must act in the future to please Him. I call it, a fair warning and last chance to avoid the eternal consequences of our serious, personal sins. So, there is this promised correction of the world that we can base some hope on for a better world in the conversion of those who have good will and are willing to repent. Given the eternal consequences, this is an act of Mercy by God's permitting Will."

When David called a break, there ensued a buzz of excited conversation. Hot dogs were roasted seven or eight at a time, people returning with them to the log benches to eat. David moved about in order to eavesdrop, trying to gather from the conversations between individuals and within small groups what needed more explanation. He made "cowboy coffee" in a big kettle sitting on a stand-up grill set over a small cooking fire. Those drank it who liked coffee black, like David did, but at least all enjoyed the aroma of good coffee drifting in the early evening's crisp mountain air. The other option was the pure spring water from the nearby stream for all to drink. Stars had begun to stud the darkening blue sky when David began speaking again.

"We who have an internal commitment in conscience to defend our neighbors and fellow citizens need to know the identity of our enduring and greatest enemy, as well as the changing nature of the conflict that same enemy has initiated. As I see it, this infernal enemy of evil spirits from Hell employed a giant army of the brainwashed Chinese slaves or at least largely unwilling young men conscripted by the Chinese Communist Party to attack America via giant commercial tankers. This army was commandeered by a Communist general determined to crush the people of the United States by imprisonment in a godless commune, first destroying their livelihood and their political and moral structures by a virus scamdemic, a narrative rammed through by their bought-and-sold Press. In return for their conquest, those funding this army, Big Tech, Soros, etc., were promised the wealth and economic profit of those they subdued. But they came to realize that the bravest amongst *we the people* were *resolved* to prove up their claim to *the inalienable human rights of life, liberty and the pursuit of happiness with their lives*, in order to remain *One Nation under God*. At this point in time," said David, "we have won the initial battle of this War to enslave free men: a war fought by Chinese soldiers captured, corrupted and driven to assault us by the diabolical spirit of fear, fear of the wrath of the 'Red Dragon' and his Antichrist forces."

"These diabolical spirits have no other choice but to quit or to cast off their masks of deception and fight us as they are: the incarnations of evil. In fact, God requires they be unmasked as the price of their humiliating defeat by the Americans faithful to the Spirit of God upon which this Nation was constituted and has been maintained. It was destined to be this National Spirit, entrusted to God, upon which the Antichrist's spirit would dash itself to pieces, as world-wide, towering waves are crushed against a Mighty Rock of Faith in God. God will send His angels to defend us and fight alongside us against the Monster from Hell. We will now be fighting evil spirits more or less directly. We need spiritual armor and spiritual arms that are guaranteed to kill the diabolical enemy we are up against. We also need a spiritual battle plan and, finally, the arms, instruction and training we will need to *win* this fight, with God's help. Altogether, this amounts to a divine grace. I am asking you to trust me, to follow me, as I try to do God's Will in fighting His battles."

To give them an example of what they were up against, he then told them again of the recent attempt to kill his body, his soul and his reputation as a Christian Patriot by means of Melissa's attempted seduction. "Beware," he said. "We are all vulnerable. That is why belief in the doctrine of Original Sin and its effects, concupiscence, is necessary for understanding our plight. As St. Paul put it, 'The spirit indeed is willing, but the flesh is weak.'[14] Our feet are made of clay."

Someone raised their hand and asked, "So can you summarize what we are now fighting and why?"

"First, we are fighting for God, as the forces of good, a 'white army' led by the Woman of Genesis and of the Apocalypse who is given the power and the mission to crush the head of Satan, the Serpent who led Adam and Eve into Original Sin, with the subsequent loss of Paradise and our first parent's perfect integrity of body and soul. He is also the Red Dragon of the Apocalypse[15], the cause of all evil in our times. The mission of our *white army*, led invisibly by the Mother of God, is to save souls, and we are, therefore, fighting against Satan and the demons who seek to lead souls to eternal damnation in Hell."

"The fight against the Chinese for control of our country that we just engaged in was about preserving, protecting and sustaining a godly, nurturing human society, which George Washington said would require Religion, the key to a society's social bond of unity needed to serve the true common good and secure this Nation against its enemies. Only the one, true Religion of God, Roman Catholicism, will be the bond of unity that will save us as a Nation. Therefore, since we are not directed by our Constitution to the *public worship of Christ* through that one Religion God established, we are left vulnerable spiritually and morally, because the evil spirits can and will take advantage of this lack of public integrity. We also fought the Civil War because that same Constitution did not settle the issue of slavery. The result of a lack of national integrity (wholeness) is that first, public morality will begin to deteriorate, then the nation's laws. Finally, evil spirits appear on the scene of carnage, usually through their Communist agents."

"Our own intelligence personnel are now telling us that we are fighting seven ogres dedicated to the assassination of Michael and myself and, probably anyone who stands and fights with us. That would be your choice. If you accept the mission of supporting us, you will fight on the front lines, one way or another. These demons in human

[14] Matthew 26:41b

[15] Apocalypse 12:3

form are a thousand times more intelligent and powerful than we are. Therefore, common sense tells us that we *must* have spiritual help from God to destroy them. Helping the ogres is their army of possessed and mind-controlled soldiers of different powers and skills. For example, the seductress in my story, a professional prostitute, was 'skilled' at seduction. Her vice was usable to them and, of course, made her one of their defenseless victims because sin caused her estrangement from God, our spiritual guardian. Observe how the enemy assiduously cultivates sexual immorality in America and the world through their Media. Like most of us, the seductress in my case was a good person whom we were able to help recover the grace of her spiritual formation. It may be useful for you to know that demons cannot act on earth except through natural bodies, alive or dead, human, animal, vegetable or mineral. Storms and hurricanes would be examples of the latter."

"Demons can cause any natural disaster. It's possible that Hurricane Katrina was Satan's doing through his human agents. Your greatest protection and power will come from the Catholic Church, whose life is God Himself, but only if you have the true and divine Faith which makes you one of Her children. So, I will give you the opportunity for instructional inquiry into the holy doctrine of this Faith, which is perfectly consonant with the Bible, before it was edited and misinterpreted by protestors inspired and deceived by the same enemy we are fighting today, an enemy who wishes to destroy the practice of the true Faith by pretending to relieve Catholics of worshipping God by attending Sunday Mass, as they shut down churches, further, telling them they cannot have the Sacraments (i.e., do not need them). All of this is designed to erase the actual practice of the Catholic Faith (or any genuine faith in God) under the phony scare of a media-managed *pandemic* and the false authority assumed by bishops: many of whom were threatened, bought off or infiltrated. In order to make themselves appear to be merely complying with civil authorities or hidden superiors, they appeared publically to react to medical advice from the enemy's groomed advisors."

"Ladies and gentlemen, as much as we have been taught to believe in an absolute separation of Church and State, this is just another one of their lies designed to prevent the infallible Truth of the Church from informing human governments of our time. If you choose to stay with me, it will be under the condition that you take the present opportunity for an honest inquiry into the true Faith simply because no one can effectively fight this battle of the spirits without at least a true *desire* to know the truth of religion, that is, our actual relationship with God. Fr. Keogh has agreed to take over this duty of making instruction and inquiry available. He is a priest of the Church, an exorcist and presently decommissioned by this diocese, making him available for our use, at his choice and discretion, of course. I and others will be a part of his education team."

Loud shouting startled them all. "I ain't studyin' any Catholic stuff! The South hated them like it did the niggers, and we *still* do!" the angry voice shouted. The outburst came from a lanky young man who stood up in the midst of the circle of listeners. Everyone shrank from his shrill words of red-hot *hate*, just as they would have from a firebrand waved in their faces.

"*Well, then, get out of here!*" David shouted back angrily. "Go fight for bigotry, if you love all the bullshit it pedaled to almost render this nation asunder by Civil War. Your bigotry is a magnet for our enemy; we cannot trust it fuming within our ranks. It will eventually betray us. GET OUT, NOW!!" yelled David walking up to him in a rage fit to kill. The sinewy young man with long, red hair, beard and mustache left *in a hurry*.

"There goes trouble again," sang Michael in a quiet, prophetical aside.

"I'm sorry," said David to the group as he paced about, fuming in anger. "I can't stand bigotry trying to justify itself. Half a million Americans died for that kind of arrogant *crap*, errors sown by Freemasonic agents," he explained. "Every one of you could have found something you did not like about this militia by now. But instead of throwing the baby out with its dirty bathwater, cutting and running, while reducing our ranks one by one, *you stuck it out*!" shouted David, The Bull. "And as one force, we united for the greater good, and we overcame *terrible* odds together!" Cheers rose from the nineteen that remained.

"I am not trying to manipulate anyone or lead them anywhere against their conscience. I am presenting, as best I know how, the actual identity of our enemy and the way *I know* we can defeat it, because it is inhuman. I fight to be victorious, and I believe God will help those faithful to Him to do just that!" David, stood up, raised his arms, clenched his fists and shouted, "So help me God!" A loud chorus of support repeated his words.

* * *

David stopped by the abandoned rectory to get some items Fr. Keogh had requested. He noticed half a dozen windows had been broken and covered with boards at the rectory. Furthermore, he learned from a neighbor that there was regular vandalism and looting taking place, probably by the same gang of hoodlums they had dealt with before.

David visited Fr. Keogh at the isolated cabin they had rented for him under a pseudonym, bringing a relief for his guards. Though safe, Fr. Keogh looked worried, worn out and bored. David told Father that he wished he had chosen to stay at the cave as he had been invited to do. His threadbare clothes and stubbly face showed David he was living on the edge of psychological and material destitution.

"You are living in a 'war zone' again, Father," David said. "Come with us. We need a priest, especially in the future." He shared with him concerning the talk he had with the remaining loyal supporters and how he had volunteered him for the role of chief religious educator.

"The Church must now go underground with Pope Benedict XVI, David," Fr. Keogh replied. "The Diocese has implemented a so-called mass straight from the devil's Anti-pope in Rome. It has an obviously invalid Consecration. So, I am probably the only priest in the diocese saying a valid Mass right now. I have gone back to the Tridentine Mass that we can trust and are authorized to say by Pope Benedict XVI, without our bishop's permission. David, the radicals in Rome have made a joke of the papacy and a joke of the Church by their in-your-face heretical antics. They bring to my mind the image of a *demonic clown.* I think this may be the Great Apostasy of the last times, David. Many souls are being lost, as we speak. It … it is killing me." The poor priest choked up. He went down on one knee, begging for God's mercy. He was so strong, thought David, and yet so humanly fragile because his total dedication drained him of all but the breath of life.

David decided the priest might rebound if he heard an exhortation that had been rolling around in his mind lately. "We know, Father, that mockery is a hallmark of Satan. And we know his followers are masters of the smear tactic which is what they planned and executed in their crucifixion of Jesus and now His Church, the Mystical Body of Christ. By inciting their so-called reformers of centuries past to sully and smear the Church, they instead stirred the Church to a strong defining action at the Council of Trent in 1545. God raised up Pope St. Pius V to restore discipline and integrity and then God raised up saints in every age thereafter, not unlike yourself, Father, all of them bold witnesses to the teachings of Christ, the Deposit of our Holy Faith. Pope Benedict has been laid low by this diabolical enemy, smearing him with the pedophile priest scandal they themselves created by staffing seminaries with homosexual *change agents*. Then they used their own Masonic bishops, along with lax, threatened or bribed bishops to cover up the homosexual and pedophilia scandals for the purpose of further denigrating and misrepresenting Christ's Church. They do all this as a means to disfigure the Church beyond recognition, just like they did to the Body of our Crucified Jesus, again to discredit Him. Diabolical agents did the same thing in the 16th century through the Pharisees of that day. Today clerical change agents, i.e., *agent provocateurs*, are allowed to teach in our seminaries as gay instructors promoting perversion. The whole sorry show is only believable as the work of Satan. You know this, and if you fall apart over their present antics, they win. If God allows them a limited reign, that is His will, but you must fight them as they are, having been given important ground on the battlefield as His priest. God does not want you to carry this thing as a burden upon your back. Am I right or not, Father?" David insistently asked.

"Yes and no, my friend. I very much appreciate your concern, in any case. But what if God wishes me to suffer martyrdom as a sacrificial lamb? I cannot shirk this role if it is given. Nor should I seek that role. I will consider all things you have said, and try as I may to avoid being their duped and hapless victim. But if God, for all this, wishes me to suffer like the Lamb of God, then I shall."

"I agree, Father. You are ahead of me in your understanding."

"You don't have to explain or excuse yourself, David. Your point is very well taken. Your motive is charitable. And it wouldn't surprise me if you had already considered my possible victim status."

"You are right, Father. I find myself pitying you as God's suffering servant, but you are also stronger than I think. I know our God is still in control. The rot, the scandal was all *staged* to denigrate the real Church as the Freemasons intend, making it out to be a pitiful, all too human, outdated institution of man obviously in need of reform. This is the same ruse they repeated in the 16th century 'Protesters' Revolt. God is allowing all this smear today in order that the few with Faith will emerge as God's Champions in the heat of battle to save the Church and through it, all of humanity. At the same time, God is separating the 'sheep from the goats'. I see that you agree, Father," David said.

David continued, "Scandal and corruption at all levels of the clergy was also the pretext for trying to demolish the Church in the Protestant Revolution. But, the Church was not destroyed; instead, God, through His vicar St. Pius V reformed the clergy and the whole Church with a 'rod of iron'. Jesus said He would be with His Church until the end of time -- so the present, apparently last-ditch attempt of the Demon to destroy what is both human and divine (Jesus: His visible head, the pope and the *ecclesia,* the Church or 'Mystical Body of Christ') will fail too. Weakness in the body of the Church's members actually serves God in cleansing His Church of the *apparently faithful* who will bail out because of Judas Pied Pipers."

"David, you are right," Fr. Keogh said, leaning back against a tree in front of the cabin as he spoke. "The Church does not reside in the weakness, nor in the sin of its members but in the perfection of Christ, its Head, Who forgives and sanctifies all who humbly repent. The Catholic Church is where the Deposit of Faith resides in the love of Christ in the hearts of men and women. This Faith is contained in Scripture and transmitted down to us for two thousand years; it is preserved by the Holy Spirit through a visible Church that is, nevertheless, Divine, like its Founder and Head, Who is both God *and* Man. Holy Doctrine is the Voice of God, and that Voice is what the diabolical forces cannot stand and want to wreck by denial and apparent doctrinal change conveyed by the heresy of Modernism. It's what I call *diabolical vomit!*"

The priest's anger told David he had succeeded in arousing the hope that fuels courage, the mother of righteous anger necessary to *fight*. "I am going to fight by speaking out," the priest said. "If they kill me, that will be the martyrdom God has chosen for me, because to stand up for the Truth is the imitation of Christ, Who is Truth. I also recall reading in Romans 12:9, '*Let love be without dissimulation. Hating that which is evil, cleaving to that which is good.*'"

"The enemy within likes to make the Church look like a joke by misrepresenting it," David said. "This causes weak conservatives to break off in schismatic disgust, while liberal leaners lap the heresy up like a sick dog does its own vomit. These 'conservatives' and 'liberals' both abandon the true Faith; they end up marching out of the Church, just like the eleven million Catholics who committed heresy in turning Protestant when they followed Martin Luther out of the Church. What a coup for Satan! Solid Tradition says, 'There is no salvation outside the Church'[16]. If we fight, the demons will fail. What do *you* think, Fr. Keogh?" David asked earnestly.

"God, in His Mercy, always intervenes in some extraordinary way if mankind has created a tragedy beyond his ability to correct," said the priest. "The risk in a *cataclysmic divine intervention* is that people will convert, but not because they believe and repent, rather because they are *afraid* of the consequences of not converting. Then, out of their culpable self-deception, they perform insincere acts of repentance and reform, which will *not* save them, because God does not accept their insincerity as worthy of His mercy."

David was happy to hear the priest preaching. Preaching lifted him out of depression by employing him in the duty of his vocation. "But at some point," said the priest, "the insincerity of these most probable reprobates is preferable to the risk of so many that might not respond to divine intervention. They are in grave danger of eternal perdition without God's dramatic intervention. In past decades and in our times, God sends His Mother with apparitions, miracles and messages of instruction, warning and admonishment. Those offend God greatly who cast off without discernment the loving entreaties (apparitions and Messages) which Heaven must think necessary to save souls. God loves

---

[16] http://www.traditionalcatholic.net/Tradition/Information/Salvation_Outside.html

sinners so much that He sends His Blessed Mother, the Queen of Heaven and Earth, even with the near certainty that she will be ignored by the majority, that is, the arrogant know-betters."

"Right," David said in agreement.

"By repeatedly turning away from the private revelations categorically rejected by the very liberals they despise, the 'I-know-better' traditionalists let their pride, which resembles that of the Prodigal Son's elder brother, hasten the necessity of God's chastising intervention because they do not believe the Virgin Mother's merciful warnings. It helps to remember, David, that in 1966 the Vatican abrogated Articles 1399 and 2318 of Canon Law making it permissible to follow various cults as long as they did not violate faith or morals. This placed the burden of discernment that St. Paul commanded in the hands of the laity. I think the practical reason for this abrogation of Canon Law was the flood of private revelations, which the Holy Office could not begin to process."

Since the priest's eyelids dropped and his thoughts seemed to wander, David whispered to one of the guards to prepare a meal. David suspected he had not eaten in days. "Did you know, David, that Islam is actually an early heresy?"

"I didn't know that," said David, feeling the need to support a possibly failing mind. "But I believe that a small minority of the people who practice Islam are the radicals who think they are allowed by Allah to abuse and kill those who don't believe as they do, even though that evil aggression could be substantiated by the Koran and Mohammed's example. But aside from the heresy of Islam, certain Muslims have been weaponized by the Communists, and these give a bad name for all who practice this twisted persuasion."

"So, you believe the goodness and godliness of the average person born into a tradition of heresy prevents most of them from being convinced that such savagery is really blessed by God?" asked the priest. "If I read you correctly there, I think I would agree, David."

David decided to continue the conversation. "I believe the radicalism of a Muslim sect was weaponized by Communists to create an army of terrorists. They trained Islamic terrorists using the example of Mohammed's ideas and actions to attack western civilization; they do so on one level by the explosion of Muslim births in targeted nations, caused by the allowance of up to six wives per husband. This 'soft invasion' coupled with the sect's brutal terrorism will eventually allow them to dominate any society. This is not the first time Islam raised Islamic armies to assault Christian civilization. Their 16th century invasion of Europe was only stopped at the Battle of Lepanto. The massive invasion of Europe and the West by their creation of desperate (pitiable) immigrants certainly fits Satan's playbook: to deceive, in this case with an appeal to humanitarian societies blind to their evil intentions."

"Actually," David continued, "I think the recent radicalization of Islam was another CIA operation; they are the enemy within. As you know, Father, I believe most CIA agents are good, patriotic men, but secrecy protected by law is a perfect hiding place for vermin, enemy infiltrators who commit crimes in the *name* of state security. Anyone can hide under the presumption of the gullible, who passionately assumes all is well because they believe it should be, and because that is what *everyone* expects them to believe. Look, they say, all is well because everyone is on stage who is supposed to be and they are all wearing their white hats. Dirtballs love the darkness of mass gullibility in which they violate foolish trust and do their dirty deeds. Secret services are also licensed to operate without significant oversight, *for security reasons*, of course. Here the vermin of the world, agents of Satan, one and all, can breed. Actually, I think all secret services were created for just such purposes," David said.

"All this may be true, David, but what goes to my heart," said Fr. Keogh, "are the wandering of my sheep into alien pastures of outright sin, from sexual debauchery to satanic worship. Sin is really the engine causing this train wreck of a world," he said. "In fact, the Virgin Mary told us repeatedly that Satan is powerless without the invitation of sin."

* * *

Dave left but returned within a week, feeling that the priest might be ready to make a decision. He was right. Fr. Keogh wrote a hasty "I quit" to the Bishop, outlining his reasons, principally citing the invalid rite of the Mass he was permitting. David smiled when he saw the phrase the priest had crossed out on his rough draft: "like the jellyfish you and your peers have become." David's truck was loaded with the priest's books and belongings. Fr. Keogh would follow with the guards within the next twenty-four hours.

One of David's men rushed up to him when he arrived at the cave and reported that the cave's location had been revealed, according to Ricky Recon, to the enemy by a traitor and a raid was imminent.

"I need to talk to Michael," David ordered to the strawberry blond courier, dressed in brown and green camo pantaloons and kaki blouse, the female uniform Angela had designed. David stood near the entrance to the big cave room speaking to Michael. "Send a detail with a walkie-talkie up the road far enough to give us a thirty-minute warning of their arrival," he said. "Since the cave location is known, after this fight, Michael, we are all going to pack up, divide into groups of five and rendezvous at a distant destination ten miles away in these mountains; let's say exactly ten miles due south of us. Now, daypack up and be ready to take up an ambush position on this cave entrance with two men. We will let their main objective, the cave, be their bait. Put Ricky Recon onto finding out who spilled the beans as to our location. I have a hunch ..."

"It was Johnny Reb alright. Ricky told me that first off."

"Well, he is a marked man, then. He dies as a traitor, either in combat or by execution. He's free to disagree with me, but not to betray the trust that all of us put in him with our lives in the balance. Such treachery is murder."

The call came. "They're on the way. You've got half an hour, tops."

David helped position all fighters, telling the non-combatants to take a bearing of 180 degrees south and stick to it for *exactly* ten map miles, then stop and wait for the surviving combatants. He marked the rendezvous point on a topo sheet for them and put someone who could read it at the head of the column. He had some of them load one of their dump trucks with food and various gear, with orders to find a good place to hide it near the ten-mile destination point and then join the noncombatants on foot. The truck was filled with extra weapons, ammo, food, water and other priority items. Each combatant carried two days' worth of food and water, plus a thin sleeping blanket.

The attackers were fifty non-government, CIA drafted and led mercenaries, all deniable assets and most with a long criminal record. They came in five trucks with one tank trailing their column.

The shooting from David's men began when the enemy's special operations unit leading the attack approached the rocky, forested complex where the Patriot cave was located. The enemy's assault force had to cross an exposed position, a grassy clearing flanking David's excellent defensive position behind weathered limestone. The enemy casualties were heavy, while David's soldiers took none.

Finally, the enemy's lone tank broke a passage through the rocks for their troops, but it did poorly amongst the boulders that dwarfed it, some twice its height. David, with two grenades, stayed atop the tallest boulders where he knew the tank would be forced to pass. As the tank passed below, he lobbed two grenades through the gunner's top hatch. The first one hit the gunner and rolled off, but the other fell into the tank's interior. Its explosion killed the gunner and all occupants.

David jumped in and commandeered the enemy tank and with it, he turned the tide of battle, calling for two of his men to operate the tank's two guns, the turret machine gun and the main cannon. Finally, the tank lost a track among the boulders, but from that position, using the 50-caliber turret machine gun, he was able to take out the most heavily armed position against them, a 30-caliber machine gun nest. In the rocks he ordered short retreats, in order to lead the enemy to the empty cave where they would take cover and make a final stand. David took their one sniper rifle and stationed himself fifty yards from the cave, with a clear view of the main entrance door. Finally, the cave door was opened by Johnny Reb. The enemy's company commander observed the battle with binoculars from behind the traitor. David nailed Johnny with one shot. "Paid *back* in kind," muttered David, as the man was slammed to the earth by the high-powered round. "Your debt has been paid. Go see the Judge."

David and his men put so much pressure on the enemy troops in the field that they all took up a defensive position inside the cave. That was exactly what David had been waiting for. He put four men each on the two entrances and another four to cover him. He jumped on top of the cave's rocky mound and quietly entered the small ceiling opening to the cave. As the enemy huddled, discussing their now entrapped situation, he dropped down two grenades and a full stick of dynamite in the direction of their voices. The concussion inside the cave killed some of those who survived the actual explosions, David figured. A few survived, attempting to escape through the known exits, but they were cut down immediately by rifle fire.

Within several minutes all was silent, and the cave was sealed like a mausoleum. Before leaving, David and Michael studied their topo maps under the skylight to plan a reasonable resettlement campaign. It wasn't easy. David had just buried his two dead men in a shallow grave that had been prepared in advance. He and Michael both longed for a final decisive showdown with the forces commanded by evil agents. They would not have the opportunity to set up a plan for that showdown, because the enemy would beat them to it.

"All they want is the two of us, Michael," David said as they slept next to each other that night under the stars after rejoining their noncombatants. He forbade campfires and loud talk and no one was allowed to wander about outside the perimeter of their evergreen canopy or to wear bright clothing.

"Then why continue to put the others at risk for our sakes?" asked Michael. "We could let them go find mop-up situations statewide, help with Patriot Radio or go to their homes and remain on standby alert."

David agreed. "That's exactly what I was thinking." The next morning they dismissed their little army with instructions to stay watchful and keep them informed. After announcing that the two couples would set out on foot to look for a wilderness home, David and the others received goodbye hugs from the many who had bonded strongly with these leaders whose decisions they had trusted with their lives.

David used geologic maps to locate the cave-prone limestone surface outcrops and surface fault traces that intersected the five-hundred-foot thick Mississippian limestone formation. They looked for caves in these and other formations, preferably near a source of potable drinking water. The food they carried ran out on the third day, so David, their silent hunter, strung his bow.

It was the morning of their fourth day, as they walked further south along the crest of the Laramie Range that David and Michael managed, with considerable difficulty, to trap and rope a small, wild horse by driving it into a box canyon. They tamed the small Pinto enough to tie a makeshift travois to it for the girls who took turns riding on it with the twins. This relieved two of the four from carrying the now, heavy six-month old twins in converted backpacks. They all admired the little horse, beautifully colored, especially in the light of sundown, where its darker reddish-brown patches "caught fire". They decided to name him "Paintbrush", after the Wyoming state flower. They were following a long limestone ridgeline, with David leading, a five-day old red beard lending him a rugged look, or so the girls thought. He led Paintbrush with a twisted vine tether, while the pony pulled Angela and the twins on their travois of woven willows.

Michael and Charlene followed David and Angela. That evening, all of them were silhouetted on a small ridge against a spectacular lemon/orange, cherry sherbet sunset. David limped slightly from a bullet that had grazed his right thigh. His hair was tangled, wild and, definitely unbrushed. He was also covered with a thick layer of rust-red dust, from head to foot, completing his resemblance to a Martian soldier, two years from home. They followed a game trail that paralleled a four-hundred-foot outcrop of Triassic red beds called the Chugwater formation, a forty-five-degree slope to their left, bare of vegetation. It was capped with a ten to twenty-foot-thick, gray, laminated limestone. Lush stands of Colorado blue spruce, some of the conifers rising forty to fifty feet high, grew in a narrow forest along the base of the rusty-red *slope of repose*. The new growth of the blue spruce forests formed rubbery soft, blue-green needles at the tip of every branch on the younger trees and on the new growth on the top thirty percent of the older ones. Dead logs, some totally rotten, were haphazardly strewn over the spongy, needle-blanketed forest floor. Everyone was exhausted and discouraged by their fruitless search for a safe hideout home and the lack of food for over twenty-four hours.

David passionately loved his city, state and nation, but he would have risked as much, with the same passion, defending the high American desert where he grew up playing cowboys and Indians. As an adult, he figured there was a protective, possessive love of the country of one's upbringing that fired every man's soul, and this was by God's design, His *Providence*, whether that homeland was in Vermont, Kentucky, Texas, California, Wyoming or Africa. No *aliens* were allowed to invade one's beloved country, and wars to expel them had been waged by peasants and their lords against the armies of the greedy and powerful in every century.

Before stopping for a rest, David daydreamed as he led the small band, picking a trail the travois could negotiate, and trying to dodge prickly pear cactus for those walking. He also avoided the needle sharp, long-bladed yucca, big rocks and the largest of the pale green, ever pungent sagebrush. The war to save America, he thought, would be, in retrospect at least, a godsend for a fat and apathetic America because in uniting those who fought with their lives for the nation and its principles of liberty, a common core of patriotic values was recognized by all and the enemy-initiated lie of *pluralism* was put to flight. Americans were once again on the same page. But David wanted more. He wanted everyone united, not only politically and socially, but also eternally, a nation united around the pillar of Divine Truth. They were, after all, like the Israelites following Moses through the wilderness of the Sinai Peninsula. He knew the nation was already settling into apathy, but they were only safe when following the one God who created them in the one universal Religion that Creator had decreed and instituted by their Messiah. Only those who received Him entering His Ark with open minds and hearts were safe and at peace. Now that royal road was considered to be an exaggeration, fables for fools, for the gullible, the nutcases, as if the passage of time with its newly minted opinions could change the truth of something as grand and revolutionary as Salvation History. What else was Religion, David thought, than the relationship of the One God with the sinful human race that had turned on Him, their Creator. But He still loved them and would save those who believed in Him.

David was "awakened" from his walking daydream by the sound of water gurgling in a shallow draw forty yards to their left, a tiny stream running along the base of the red bed slope they were following. They rested by a stream that wound slowly through the foot-high grass. David pulled individual grass shoots from their tubular stalks, chewing the sweet milky root-end, while gazing up at the sky's cobalt blue vault with its high, wispy-white cirrus clouds that he knew were swept by the high velocity westerly winds of the northern hemisphere's mid-latitude jet stream. They all dozed off for an hour under the warmth of the afternoon sun. An hour later, a slight sound, like a distant snort, awoke David. Without moving, he caught something in his peripheral vision; slowly rolling his eyes right, he saw that it was the twitching of a mule deer's big ears. Four of them were grazing beside the creek only thirty yards away. He very slowly and silently knelt, knocking an arrow, drawing taut the waxed string on his short, break-over recurve bow until the soft web between the knuckles of his thumb and forefinger locked into place on the back of his jawbone. "Twuanghh." He released without moving his hand, his eye following the arrow's true-arc flight until the aluminum shaft passed through the neck of the two-point buck.

Michael woke with a jolt at the twang of the bow string. He helped David gut the animal, running his short, razor-sharp fixed blade knife up the belly, just beneath the hide, so as not to puncture the gut sack, finally rolling it out as an unperforated whole. They removed the lungs, heart, windpipe and esophagus separately. Meanwhile, David had removed the scent glands from inside of the hind legs, since they could disflavor the meat if left intact. They dragged the carcass into shade and propped open the gut-chest cavity with stout sticks to allow rapid cooling of the meat, an essential key in preserving the good flavor of freshly butchered meat. Afterwards, the carcass was strung up on a thick, seven-foot-high tree branch using a pulley and a short rope run through the buck's hind-hocks. Then, to cool the meat even faster, they skinned the carcass, starting at the hind quarters, peeling down, decapitating last. David later stretched and scraped the hide, using it as a surrey over the travois to shade mother and twins, flesh side up.

After that, they spent a lazy day in camp, washing clothes, bathing and shaving. All finally rested on the ground around the cooking fire, the central gathering place in the evening, where coffee, tea and quiet conversation made the long night more bearable. David liked to tend the fire as it grew smaller, even when twigs were the largest chunks of fuel the tiny fire accepted. He would gently blow until flames leapt above the red-hot coals. At bedtime, they would build up the fire and encircle it in a ring of sleepers who turned themselves like hot dogs throughout the cool night to keep toasty warm.

Before retiring, the two men scaled the highest point of a local ridge and decided the tawny limestone of the Madison Formation, being many millions of years older than the Chugwater, should outcrop to their south, since the formations around them were dipping north. Therefore, they would head out in that direction before noon tomorrow, even though they couldn't see the pale tan of the Madison yet.

Coyotes came that night, attracted by the smell of the deer carcass, their gray coats streaked with strands of silver, barking, howling and whining like the dog-eared canines they were. It was the constant whimpering of the pack that finally unnerved both women, who screamed at their men for relief. Paintbrush was jumpy too, so David drove them away with a flaming branch. When they returned, skulking silently through the brush, David ran an arrow through one of them to feed and quiet the rest. But that restless night was filled, nevertheless, with their distant whining, howling and yipping, sounding at times like a teenage drinking party, David thought.

They roasted the best of the venison loin for their evening meal, and David expected the aroma would travel far enough to attract a more powerful predator. His anticipated visitor arrived without the slightest sound at 3:30 AM. The mountain lion snuck in silently, but when it caught the carcass with its teeth and pulled, a string David had tied to the carcass toppled a small log onto his shoulder, waking him. Ever so slowly, David sat up, knocked an arrow and sent it through the cat's chest cavity.

Now he could sleep without worrying about carnivores raiding the deer carcass, since the lion's presence and scent would keep the coyotes and feathered predators at bay. Skinning the cat would be tomorrow's decision: the only question being whether the pelt's weight would be worth packing. He built the fire up again, curled up around sweet mother and babies and slept soundly until midmorning.

A half-dozen noisy stellar blue jays woke David around eight in the morning. They were big birds, sunlight flashing a scintillating midnight blue over their wings, trimmed in black. Two shadows suddenly passed over the camp. Looking up David saw the universal garbage disposal units of the West, four huge turkey buzzards circling; then, far above them, a bald eagle appeared. The turkey buzzards disappeared, acknowledging the King, with its regal seven-foot-wide wingspan and deadly talons.

David and Michael butchered the deer, packed it on the travois, and ate a quick venison breakfast. The band set out to the south at 11 AM, planning to stop in four hours to further dry the meat in thin strips over a fire to preserve them. They traveled fast, and by 3 PM they stood on the edge of a five-hundred foot deep, narrow canyon, its vertical Madison limestone walls rising three hundred feet above a shallow, five-foot wide stream below. Bald eagles nested up high in the chalky, limestone walls. The eagles were easily identified by their white neck and head plumage, as well as their large, curved yellow beaks and large, sharp claws designed for tearing raw flesh. Four-foot-high masses of sticks formed their nests, which bulged from the wider sections of the vertical fissures in the pale tan limestone walls. Young eaglets with fluff feathers squawked loudly from atop the huge nests, their gaping bright orange beaks open and ready for shredded bunny rabbit breakfast or maybe chunks of squirrel or rattlesnake. Large, white poop-washes brightened and marked the walls below each nest.

Twenty-five yards from the stream, David and Michael found a double cave with a ground level entrance and inside two twelve-foot square cave-compartments, connected by a two-foot high, five-foot long passage. They spent three hours making a functional cave home, after helping the girls cut up the remaining venison into strips for drying, hanging each strip over a slender horizontal pole propped between two forked sticks planted securely in the earth. Two three-foot long fire trenches dried two poles of meat. Finally, a food called pemmican by the Indians was ready for storage.

David was content that the bishop had promised to provide Fr. Keogh with a place to live in some parish, despite having no diocesan status. Secretly, the bishop sympathized with Fr. Keogh on the invalid mass, but he did not have the fortitude to stand up and condemn it, knowing the Vatican's Jesuit Mafia would make his career resemble a rusting tin can in a mosquito infested junkyard located near a backwater bayou. David pitied the bishop and all the clergy caught between their conscience and the unjust annihilation of the Faith they were sworn to uphold as ministers of the Church. David figured the bishop had also given Fr. Keogh credit for years of faithful service and the loss of his parish over a matter of principled conscientious objection.

Angela and Charlene sat by the stream, sharing their feelings as fugitives hiding in the rock caverns of their own country. "What are we really fighting for, Angela?" Charlene asked. "That question continues to be confusing and nebulous. That's when my motivation to sacrifice for the cause deflates like the jet of an untied balloon going crazy: Bth, thi thi."

Angela laughed, and Michael, lying nearby, said, "*Very* good, Charlene. What else can you do?"

"Bet you can't do it," teased Charlene back.

Michael's verbalization of the flabbergasting blurt of a balloon shooting off like a crazy monkey on a pop bottle rocket, as David put it, set them all four laughing like children. Even the twins started babbling and kicking upon the rarity of adult laughter.

"But Charlene brought up a serious question about motivation," said David after the fun had died down. "We all experience the same dryness, and sometimes it is grievous. I view the problem like this: We are not the Playwright, just His actors or stagehands. So, the question is not, are we feeling fine but are we playing our part well; are we being good actors for our Master Playwright?"

"But that question cannot be answered except by knowing what God desires, what pleases Him," said Angela.

"Right," David said. "Our catechism tells us that our purpose in this life is to 'know, love and serve God'."

"So, what does God want, if we are to serve Him?" Michael asked, sitting down on a big flat chunk of layered gray limestone with a white ring deposited at former water levels, along the side of the rock facing the stream.

David, the teacher answered, "Michael, the old Baltimore Catechism tells us that what God wants is not about God, Who doesn't need anything, but about us. So, when asked, 'Why did God make us?' the catechism's answer is '*In order to share eternal Happiness in Heaven with us*'."

"So, He wants eternal happiness for us," summarized Charlene, "and in order to accomplish this, we are ordered to know, love and serve Him, probably helping others to do the same," she added.

David continued, "We find our way to Heaven by following the

Great Commandment, to love God and love our neighbor as ourselves for His sake, which the rest of the Ten Commandments detail. In obedience to these Commands given to Moses directly by God, we know, love and serve God in order to possess eternal happiness which He wants to share with us. Only by obeying God with Faith in Christ is this happiness possible, because our part is fundamentally to obey. This humble obedience prepares us to accept the good news of the Gospel, Jesus, the Christ, our Savior, who will perfect our obedience."

"What comes around, goes around," said Charlene.

"Ok," said Michael, "but the question to me is, *how* do we and others know, love and serve God?"

David answered, "We *know* God by having Faith in Him and therefore what He reveals to us; we *love* God by doing all He commands, as recorded in John's Gospel; and we *serve* God in performing the acts which Faith and Love direct us to do."

"So, we believe the Bible?" asked Michael.

"Actually, we believe the truth, Jesus Christ Himself, Whom the Bible partially reveals to us in recording Jesus' major teachings," David said.

Michael complained, "But we can't go around selling people the truth that we can't vouch for ourselves. You and I have never even seen Jesus; nobody has for two thousand years. So, the question is, why do we believe in Him and how?"

"How and why do you believe the truth that 2 + 2 = 4, Michael?" David asked his friend, looking directly at him, the two girls watching one of them from either side, as if cheering for two boxers.

Michael stuttered, "Uhhh, uhh, I … well, …"

"It's self-evident," David said calmly. "That's why you believe it. And, if God the Father reveals His Son to us, like He did to Peter, then this revelation cannot be doubted because it would be a self-evident certainty. You could reject it, but that would be a conscious *decision* to deny the known truth, what they call the sin against the Holy Ghost. So if the Father infused this truth in all, its rejection by unbelief would merit damnation."

"Do you believe in Jesus Christ?" David asked Michael, the hesitant. Michael wavered in the face of his own questions, rooted in doubt.

Charlene looked worried for Michael, waiting and hoping. David took his friend by the shoulders in his powerful grip and squeezed until he looked up at him. "Have you begged God for the gift of Faith, like you promised, Michael?"

Michael lowered his head, "Not very … no, no, I have not, David," Michael said looking up at David, pleadingly. "I kept thinking that would come automatically with my joining the Church."

"I can lead your horse to water, but …" David paused for effect. "Do you even want to believe?"

Michael thought for a while, then looked sheepishly at David and whispered pitifully, "I don't think I believe what I don't love." He raised his eyes to David, begging for understanding.

"But how can you love what you do not first know?" asked David, his eyes not releasing his friend. "And how can you believe in what you do not know, which is what you cannot see without Faith? So, your answer does not work, Michael," David spoke firmly, his eyes unyielding. But he also looked at him with compassion. "Faith comes first; God is unknowable without it, and it is a gift from God, something you must beg God to simply give to you. I think you once trusted someone, Michael, and they betrayed you. Now, you must abandon the pride that keeps you holed up. My strong hunch is that self-pity prevents you from having the freedom to trust and come to know God. You think you must first believe that you are loved, before you come to know?"

"Yes, how do I *know God loves me*?" asked Michael.

"You know God loves you because of all He has given you: a good friend like myself, which is rare and now this beautiful woman, Charlene, and so much more, like your health, your courage, your values, and your wealth. Surely you can choose to love God in return. His Love will never betray you; you are safe, and you can let yourself come to know and believe the Truth which is God." David stepped across the tiny stream and turning to face Michael, he extended his hand and said, "If you love me, my friend, walk over the water." The girls muffled nervous giggles, but still stared, expectantly, at Michael.

Michael stood up, a manly look on his face that relieved them all as soon as they saw the set jaw, but whatever resolve he had, seemed to trickle away, like the stream before them. The noon day sun blazed down from straight above on the two, still facing each other over the tiny stream of water.

David said, "So, let's talk about this group of believers called Catholics and their fathers in Faith. Do you think, without the help of God's Holy Spirit, they could keep the same doctrine, generation after generation, for two thousand years while retaining their normal, erring, fallen human natures, prone to bickering and disagreements?" asked David.

"No way," said Michael. "It would get screwed up. Okay, I acknowledge that you answered why I must know and believe before I can love, but the more difficult question for me is *how* do I believe in Jesus?" A 'light bulb' seemed to light up Michael's face, his blue eyes began to shine with understanding. "Yes, it was *God* that had to preserve the Truth in that Church of mere men, as you have said time after time, David." Slapping his leg, Michael continued. "He will give me the Truth, so I can believe in Him, so I can love Him. God Himself told me *how* to love Him by just obeying the teaching of His Church, right?" They all nodded. "So, I don't really have to have a special knowledge of *how* to love Him, because God is offering me Faith, which makes love possible. All I have to do is acknowledge what He has offered to me and I do."

"Yes!" shouted David, raising his fists jubilantly before thrusting them across the stream again to shake the hand of his Christian brother.

"You always seem to pull me back from the brink of foolish despair," said Michael. "Why am I afraid to think on my own? The Church is *how* I can know and love and serve God. Got it!!" Michael laughed, thinking of his amazing recalcitrance.

Michael stood motionless. Time seemed to stand still for him, yet the stream of this life continued, babbling contentedly. Michael shook David's hand and with his friend they nimbly stepped across the stream. Another battle won, together, thought David. He turned to Michael and said, "Let us walk together in the Faith and Love of God, with the Hope that gives us Eternal Life."

"I accept," said Michael. Applause broke out. All smiled with joy and relief, a tear budding in Charlene's eye. "So, I guess we better throw down these guns and study doctrine and start witnessing," Michael said boldly and seriously.

"Yes," said David, "as a matter of fact, Michael, that is what I have been waiting for. Without realizing it, you have just pointed out the way for both of us to fight this war properly in the future."

Michael turned to David, "I think some very deep desire in me has always craved what you had." Then, to the astonishment of all of them, Michael folded his hands, dropped to his knees and bowed his head, praying in a low voice, "Thank you, God. *Thank you* for helping me and waiting for me until I was finally humble enough to drink the water I had been led to so often."

Angela came up to David and took his arm in hers; they walked toward their new cave-home, tears now brimming in Angela's eyes as she looked at her man, smiling. "I am so happy to be your wife, right now!" she said as she lay her head against his arm. The twins in their arms began crying. Both needed to breast feed at once and Angela had learned how to do that well. Her milk was plentiful and rich, so the twins were fat, healthy, happy and *heavy*!

They ate well that night before the two men left the next morning. All were in a festive mood. Just inside one of the cave entrances, they roasted the last of the venison steaks over a fire of coals. After supper they worked for hours cutting what remained into thin strips for drying. With plenty of food stored for their wives, David and Michael went over their trip plans and schooled the girls in the operation of their personal revolvers. They instructed them to shoot dead any uninvited stranger or wild animal that entered their cave after firing one warning shot. Two practice shots and reloads finished their schooling. They were to hang the pemmican outside for further drying, but only in the daylight or when they were present. They were to store it deep in the cave, off the ground, with a light cover to keep the deer flies off at night.

David and Michael would leave the next morning before sunrise, taking Paintbrush and empty containers to fill with food and other supplies. That night the two men relaxed outside the double-cave entrance. Taking the lion pelt in his hand David said, "One day I'd like to put this somewhere near the big grizzly hide lying before my woodstove in the living room. But for now our main mission as I see it is:

1) We are going for food and other necessaries. Make sure you have our list on your person, Michael.

2) We need to check on Fr. Keogh.

3) We also need to visit with Ricky Recon to get up-to-date news on what the enemy is up to and what the forces of patriotism are doing to secure law and order."

David added, "I'm always worried about Fr. Keogh's safety. We need to let a few trustworthies know our cave location, marked on a map, in case the other communications fail and those in the know need to get ahold of us."

The next day, after walking for an hour, they took cover as a small plane flew overhead. They wore army issue camo clothing, including wide brimmed floppy hats. Shades provided some anonymity. Each carried maps, an AR-15 automatic rifle, ten clips of twenty rounds each, three canteens of water, five days of food and a compressed, camo space blanket.

"If possible, we need to identify and locate our preternatural enemy," David said, "targeting them where they are most vulnerable. But the real war is to be fought for souls. The sin of unbelief, Michael, will eventually defeat many."

"Sorry to switch tracks, but where is Fr. Keogh? Ricky? Where is anyone?" Michael asked.

"I only know the friend Fr. Keogh was going to board with when the cave home failed, and we left him. The friend's name is Frank, and I have his address," David said. "We'll start looking for Father there."

They walked fast, with long strides. Ten hours later they stood talking to Fr. Keogh.

"I has been pretty hectic and confusing for me, David," said the priest, who, in the last month had grown a considerable red beard. He was physically and psychologically stronger, it seemed to David. "I need a place to say Mass and a trustworthy assistant, David. Without a congregation, I am like the fish out of water."

"Your best congregation now might be gathered around a log cabin in the woods rather than in towns," said David. "You might have to say Mass outdoors."

"That sounds good to me. If possible, I'd like to be near St. Joseph's in Silverton. I have always loved that church. It's where I was baptized, you know. I think the pastor would let me say a Mass in that church occasionally, but only if the bishop okays it. I'm still considered a pariah by many in the diocese, which is still effectively controlled by the phony 'church of man' diehards. The masonic club is still ruling the roost in Rome, too, you know. But, our bishop, though cowardly, keeps his own counsel and hopefully an open mind too," said the priest. "If he can move me quietly, he might do it."

"I've got something you will like to hear," David said. "I came upon this little book a year ago and just re-found it a few days ago when we visited our old cave home." David showed Fr. Keogh a small, well-worn paperback. "Let me read the introduction and a short a passage to you, Father." The priest nodded and relaxed in Frank's favorite recliner.

"FAITH IS GREATER THAN OBEDIENCE - AUSTRIA 1922-1977

Words of the Savior to Professor Drexel

Original messages from 1970 to 1977

The Editor's Preface

In 1922, Fr. Drexel had a private audience with Pope Pius XI; he taught as professor in the Vatican University for Missions and was later used as an expert in racial questions at the Vatican. For the first time in November 1922 and from then on in all the nights of the first Fridays of the month, Our Lord appeared and spoke to our deceased friend, who spent those nights in prayer. The phrase which was selected as the title of the book are the words of the Savior, and they may solve the painful conflict between *faith* and *obedience* under which many priests and faithful suffer today: Nobody can claim authority in his office, and demand obedience in the name of the Church, when the faith of the Church is lessened or destroyed! Whether unbelief and its practice is dictated by the interior or exterior enemies of the Church

-- the clear teaching of the Acts of the Apostles is still valid: "We must obey God rather than men." (Acts 5,19)

"Now, Fr. Keogh, I quote Jesus' words to this Austrian priest," said David.

> *"Severe trials are trying My Church ... Therefore it is necessary that men and women fight and pray indefatigably and imperturbably, defending and clinging to the* ***faith****, making sacrifices, and maintaining in this way hope, trust and confidence among the faithful and in the people. Did I not praise the blessed ones who suffer persecution for the sake of justice?* (Mt. 5,10) *Have I not said: He who confesses Me before men, I will also confess him before My Father who is in Heaven?* (Mt. 10, 32) *But the greatest pain to My Heart was given by those who should be shepherding the faithful -- and these are the bishops, who have become silent, indifferent and cowardly. Not only a few, but many of them, are afraid of men, and are removed from the fear of God. This is the reason why the wolves could break into the flock, bringing such confusion and devastation and destruction upon the Church.*
>
> *Therefore, do not let yourselves be oppressed by the apostasy and heresy of many. All those will crumble in their own sin, and becoming unhappy in their inner soul, they will come back to Me -- or perish eternally. ...*
>
> *These confusers and seducers speak and write much about a* ***new church****, of a church that is no longer a religion, but is purely human. I tell you:* ***This is the church of Antichrist.***
>
> *...In this new church one can no longer find the cross of My redemption which is salvation, but their happiness lies in sensuality.*

> ***This new church is the living Antichrist, the real Babylonian harlot, as My disciple and apostle John has written in the Apocalypse."***[17]

David closed the paperback and handed it to the priest. "You are right. From that summary, I do like it," said Fr. Keogh. "It's consoling that Jesus understands the plight of His faithful, as few and as muffled as we are."

After conferring the three of them selected a cabin site for Fr. Keogh on the topo map purchased at Badger's place. Badger was doing a brisk business. In fact, he had become so rich, he splurged and bought himself the 1965 Chevy pickup he had always wanted, but he had to go to a junkyard fifty miles away to find it. He had it painted cherry red, metal flake.

David gave the order and provided the money for skilled builders to construct a cabin for Fr. Keogh on five acres of private land he had purchased next to six sections of federal land that could be used for recreation; the land was only two miles from St. Joseph's Church. David also had a smaller cabin for two built near the priest's cabin in order to house two 24-7 security guards, doubling as the priest's assistants.

While Michael purchased food for the cave-dwellers, David stumbled upon a makeup artist also housed by their host. Mr. Stevens was an artist who showed David how to hide one's identity by disguises, and he gave him the materials to do so. David thought this might help them evade their would-be assassins someday.

Upon their return to the cave, everyone bathed, using the soap and the "shower curtain" Michael had found. The men made presents of two colorful bonnets for their girls. A beer and a cigar they gave to each other. Drying themselves beside two boulders, the guys sang, split a beer and a cigar, while the girls bathed. But the opacity of Michael's shower curtain by the stream was severely compromised by silhouettes of the female bathers when set against the light of the evening's sunset. Both

---

[17] *Faith is Greater than Obedience: Words of the Savior to Professor Drexel on March 2, 1976*, by Albert Drexel, publisher unknown, 1985, 106 pages.

men made sure the other admired only the tip of his cigar, their backs to the women at all times.

Everyone was happy, dirt poor, but no longer dirty. The clean, naked twins celebrated by kicking up a storm and screeching loudly as they dried off, probably imitating their dad who was singing sentimental (soupy) ballads in their honor. Late that night David and Michael decided that in a month or less they would all move closer to Fr. Keogh's new mission cabin since David had purchased another five acres with the idea of dividing it between the two couples later, if they ever moved back.

* * *

Three weeks later they left, taking Paintbrush, who pulled the travois loaded with the twins and most of their worldly possessions. The girls walked, talking excitedly about everything in their happiness to be gone, as if it were a permanent vacation. Late the next day, deep in the woods, they found Fr. Keogh already inhabiting his newly built cabin. He seemed years younger, more cheerful and more energetic. The priest talked with the girls about the skills of cabin life, giving demonstrations whenever possible. In the meantime, David and Michael, knowing winter was a short month away, filled Fr. Keogh's wood box and stacked a winter's supply of split firewood outside the front door. The two men then tested the small woodstove David had packed in from town behind Paintbrush, whom he decided needed a proper harness to pull a wagon. They filled Fr. Keogh's cabin with all the food and supplies Paintbrush could bring in his new conveyance, planning to buy more for themselves after their visit ended in a few days.

Fr. Keogh celebrated his new life of service and his gratitude for everyone's generosity by hosting a grand breakfast, a feast for all: sausage, bacon, eggs, buttermilk pancakes and biscuits, butter, honey, coffee and Angela's slow-cooked vegetable medley, a blend of diced, soft spuds, green peppers, onions, mushrooms, jalapeno pepper, and tomato sauce, all topped with grated pepper-jack cheese. When Fr. Keogh said the blessing, David saw gratitude in his eyes for the preparation of a delicious meal, but also for the Christian fellowship that surrounded it, one founded on the love of Jesus Christ. It reminded David of accounts of the early communities of the Church, where the religious bond was the Church, more or less one with the human community that lived strictly by the Catholic creed. David decided Fr. Keogh needed a daily visit by a cook/housekeeper. He determined that the guards could temporarily double for this duty, while they looked for someone more suitable and more permanent.

The next morning Charlene was asked by Angela to baby-sit the twins while the parents took a two-hour walk. The perfectly round, straight lodgepole pines towered over David and Angela, partially shading them as they walked over a pine needle forested ground. The clearings in the forest were covered with long grass and a few currant bushes and, even at this elevation of eight thousand feet, a few small sagebrush. As they walked single file out of the forest, a beautiful panoramic view made them stop, as a doe and fawn slowly moved out of sight into the aspens. At the forest's edge, a gently inclined plateau came into view; green grass grew from a thin cover of earth deposited over the limestone bedrock. This landscape took up their entire view as David tried to take it all in. Groves of aspen, their small leaves fluttering and twirling in the breeze like the hem of a skirt, trimmed the edge of the forest around the square mile clearing. The aspens were punctuated by a few stately, one-hundred-foot Ponderosa pines.

In this "Meadow", by which they referred to it thereafter, Angela later rode Paintbrush bareback, with some speed and grace, David had thought, concluding that the two must like each other. David showed Angela St. Joseph's church in the distance. They walked together over the Meadow south for half a mile, coming to a long, low, exposed limestone ledge, studded along its length with stunted, wind-withered Ponderosa pines, their eight-inch needles glistening in the sun.

David, as always, studied the subtle features of the landscape, taking this opportunity to bathe his eyes and his soul in the mystery of the mountain country he had grown up in, like a tree grows, gaining mature stature, slowly but surely. With the eye of an artist, he studied everything: how the lush protected patches of vegetation always favored the north lee of every rock and shrub, and how the wind-exposed trees were gnarled but the protected ones stood straight and tall.

David sat on the gray limestone ledge with Angela, dwelling on the mystique of the mountain's misty morning, with its grassy parks here, draws and bluffs there, hills and ridges. This morning, a soft gray mist enveloped them, veiling everything in a soft blanket of very fine moisture. Then a gentle breeze rose to push the ground-fog away, refreshing them; the sun warmed their bare heads. David remembered a countryside somewhat like this one which had become his home during daylong hikes as a youth of twelve. Wandering over the hills and prairie, he had explored the high desert of Wyoming on foot and in his imagination "witnessed" sweeping U.S. Calvary and Indian battles; yes, these were the "foothills" he cherished. Once Fr. Keogh had followed David's gaze when in the country and he remembered on earlier occasions reading the same longing in David's eyes for another world where he could, at last, find peace.

The priest had pulled a small Bible he always carried from his knapsack and said to him, "Come sit, David. I have something to read to you." David remembered feeling privileged to sit beside the priest while he read to him from Genesis chapter 49, verse 26: *'Jacob said on his death bed, the blessings of thy father are strengthened with the blessings of his fathers: until the desire of the everlasting hills should come'* ..." Fr. Keogh continued, "A gloss explains the meaning of the phrase, '*The desire of the everlasting hills.*' It reads: 'These blessings all looked forward towards Christ, called *the desire of the everlasting hills*, as some mysterious thing longed for, as it were, by the whole creation.' Even though we know of Christ," said the priest, confidentially, "from literal public Revelation, by what He said and by the witness of His Apostles, who actually saw Him, we still long for Christ *personally*, because we desire to see Him forever. In other words, the fullness of Revelation, is the Beatific Vision, the mystery we long to *experience* concretely. The Patriarchs of old longed for this too, but they had only a dim notion of their Savior; they called this longing *the desire of the everlasting hills*."

On that occasion David remembered Fr. Keogh had a second time looked at him saying, "David, all mankind secretly longs for Christ, the *Anointed One*, but only some know Him positively, by fidelity to His Word, as He really is, embracing Him in *true doctrine*. He is the Alpha and the Omega, everyman's beginning and end, as individuals and as a race. We were made to be with Him forever, because He made us for

Himself. So, despite man's fall from grace through Adam, in the very core of our being there is a deep longing for reunion with our Creator. But we must be as pure as we were at our creation/conception in order to be able to see Him, to be in His Presence and to be known by Him, that is, as a true image of the Son of God. Therefore, God's Mercy allows *Purgatory* to prepare us for Heaven. Many, even without knowing it, search for happiness and fulfillment by pursuing 'strange gods', some in fads, others in false religions, and others in what they fear will take from them their idols of comfort and well-being. These will not possess the Beatific Vision, which will satisfy all our desires according to God's holy will. In His Presence, all our hopes will be realized; all our wounds healed. All things must return to their origin in the Creator," said the priest, "in order for the creature to realize his final end or *purpose* for being. Of course, each person's mission is accomplished in the context of their particular circumstances. David, know that your longing and sadness is beautiful and holy. It is the natural expression of a soul longing to be one with his Creator."

David recalled his response, "Yes, Father, I long to serve Him in this life, in death and forever. I have always wanted to save souls, since childhood. The Saints tell us that, above all, Jesus on His Cross and even now in Heaven thirsts for souls, and I feel that I am one with Him in that thirst. I want to sacrifice my whole self to fulfill His desire for souls, but I realize I am far from *doing* that; it is a wish, because I am too weak and selfish."

"David, you must remember that it is our intentions that express the moral and spiritual content of our works; this offering is what is valuable to God, not the successful accomplishment of those intentions. He is God; He makes up for our limitations, even our failures. Remember, '*man proposes but God disposes*'; our 'success' is measured by the world's standards. An atheist might easily accomplish the same human goal you strive for in giving to the poor, for example, but it would have no value before God because the spiritual and moral value of an act is in the purpose or final cause for which it is done. Therefore, the widow's mite God accepted over the rich man's tithe of much greater monetary value. Therefore, place no value in your accomplishments, nor assume they are devalued because of your failures. Do not become discouraged when your projects fail. You must work for the glory of God, and only indirectly for yourself or other causes. Pursuing a sense of accomplishment is a selfish motive not worthy of a Christian. God will bring to fruition what His inscrutable Will desires. Your offering to Him should be works of Faith; that is all He desires of you, not whether you win or lose, because, of course, He is sufficient unto Himself. Continue on, David. The Lord is your Shepherd and your Guide. He has truly blessed you. But do not take your eyes off Him for a second, like Peter did when he was walking on water, or you too will sink into the deep. There are very *dark* waters beneath us, very intelligent, powerful, fallen angels, full of wickedness and hatred of all that is good. They roam about like ravenous lions, looking for vanity, complacency, pride and idleness, all tasty food for Satan. This exorcism should always be ready in your scabbard." He remembered they had prayed together the prayer they both knew well:

> *"St. Michael the Archangel, defend us in battle. Be our protection against the wickedness and snares of the devil. May God rebuke him we humbly pray and, do thou, O Prince of the Heavenly Host, by the divine power of God, cast into hell Satan and all the evil spirits who wander now throughout the world seeking the ruin of souls."*[18]

"We are in the Church Militant here on earth," Fr. Keogh had said. "It is good for us to long for our rest in the Church Triumphant in Heaven, inasmuch as that strengthens us in persevering *hope*, the virtue which brings us home; it gives birth to courage."

During this reverie, David had slowly walked with Angela to the highest point of the long, low limestone ledge that divided the expanse of this two-square mile field of grass. As they stood together on the arch of that gentle limestone brow, they saw St. Joseph's church far below them in a broad, grassy swale. It had the appearance of an ancient stone castle. Local granite, the oldest in the world, had been used to sheath the church's exterior; its design had a medieval aspect, presenting from this

---

[18] In 1886, Pope Leo XIII added this Prayer to Saint Michael[1] to the Leonine Prayers, which he had directed to be prayed after Low Mass two years earlier. *Wikipedia*.

distance what seemed like a beautiful gem set in the lush green vale. In David's moral vision, the Church was the throne of a Virgin ever pure, ready to bear a child of eternal spiritual fruit. The Maiden was clothed in the glorious wisdom of Timeless Ages. He imagined the Virgin gazing out of her castle window upon the endless fields of *eternity*, beckoning to the elect, her sons and daughters, to come home.

Chapter 3

SEVEN ASSASSINS

Late one afternoon a messenger walked up to the priest's cabin with a note signed by the pastor of St. Joseph's parish. It was an invitation for Fr. Keogh to say daily Mass at 9 am on the next day, Friday, at St. Joseph's, because the pastor was unable to say his usual Mass at that time due to a last-minute call to attend a parishioner on her deathbed near the furthest edge of his parish, which truly was an unusually large parish. He would have to go tomorrow, since it was too far to make the round-trip in one day. The messenger waited for a response. Fr. Keogh eagerly accepted the invitation, without seeking counsel.

David, ever suspicious of evil designs on the good priest, examined the typed but signed note, skeptically. Without evidence that proved it a forgery, David acquiesced in Fr. Keogh's joy at this rare *opportunity* which David found suspicious. They all planned to attend his Mass the next morning. David was inexplicably disturbed; he remained restless and worried, confiding only in Michael. David estimated that it would take them a leisurely hour and a half to walk there, so he agreed when Fr. Keogh suggested the two families leave no later than 7 AM, a half hour after he himself would leave.

Fr. Keogh left at 6:30 A.M. David's group managed to set off about 7:00 A.M. The group stopped briefly at the Meadow rocks for a rest. St. Joseph's Church lay as if in sweet slumber, a mile and a half away in the valley. The sun, rising behind the church, seemed to set it ablaze with a golden halo. The air was crisp and clear. David detected tension in himself and, it seemed to him, in the very atmosphere. He felt he would very soon be immersed in a struggle with some evil. He knew only one remedy; dropping to his knees near the rocks, he prayed that Jesus would send His Angels and Saints to help him in whatever trial he must face. He prayed that his spiritual Mother, whom Jesus had given him from His Cross might intercede for him, in order to procure protection for him and all those with him from any shadow of evil. Because Jesus loved her so much and because she was the Woman in Genesis destined by God to 'crush the head of the Serpent', David was confident in placing his care in her hands. Mary was held as the chief *mediatrix and intercessor*, appointed and established by God to obtain grace for mankind from the Father through Jesus Christ.

That very morning David had detected a lustful thought arise in himself as he woke Charlene. Even though he banished it immediately, he realized anew how flawed he was in the fallen human nature he and all mankind had inherited from Adam, a guilt inherited because Adam was the father of the human race and because all the members of that race had ratified that original sin by their own actual sins. Yet the Virgin Mary, the Church declared, was conceived *without* Original Sin. This *Immaculate Conception* prepared her worthy to be the Mother of God. This term can be understood only by those who believe that Jesus is divine, born by Mary, His entirely human Mother. Now, because of his inherited weakness to sin, David feared to meet the foe alone, so he asked God in prayer to be "*placed beneath the shield of the Immaculate Conception*", the title under which America is consecrated as one nation under God.

"Angela!" David called out.

"Yes?" said Angela, quickly coming up to him, ready to help.

"Sweetheart, I feel that we must do some penance as we approach the Holy Sacrifice of this Mass," said David earnestly, beseeching her help with a woeful expression.

Angela gathered all, and they briefly prayed together. Immediately afterwards, Charlene spoke to David, bashfully, as if ashamed of herself. "David," she said timidly, "if you would like to enter the parish grounds incognito, I confess that I borrowed your disguise make-up today and brought it with me." David looked keenly at her, wondering if she could have read his mind. "It was one of my jobs in high school," she said.

"When we had a play, I made up the actors. I brought it all, hoping we could have some fun using it today." Charlene opened a bag. "I thought it would be amusing for us to come made up as penitents, you know, pilgrims. You and Angela could be lepers. The rest of us could be cripples, maimed and distorted like the sinners we are."

"A fine idea, woman!" David proclaimed loud enough for all to hear, clasping her shoulders and smiling broadly at her suggestion. "One question, Charlene," David said, lowering his voice. "I noticed something in your bag that looked like one of those toy squirt gun cannons?"

When Charlene's laugh turned to giggles, she pointed an index finger at Michael, who came over, not knowing what was going on.

"Michael, would you like to explain," said David, with growing curiosity, as Charlene held the water pistol at arm's length in front of Michael's embarrassed, rapidly reddening countenance.

"Okay," Michael said, taking the toy gun. "I always like to be well armed, right? Now we are." He shot Charlene with a short blast. Then holding up the half gallon toy bazooka, he said, "It's full of holy water that Fr. Keogh blessed for me last night. I was probably going to tell you," Michael said sheepishly.

After Michael shot everyone at David's command, Charlene created two lepers and a band of crippled, penitential pilgrims. They all set out, praying the fifteen decades of the Rosary as they walked along, heads bowed under makeshift cowls. Their prayer intention was stated as *the conversion of all on earth to the one true Faith and our special protection today*. Forty-five minutes later, after the Glorious Mysteries had been said, Angela began to sing the Rosary's concluding prayer, the *Hail Holy Queen*. Her voice, it seemed to David, had an unusually angelic quality this morning, a harmony that was other-worldly, even beyond her superior natural abilities, as if another *Beautiful Woman* and her angelic companions were singing with her. The singing of the tiny band of pilgrims also seemed to have a volume above their ability to produce alone. In fact, David thought, the singing seemed perfect in every nuance; it was as if the singers were accompanied by a vast but invisible choir of angels, hovering in the sky just above them. David saw Angela's face lifted heavenward. It seemed to glow as she sang of the Blessed Mother, along with the angels she was named after. Today,

August 15, the Church celebrated *the Assumption of the Blessed Virgin Mary into Heaven.*

As they neared the church yard, David and Michael, for no apparent reason, became somber, nervous and intensely watchful, withdrawn into a self-defensive mode. They had a strong temptation to be overwhelmed with fear. Angela, seeing her love under silent duress, also became anxious. Three hundred yards from the church, the first clap of thunder sounded, without warning, like a cannonade fired just above and behind them. They all clapped their hands over their ears. Charlene jumped; when she looked overhead, she screamed. Frightful, ugly, pitch black, roiling clouds *growled* close above them, like monstrous, chained mastiffs, viciously seeking to tear them apart. David thought in desperation, 'I have never experienced anything even close to this. It's unnatural, *diabolical.*' He remembered that there had been no weather-warning that morning on the radio.

* * *

Little did David know how right he was about the diabolical, for Satan, drooling, red faced, in a towering rage, rode the clouds above them, hidden in a giant thunderhead descending on the helpless little church below. Satan had stationed his seedy ogres, evil minions one and all, outside the church building below, a building made holy by the Sacrament of the Lord, which it enclosed like an architectural tabernacle. These creepy, dead dogs of Lucifer could not enter the church without the "invitation" of a crime or a sacrilege, which they all knew this filthy, impoverished, flee bitten, worthless little priest was incapable of, with his better than thou sanctity, a sanctity they *detested*, ridiculed and spit upon.

This gang of seven diabolical ogres, minions of Satan, scoffed as they gnashed their sharp teeth, thirsting for bloody *Vengeance*! They had been given absolute orders, commands from the Chief, to murder these miserable Davidians, creatures that had so far been protected by their angelic cheerleaders up there. The villainous sarcasm of these seven, thinly disguised, diabolical assassins dripped from their lips, like poison from a rattlesnake's hollow fangs. It was indeed a deadly contest between champions of good and evil on which the future fate of many hinged. But to the ogres the two sides seemed laughably unequal, and so they believed the outcome was foreordained in their favor. The seven ogres and their master, Satan, were so confident of victory, they were *popping* with pride, baring their terrible, putrid-yellow fangs in malicious anticipation of a meal for their *insatiable hatred* for these human *worms*, so far beneath them, yet preposterously and unfairly capable of receiving the eternal bliss they themselves had lost forever due to their pride, a pride in their intelligence and other natural perfections of which they preened themselves like birds of prey, above all because they defied their Creator with infinite malice. Why, they whined, didn't *they* get a second chance like humanity did? Why didn't God bend over backwards for them *too* with His offer to trade mere repentance for infinite Mercy. Instead He had snatched from them so many sinners, who should have been theirs.

Cloaked in large cowls and flowing, black, rotten robes full of worm holes, these eternal whiners hoped to *deceive* these merely *human idiots* as to the preternatural monstrosities they were. Their pride and pleasure was in being *evil.* They waited to pounce on these inferior creatures like savage animals, each with his own unique, perverted nature and corrupted character: therefore, one resembled a leopard, the others, a snake, a dog, a bear, a condor, a deadly spider and a ravenous shark, even though they appeared to be humans. Apparently, these seven assassins formed a small band of itinerant mendicant monks, each one leaning slightly against the thick stone walls of the small village shops across the street from the oldest church in all the land. Large wooden beads *resembling* a fifteen-decade rosary hung in a large loop from under their hooded black cloaks, from waist to bare mid-leg.

These proud seven waited, watching for that man, his companion and their slutty consorts; they waited to devour them whole, but only after tearing them to pieces alive with their horrible teeth, spilling their steaming guts onto the earth! Then, they intended to *ritually decapitate them* with long razor-sharp fingernails at the tips of huge bone crushing fingers. A similar fate would follow for their sorry little black robe, for whom their hellish 'King' might direct them to deal out an even more gruesome fate, since his most Horrible Majesty imagined that priests usurped *his* place as man's natural leader and savior, thus impeding his grim harvest of souls for Hell, an unendurable home, where he (Satan) feasted all day on souls, each one tormented by the certain knowledge of their very *own eternal loss*! Satan greedily gobbled up the habitual sensuality of these souls, damned because they had served it or some other personal idol with their pride while on earth, procuring for their senses special vanities, thus hanging themselves on a gibbet of their own choosing, like Judas.

Suddenly, David and his band, now in the outer courtyard of the church, clapped their ears in pain and alarm as they heard and felt the wildly clanging church bells in the tower far above them. David yelled at Michael who was nervously playing with his squirt gun, "Something's wrong!! Fr. Keogh is calling us. That was an *alarm*!" They ran the remaining eighty yards in seconds. Seven deadly demons followed them with evil glinting eyes but apparently deceived themselves, seeing only two disgusting lepers, instead of the worthy warriors they were expecting. The holy angels secretly assisted this deception, as did St. Michael, his exorcism prayer still on David's lips as he ran like the wind, finally reaching the church doors.

Fr. Keogh met them inside, his eyes wide and bloodshot with alarm. "David, I prayed you would come when I rang the bells out of tune and at the wrong time."

"Father," David broke in, "what's wrong?"

"A giant man in a dark cloak with terrible, inhuman teeth and eyes, threatened me and the whole congregation just now if I dared to say Mass. He told me to cancel Mass, immediately!"

"What was the threat, Father?"

"Death, instant torturous death."

David looked around. "Father, how big was this man?"

"Huge! He was probably eight feet tall, David, and muscular, maybe four hundred pounds or more. I know, that's hard to believe."

David looked around. He saw a giant, cloaked in black, leaning slightly against the white latticed arbor of a residential gateway across the way. The giant was watching them, as David peeked through the doors; he turned to Michael, as if he hadn't seen anything and whispered his plan out of the side of his mouth.

"Father, please go prepare for Holy Mass, but first instruct three men to close these double doors and lock them behind us. Then tell them to only let Michael and me or known parishioners in. Tell them we will shout, 'Blessed be the name of Jesus' when we need the doors opened *immediately*."

The priest turned to go without asking any questions, since he trusted David implicitly, and he prayed for him intensely from that moment, sensing extraordinary danger.

After instructing Angela and Charlene inside the vestibule, David and Michael went outside to sit on a black, wrought-iron bench under the apple trees that surrounded the small, half-round, cobblestone courtyard in front of the double entrance doors of the church, ten yards away. They pretended to joke and horse around with some abandon. After some minutes had passed, they idly got up and waltzed down the narrow street, idly looking into the shop windows, apparently trying to kill time. Then they turned up the inclined sidewalk where they would pass in front of the giant "monk" who was still leaning against the white arbor laced in dark green ivy. Michael, taking the inside of the walkway, playfully shot David a couple of times with the ghetto blaster squirt gun, both laughing raucously. Wicked eyes followed them, deadly serious but not suspecting who they were. Before passing the giant, Michael laid the gun in the crook of his arm, barrel pointing down and toward the street, as if to assure the stranger that he had no intent of any monkey business in his regard. They both bowed their heads, as if to modestly defer to the presence of a religious.

But just as they passed, David slightly nudged Michael, who wheeled swiftly and squirted a full, hard blast of holy water through the facial opening of the ogre's cowl. The demon threw his giant hands to his face and screamed a blood curdling cry of agony and despair, reputedly heard miles away. The dead body inhabited by the demon, like a black widow inhabits an empty skull, went limp as the demon fled, severely "burned" by the holy water.

David and Michael ran furiously for the doors of the church, as six other "monks" pursued them. They were inside, after shouting the entrance code, seconds before a tremendous force hit the doors. It would have been a greater force if Michael had not squirted the outer doors liberally with holy water before the "monks" reached them. Five men braced the thick wooden doors from the inside, waiting for the next assault, but it turned out to be relatively weak and half-hearted. David asked the men if they would attend Mass while standing guard at the doors, in case there was another attempt to break in. David knew these demons would be waiting for them after Mass, but he did not yet have a plan for that engagement.

* * *

It felt safe inside the church, even as thunder rumbled outside as if wanting to invade the house of the Lord. Violent thunder shook the church like waves when they pound full force against the hull of a ship at sea in a great storm. Fr. Keogh began the celebration by heavily incensing the altar and the entire nave and vestibule of the church with the smoke of blessed frankincense, chanting the Church's ancient ritual of exorcism.

"The traditional Mass is said in Latin by the priest," David whispered into Michael's ear, by way of this opportunity for instruction. "Even the real Vatican II Council ordered Latin preserved in the Mass." They knelt in the fifth row of pews. "We can read the strict English translation of the Latin," he said, showing him the parallel Latin/English texts in their St. Pius X missal. "See, here, the Mass begins with Psalm 42. It has the Latin on the left, the English on the right."

> **Psalm 42**: *'Do me justice O God, and fight my fight against a faithless people; from the deceitful and impious man rescue me. ... Send forth Your light and Your fidelity; they shall lead me on and bring me to Your holy mountain and to Your dwelling-place.'*
>
> It was a High Mass, so they stood for the recitation of the "Gloria":
>
> "**Glory to God** *in the highest. And on earth peace to men of good will. We praise You. We bless You. We adore You.*

We glorify You. We give You thanks for Your great glory. O Lord God, heavenly King, God the Father Almighty. O Lord Jesus Christ, the Only-begotten Son. O Lord God, Lamb of God, Son of the Father: You Who take away the sins of the world, have mercy on us. You Who take away the sins of the world, receive our prayer. You Who sit at the right hand of the Father, have mercy on us. For You alone are holy. You alone are the Lord. You alone, O Jesus Christ, are most high. Together with the Holy Spirit in the glory of God the Father. Amen."[19]

"Now comes the reading of the Gospel, then the priest's homily, followed by the Creed, which states our core beliefs," explained David.

Fr. Keogh stepped up to the lectern and began, "Before reading, interpreting, and discussing the Word of God, I would lead us in seeking divine inspiration. Therefore, we will pray the same prayer we pray before reading Holy Scripture:

'Come Holy Spirit, *fill the hearts of thy faithful and enkindle in them the fire of Thy love. Send forth Thy spirit and they shall be created. And Thou shalt renew the face of the earth. Let us pray. O God, Who didst instruct the hearts of the faithful by the light of the Holy Spirit, grant us by the same Spirit to have a right judgment in all things and ever to rejoice in His consolation. Through Christ our Lord. Amen.'*[20]

"The **Gospel** according to St. John, Chapter 1, verses 11-14," said Fr. Keogh in a strong voice:

'He came unto his own, and his own received him not. But as many as received him he gave to them power to be made

---

[19] The Gloria is one of the oldest hymns sung by the Church. It was first sung by the angels the night that Christ was born in Bethlehem. https://epicpew.com/gloria-history-mass-hymn/

[20] https://catholic-link.org/quotes/come-holy-spirit-prayer/

> *sons of God, to them that believe in his name. Who are born, not of blood, nor of the will of the flesh, nor of the will of man, but of God. And the Word was made flesh, and dwelt among us: and we saw his glory, the glory as of the only begotten of the Father, full of grace and truth.'*

Fr. Keogh began his homily. "In verse 11 we read, *'his own received him not.'* The author refers literally and specifically to the chosen race of Israel, who rejected God in their rejection of Jesus, the Second Person of the Trinity made Man, their true Messiah, whom they did not recognize especially because of the arrogance and presumption of their leaders, the ecclesiastical hierarchy. Now that we of the Church have become God's chosen people, *we too can reject God* by the same sins of arrogance, hypocrisy, and presumption. God respects our free will, the only faculty by which we can love Him by acceptance or hate Him by rejection. Be *very* careful not to presume on your good fortune in possessing the gift of divine Faith, which is greater but similar to what Israel received as God's chosen people. Pride and its consequences were modeled for us by Lucifer's fall and by the Pharisees of Jesus' time. Both had the greatest of Good offered to them by God, but they were too proud to be *grateful to Him*, seeking rather to *possess His gifts as if they were their own*, thus essentially rejecting these heavenly gifts. Remember that your knowledge of the Faith and so much more are *unmerited gifts*. Yes, God comes to us as Catholics in the fullness of truth, but we are not saved by the fact of His selective generosity, any more than the Israelites were saved by the fact that God chose them, from all the peoples of the earth, to bear in their generation, for the sake of all peoples of all times, the 'seed' of Jesus Christ, the 'fruit' of Mary's most pure womb, the Messiah, the Word of God, the Savior of mankind. It was out of pride that they rejected their personal Savior and by their office and leadership, the Savior of their Nation."

"We all know that if we are *offered* something good, we will not *possess* this good unless we accept it, with gratitude. If we think it is ours by right or it is ours because we have earned it, or because it was prophesized of old to be reserved for us, then it will not in truth be ours; if something is given but not accepted, it may be taken away and given to others (e.g., the Gentiles), perhaps less worthy or prepared, but who will at least receive the Gift with *gratitude*, considering it an honor and a great good, *wholly unmerited* by them. Here we recall the parable of the King offended because the invited guests made excuses for not coming to the wedding feast, so he invited the poor off the streets."

"However, God will keep His promises to His first love (the Jews who believed in Him, i.e., those with true Faith), provided they are shriven of arrogance and ready to receive Him worthily. Those Jews in the past who suffered for God's name, unwittingly as martyrs for the Faith, will be saved. True, in some sense these will have given their life for God. And so, the true Jews of every age will be allowed to accept the true Messiah at the end of time in a similar way that the Patriarchs worshipped Christ by foresight; He Who was their true Messiah. The Church has declared infallibly that a baptism of desire is provided for those invincibly ignorant."

Fr. Keogh preached in a high, sonorous voice, which *penetrated*. "'Many are called, few are chosen' said Jesus.[21] And who are chosen but those who choose to receive Him with gratitude and become dependent upon Him, those who believe in His name and all that name represents, which includes His divinity and everything that He taught, because as the Creator of all that is, He becomes the Author of Truth Itself."

"And to those who believe, the Bible says, 'He gave the power to be made sons of God,'[22] and this means, of course, adopted sons of God, *as if* we were truly God's sons, not as naturally so and therefore deserving but through *unmerited adoption*. Sons by Nature would be impossible. Isaac blessed *Jacob*, his younger son, as if he were the elder, the first born; by *God*, Jacob was indeed the firstborn, in the spirit. So, it was by *God's* election, not by nature (order of birth) that Jacob received the blessing to become Israel, the father of God's chosen people, from whom Jesus was descended. For as the Bible relates, Esau was the first-born, but Isaac, the father, by God's divine Providence mistook Jacob for Esau, to whom the blessing of the firstborn was customarily due. Likewise, Christians are identified with Christ, their guilt as sinners *passed over*

---

[21] St. Matthew 22:14

[22] St. John 1:12

as the firstborn of God, adopted because of their Faith in God. We are elevated by God's free election to be seen in the likeness of Christ, as other christs, i.e., Christians, but we are so chosen because of our true beliefs. Nevertheless, it is God's choice that we are adopted *sons of God*. Furthermore, we might believe in Christ and be candidates for adoption, but if we do not practice what we believe, we will still be chosen as Christians but condemned for not using the graces (talents) we were given. In so doing, we would have been Christians in name only, not actually remaking ourselves in the image of Christ. Rather, we would resemble Esau, who received no actual blessing, only his invitation by birth. Esau was unrecognizable as conformable to God's Crucified Son, the Lamb of God. Historically, Esau (the Edomites) were enemies of Israel. Cradle Catholics are the seed in Jesus' parable that fell on various soils. When we actually believe in all that Christ said and did, and take up our cross to follow Him, we are like the seed which falls on rich soil, but we must do more than pronounce His name or profess 'Jesus is Lord' to be saved. If we *believe* in someone, it means we believe in who they *are* and will follow them. Even if we acknowledge that Jesus is both God and Man, we are not yet saved. What *I actually say and do* reveals who *I am*, and to *believe in me* is not just to believe that I exist or to acknowledge me or to believe I am who I say I am, much less is it just to believe in me by pronouncing my name, but it is to first *identify me* by attributing to me, correctly, *all* that I actually said and what I meant by that; then, to follow me by doing as I command; as Jesus said to his Apostle Phillip who asked, 'Lord, how do we love you' and Jesus answered, '*keep My commandments*'[23]. Yes, obedience is to love and serve."

"For example: if you know from what I have actually said that I believe in the existence of angels, you will know, if I am not lying, that a person taking my name but contradicting that doctrine is *not* me. We know what Jesus said; it has been preserved by *His Church* and the Bible, which are, together, the treasury of divine truth. Those who impersonate Christ, by confusing what He taught, are heretics and deceivers; if not by intention, they are, in fact, 'false prophets', snakes in the grass. It is our responsibility to recognize these false christs and not follow them;

---

[23] St. John 14:15

for all Christians are vulnerable guppies because of their fallen human nature but supernaturally wise in being sons of God."

"*God's* Church, divinely instituted for all time by Jesus *through the Holy Spirit*, preserves *all* that Jesus *actually said and meant*, interpreted for us by the same Holy Spirit, the third Person of the Trinity. Only the Holy Spirit can preserve the Word of God over the ages in the hearts and minds of fallible, wayward men, because He is God. To believe in Jesus, we must believe in what He said and meant to say, not just *that* He said 'something like that', to be interpreted as the individual pleases. This makes the individual 'like unto God', Lucifer's error, and such is the 'heart' of heresy. The human heart is not God, Whose Holy Spirit knows for certain what He meant."

"When we read Scripture, we must always consult the Holy Spirit He sent. Private interpretation of Scripture is the essence of the Protestant heresy. Jesus says that He Himself is the Head and we are the body of His Church. Jesus' one true Church brings the Truth to us, perfectly preserved by the Holy Ghost, two thousand years later, not what various self-authorized sects say Truth is. True, the Catholic Church is full of fallible sometimes diabolically wicked men, but God can dodge them or make use of them as His instruments in the ecclesiastical hierarchy He has established. Otherwise, God would have instituted a Church powerless to perpetuate His Truth, which is impossible of a loving God. He would also, thereby, despise the very concept of truth, which by definition is one in meaning and divine in origin. Many today, in saying the name of Jesus claim to be Christians, but they have not received Christ by their submission to what He actually said and meant, namely the *Deposit of Faith*. We must first *know* God in order to *love and serve Him*. He came, but it is largely true even today that His own chosen people know Him not; in fact, many reject Him."

"Can the elect correctly interpret Scripture? Note that our Scripture says: "*the sons of God … who are born, not of blood, nor of the will of the flesh, nor of the will of man, but of God*"[24]. Yes, the elect can correctly interpret Scripture though the assistance of the Spirit of God Whom they received at their baptism. This proves that God can have His

[24] St. John 1:13

elect. On the other hand, heretics are born of the flesh, of their own will, but not of the Holy Spirit. The elect generally have the right Spirit of judgement, but also Scripture itself, being the Word of God, is intrinsically understandable to the elect, because they 'are of' God, the *sons of God*, wholly reborn as 'a new creation' upon receiving their Redeemer, who is also their Creator. Only pride rejects one's Savior, as I have said, but if these proud repent and humbly ask for Him, He will swoop down like an eagle and take them up to Himself, no matter what the circumstances of their fall from grace, for He is the God of eternal Love and infinite Mercy, capable of making something from nothing, physical or spiritual, restoring what is lost. Say to Him with me *now*," Fr. Keogh raised his voice and his arms, like Moses mowing down Amalec, David imagined. Fr. Keogh looked out upon his congregation for a moment before leading them in a prayer of submission: "I *am* nothing and I can *have* and *do* nothing without You, Lord."

The whole congregation repeated that prayer with their priest, either out loud or silently, like Michael with only his lips moving, but eyes believing. "Now, if you said that prayer sincerely," said the priest, "you are empty of pride and you are ready to receive Christ in Holy Communion." Fr. Keogh left the pulpit.

Michael turned his head and whispered to David, "This priest helps me believe by understanding. It's like Jesus is talking to me, and I can't help but believe."

David nodded in assent and whispered to the friend he loved, "That is a sign of Faith. Now comes the Creed where we profess it."

Fr. Keogh and the congregation stood to recite the Apostle's Creed:

> *I believe in God, the Father almighty, Creator of heaven and earth, and in Jesus Christ, his only Son, our Lord; who was conceived by the Holy Spirit, born of the Virgin Mary, suffered under Pontius Pilate, was crucified, died, and was buried. He descended into hell; the third day he rose again from the dead; he ascended into heaven, sitteth at the right hand of God, the Father almighty, from thence he shall come to judge the living and the dead. I believe in the Holy Spirit, the Holy Catholic Church, the communion of saints,*

> *the forgiveness of sins, the resurrection of the body, and life everlasting. Amen.*[25]

Turning slightly to Michael, David whispered out of the side of his mouth, "Let's go to the vestibule and check on things."

"Those guarding the double-doors said all was quiet."

So, David turned to his friend and continued in a low voice. "Now the priest, in our behalf will offer to God what is ours, by His Providence, bread and wine, but wholly insufficient in itself for the Transubstantiation and divine Sacrifice that is taking place. We call this part of the Mass *the Offertory*: where man presents common, unleavened bread and grape wine to God, representing the fruits of our labors, just like the insufficient five loaves and three fish given to Jesus by the disciples before a hungry crowd of five thousand. Jesus blessed the small amount of fish and bread and it was multiplied enough to feed the multitude. In the Eucharist, Michael, Christ transforms the little we offer into the Spiritual Food of His Divine Self for the multitude of those who worthily come to receive Him in Holy Communion. Catholics believe Christ gave Himself to the multitude of all times at the Last Supper, through the ministry of His Apostles and the divine Church He instituted. But many left Him, unable to believe Him:

> *'Then Jesus said to them: Amen, amen I say unto you: Except you eat the flesh of the Son of man, and drink his blood, you shall not have life in you. He that eateth my flesh, and drinketh my blood, hath everlasting life: and I will raise him up in the last day. For my flesh is meat indeed: and my blood is drink indeed. He that eateth my flesh, and drinketh my blood, abideth in me, and I in him. … After this many of his disciples went back; and walked no more with him.'*[26]

---

[25] The **Apostles' Creed** (Latin: *Symbolum Apostolorum* or *Symbolum Apostolicum*), sometimes titled the **Apostolic Creed** or the **Symbol of the Apostles**, is an early statement of Christian belief—a creed or «symbol». Wikipedia

[26] St. John 6:53-56, 66

"How about Abraham's offering of his own son, Isaac?" whispered Michael.

"Right on!" exclaimed David softly, in admiration. "Abraham's offering, as great as it was, was also insufficient to erase man's offenses to his God, therefore, Isaac, an archetype of Christ, was spared, a beneficiary of Salvation (while Christ was not spared), but Abraham's offering was not spurned, because his gift of faith to God was accepted and credited to him as if his willingness to sacrifice Isaac was acceptable as justification, so that we still call him 'the Father of Faith'. The 'Lamb of God' would come in God's time to save mankind, including Abraham and Isaac. Abraham's sacrifice of his only son and heir in Faith was in fact a great petition to God for a Redeemer, to be fulfilled by the eternal Sacrifice of God's only begotten Son on the Cross. Only Jesus, the God-Man, can effectively be the Sacrificial Lamb of God who satisfies God's Justice, which is *infinitely offended* by our sins." David was so happy he had a disciple who was willing to listen and learn and who could now stand beside him as an apostolic warrior.

After they took a seat in their pew again, David whispered, "Now is the time for the Consecration, Michael, when the bread and wine are *transubstantiated* by the Power of God to become the *substance* of the Body and Blood, Soul and Divinity of Jesus Christ, under the *appearances* of bread and wine. We mortals cannot see the reality with our senses, any more than the Apostles could see how Jesus fed five thousand with a few loaves and a little fish. Belief is credited to the fact that we are reborn as 'sons of God', just as St. Paul said. Faith in *Jesus*, the *Word* of God, is divine, Michael, *supernatural!* This sacrament proves that. It's hard to believe that what God said is *actually* true. It is the personal identification with Christ *Himself*. It is the supreme test of one's Faith in Jesus: His Divinity, His Power, His Real Presence. By this we actually acknowledge and receive Him, God and Man, Flesh and Blood, Soul and Divinity."

"The choice is this: we either believe and trust in God's Word as recorded in Scripture, or we trust in our senses, our human ideas and reason. The Faith to believe comes from the Father in Heaven for those who *ask for it*. Remember Jesus' words to Peter, '*flesh and blood has not revealed it to thee, but My Father who is in Heaven*'[27]. Belief in the Real Presence is the defining belief of a member of Christ's Catholic Church. It is *de fide*. A valid Consecration can only be done by a legally ordained priest who believes what he is doing and is given the powers of Christ in the Sacrament of Holy Orders."

"If Jesus can feed the Five Thousand, I'm a believer, like you," said Michael, secretly warming David's heart.

Facing God, with his back to the congregation he represents, Fr. Keogh elevated the Host and said: "All of you take and eat of this, ***For this is My Body.***" Then he said, "... take and drink ye all of this (the chalice of wine), **for this is the chalice of my Blood** *of the new and eternal testament, the mystery of Faith; which shall be shed for you and for many unto the remission of sins.*"[28]

Those who received Holy Communion from Fr. Keogh had to kneel and receive on the tongue only, the traditional *norm* of the Church. A paten was held beneath their chin to catch any crumbs, for each particle of the Host contained the entire Body, Blood, Soul and Divinity of Jesus Christ.

"Fr. Keogh never gives Communion in the hand," David explained in a whisper to Michael before he entered the receiving line, "because each crumb that may fall to the ground in being handled is the entire substance of Our Lord, Jesus Christ, which makes the practice of Communion in the hand sacrilegious." After the final blessing, Fr. Keogh told the congregation that all who would process around the Church with him, in honor of the Real Presence of Jesus Christ in the Eucharist would receive a special blessing.

Before the procession began, the priest said "Benediction," where a consecrated Host, was held in the center of a gold "monstrance". Much incense was used before Fr. Keogh blessed the people by making the sign of the cross over the congregation with the monstrance. Before greeting the people, the priest called for Michael and David to follow closely behind him.

"Be ready," Fr. Keogh said. Then he turned to David and said with

---

[27] St. Matthew 16:17

[28] https://www.linktoliturgy.com/liturgy-of-the-eucharist-part-2

a confident smile, "This should take care of your problem with the demons. Thanks for your many favors to me."

The remaining "Dark Monks" were waiting for them, six black figures standing abreast, hands folded, as if in prayer. Fr. Keogh came through the ornate double doors. David and Michael stepped to the right and to the left of him, each holding a blessed candle. Father Keogh had the faculties of an exorcist. Like all powers dispensed by the Church, they were based on the infinite merits of Christ held in the Church "Treasury". Fr. Keogh commanded all the "monks", whom he had just put under the power of exorcism, to kneel. Then he commanded them to remove their cowls out of respect for the Sacrament. As each did so in turn, he blessed them with the Real Presence of God in the monstrance. David saw each one physically shrink, becoming totally submissive and terrified, as if before their *Absolute Judge* who reminded them of their eternal sentence of doom. Intense fear warped their visible forms, eliciting from each one of them frightful screams and groans of horror. The priest continued his exorcism in Latin, making repeated signs of the cross over each one of them. The wicked growls and screams of despair, some reportedly heard a mile away, accompanied the complete exorcism of the demons inhabiting each body, bodies which returned to that state in which they had been before possession. After the demons exited from the material forms they had inhabited, they left behind only putrid heaps of rotted flesh, dry bones, or the recently deceased bodies of damned souls abandoned by the demonic spirits that had given them the motions and appearance of life. Michael's eyes were widened permanently by the signs of the demonic and the priest's real-time demonstration of Almighty God's power over them.

After the procession of the laity led by the priest had ended, David noticed in Michael a demeanor much different than before, one showing a profound respect for the sacred, a greater awareness of the ongoing battle between angelic spirits of pure good and pure evil raging around him. The conviction of his own helplessness settled over him. David prayed that all people could have this humility for the good of their souls, just as Michael now seemed to be a humble, grateful suppliant, rather than the proud warrior he had thought himself to be.

When David saw Michael wrapped in awe, humbled by the

supernatural, he saw them both as actors upon a stage. Walking home now over a sunny meadow and a faultless blue sky, David reflected on their role of apostolic warriors, a kind of Paul and Barnabas team, shredding error with the sword of truth, their Faith a trusty shield against the flaming arrows of unbelief and heresy that both flattered and intimidated the people of the world, keeping them from pastures of the Everlasting Hills, where their Divine Shepherd would lead them. He and Michael would have to summon more courage, hope and charity for God and neighbor than ever before and be willing to lay down their lives as martyrs for souls secretly yearning for the safety of Salvation. God smiled on David and eventually blessed this enterprise, in the meantime exercising him with obstacles and trials, as his strength could manage and his Faith merited.

At 3 AM that night a great and frightful earthquake occurred, in which both David and Fr. Keogh detected the impending Wrath of God. They suspected that the Warning was imminent. The priest gathered all in his chapel, where he lit a blessed beeswax candle for each person. Fr. Keogh had some instructions to impart, for which they all sat around his beautiful round oak table, a three-hundred-year old heirloom shipped to him at his ordination from County Donegal, Ireland.

Fr. Keogh began, "All just anger is motivated by the desire to correct an injustice. Therefore, God's just anger or 'wrath' is due to His Justice, offended by sins against His Love for us. The sins of mankind caused their eternal fate to be in jeopardy. Out of Love for our eternal destiny, God is determined to help us by a correction determined by what will capture our attention. I think we all realize that the world we live in has reached a level of sinfulness that requires a swift kick in the butt, and that would be this frightful Warning."

"But we may justly appeal to God for a mitigation of His wrath after our repentance, because we naturally seek deliverance from the full punishment for our sins, however much deserved, because we rightly fear we cannot endure it. When we see genuine contrition, we are inclined to be merciful, just as contrition for sin moves God to forgiveness. Perfect contrition (sorrow primarily because we have offended God) is difficult for us, if not impossible. Jesus provides the equivalent of perfect contrition in the Sacrament of Penance, where through the divine power delegated to the priest, the merits of Christ procure forgiveness and mercy for the penitent by way of Jesus' perfect contrition for us before the Judgment seat of Almighty God, while the penitent brings only imperfect contrition to the confessional."

"I will now hear your confessions in the far corner of this room," said Fr. Keogh. "Remember that *only* in this Sacrament of Penance will God absolve us from our sins even when we have only imperfect contrition, i.e., sorrow for our sins because of the punishments due to them."

All bowed their heads in unaffected sorrow, recalling their sins, long passed and those more recent. Everyone's confession was finally heard. After everyone had gathered at table again, Fr. Keogh said, "We are finite beings, but we have immortal souls which have offended an infinite God. We are unable to repair or remove the offense; therefore, we are blessed to have a Savior who is both God and Man at once. As Man, He assumed the guilt of all humanity, but suffered for it and paid its eternal price as God only could. Jesus overcame the death of sin because He is *Eternal Life itself*."

The priest prepared them for the Warning by showing them how they should lie on the floor face down, arms outstretched as if on a cross, in order to show conformity with their Savior, ready to receive His Warning with humility. Fr. Keogh then read from the last book of the Bible, the Apocalypse, chapter 6, verses 12-17, which described the opening of the 'sixth seal', which in his opinion described the terrible Wrath of God's Warning. He led them in various prayers and readings for an hour. Finally, in anticipation of the Great Warning, he recalled the instruction: "Do not go outdoors, even out of curiosity, because we are not meant to witness the wrath of God. Such curiosity or arrogance, we are assured through prophecies, will be punished by immediate death."

The Warning came with the sunrise; it lasted only five minutes, but as the seer of Garabandal said, 'dying is preferable to it'. Those who desired to please God, benefited from the Warning's correction of their consciences by repentance, because they had love for the truth and the good. Others, being totally unprepared in their hardened unrepentance, died of shock or heart failure (as prophesied). There was weeping in the cabin because of fear mixed with sorrow for past sins, but when it was over, there were also tears of relief, because a stress, endured beyond anything in nature, had ceased.

Hours later, Charlene and Michael asked Fr. Keogh what happened to the demonic ogres dressed as monks. "They were banished to Hell, instantly, by the Presence of God, because they cannot endure the Real Presence of God, which for them is far worse than enduring their just desserts in Hell. This analogy may help you understand," said Fr. Keogh. "In the presence of Christ, a demon is blinded by His Light, and there is no greater pain than intense light to the eyes. Imagine the light in an eye exam or someone coming into full sunlight after years in absolute darkness. That is why being in the state of sanctifying grace is a protection against molestation or possession by evil spirits who cannot endure the presence of God in our soul. When in possession of sanctifying grace, demons are afraid of you; even though God may allow them to tempt you, they cannot hurt you without your permission through sin; for them to attack you would be like a rabbit attacking a mountain lion. Even they are not that stupid," Fr. Keogh concluded, leaning back in his recliner to rest after many hours of vigilance. David noted that when the priest was preaching, he seemed to glow like a lava-lamp with vital energy, but at rest, that animation faded like the coals of a dying campfire. David concluded that his spirit was alive, even while his body was dying.

Chapter 4

HIS WORD IS THE WAY

David, Michael and Fr. Keogh sat around the Franklin wood stove talking, long after the girls and the children were in bed. Each couple had separate, curtained-off bedrooms temporarily set up within the priest's cabin; this was not only a necessity before their building plans materialized, but they still needed each other's company after all they had been through in the last few days. David knew the priest preferred his solitude, so in the warmth of the stove he laid out their plans, both immediate and long-term.

"Father, after building cabins for our families, Michael and I want to travel from city to city fighting ignorance, educating poor souls in the truths necessary for their salvation. Of course, we hope to move them toward conversion to the true Faith," said David, as he and Michael conversed with Fr. Keogh across his oak table heirloom. "I would like to believe that the Great Warning of a merciful God which we have just experienced would be enough for the people of this land, but I think we know that they will still need much help correctly defining and making fruitful this great experience. Satan's minions, aka BIG BROTHER's Mainstream Media, is already styling the Warning as a natural event people should forget."

"I agree with you, David. The need for conversion is very great now, because without it we approach the Great Chastisement, in which at least two-thirds of mankind will die and meet their eternal Judge. We can't even imagine over 4.5 billion people out of seven or eight billion dying within six days!" exclaimed Fr. Keogh. "How can I help you, David?" he asked, leaning forward.

"We both need sound, doctrinal training," pleaded David.

"I volunteer," said Fr. Keogh.

"If you want a larger room for gatherings, instructions or Mass, we could build onto this cabin for you, Father. We will draw up some rough plans for add-on options, for your approval, of course."

"First let's look at those plans, David; then I will decide," said the priest.

The two newly commissioned *lay missionaries*, as they preferred to be called, went to visit Badger. They kept a nest egg of stored gold for future eventualities at his place. David and Michael liked to spend gold in the local economy, for its better health and independence, so they bought a small wagon and harness for Paintbrush to pull. They also purchased with a single gold coin plenty of feed for the pony and their other animals at the cabin, a pig and a milk cow, plus grain and other necessities for Fr. Keogh and their own families in lieu of their future absence.

Badger was told by the men that Angela and Charlene had drawing rights on the gold, as needed. They put a generous portion of gold in a fund for local, real-time charity cases. Badger volunteered to manage the fund in their behalf as his charitable contribution. They returned to town several more times for interior building materials, while the timber for construction of the cabins was cut from their own Lodgepole forest on their recently purchased land, thinning it for its health and longevity. They had given their mining mules to two destitute families who had the land to make good use of them for plowing.

While in town for the last time, upon visiting an orphanage, they were especially taken with two orphaned children. The Second War for Independence had taken a significant death toll in Wyoming leaving many orphans. When they arrived at the priest's cabin with a load of building materials, the two orphaned boys, each from different families, were given to their new mothers, Angela and Charlene, who embraced them, remarking with fond surprise at their heart rending, needy hugs. As the days passed, the boys learned how to help their mothers in all their many chores.

Because everyone needed privacy, especially with the sound of playing children, the two men built a quarter mile from the priest's cabin and an equal distance from each other. Before they left the cave of the eagles, they had given it to a homeless, six-member Indian family, who insisted on buying it from them for several tanned deer hides, which David accepted graciously, mostly for the sake of their dignity. Later he used the hides to make moccasins for his and Michael's families, while showing them all the rudiments of working leather.

The two "missionaries" first practiced their team-teaching locally in required classes of instruction under the supervision of Fr. Keogh. They sometimes found their own wives to be powerful witnesses, especially in regard to the women and young children. The two future missionaries concentrated on assisting the priest in building up his parish, since priests educated in the true Faith, were the focal point and the foundation of all Catholic religious activity, the *alto Christus*. Jesus had delegated His priests, bishops and Apostles, especially Peter, to act in His place, telling them: "*And I will give to thee the keys of the kingdom of heaven. And whatsoever thou shalt bind upon earth, it shall be bound also in heaven: and whatsoever thou shalt loose upon earth, it shall be loosed also in heaven.*"[29]

"Why would Jesus say that if He intended only to spiritually minister Himself, without *delegating* His priestly powers?" David asked this rhetorical question in one of his instruction classes. "For Jesus to verbally delegate the authority only He had to the Apostles (and those bishops of the Church who followed in their footsteps), but intend what He said to be merely rhetorical would be to contradict Himself (lie) and deliberately confuse us. But God does *not* deceive anyone or contradict Himself." David noted that such lessons were also arguments for those who subscribed to certain heresies he might have to face as a missionary; he saw their present catechesis as equivalent to storing ammo for future apologetic 'warfare'.

One month later, after they had been thoroughly instructed and tested by Fr. Keogh, he blessed them before they hit the road as disciples of Jesus acting under His authority in offering daily instructions in the one true Faith wherever they went to any and all who would listen,

[29] Matthew 16:19

'shaking the dust from their feet' in witness to those who rejected them or their Gospel message. One day on the road they came up with the idea to put their fame as patriot warriors to good use by setting up a privately owned, nationally syndicated talk show with an up-front, Catholic, apologetic objective. They would draw an audience with their war accounts, and in the last half of each hourly broadcast listeners would have the option to stay tuned for an argumentative dialogue between the two of them, David taking the role of the Catholic and Michael the role of a different non-Catholic creed or point of view each broadcast: the creeds of different Protestant sects, Muslims, Buddhists, Hindus, agnostics, atheists, skeptics, communists, etc.

After their idea became a reality, the dialogues dramatized on the air became lively disputes, the Catholic side always prevailing by force of logical persuasion, fairly won. After each program, the audience was asked to rate the factual accuracy and the fairness of the presentation of each side and finally the objective, rational winner of the theological debate. As time went on, they selected three expert, impartial judges, who also rated fairness and decided who, at least in their opinion, best presented the truth of the matter. David wanted to demonstrate the fairness of their show and that Truth may be arrived pleasantly by way of rational discussion, because *reason* was a universal, God-given faculty of mankind. Next to the goal of conversion to religious truth, losing a debate contest for them was of secondary importance, but knowing that for an audience, the excitement of a debate might be critical to their listening at all. Eventually, the weekly broadcast disputes came to be as popular as the duo's war accounts.

David was amazed at Michael's scholarly ability to master the opposing creed's point of view, so that listeners of that persuasion would often compliment him and even invite him to their social functions, which he never failed to politely refuse. David knew that the Freemasons, even though pretending to embrace all religions, in fact, worked to substitute *Nature* for God, in order to further atheism, displacing all religion and the Creator with rule by the god of "nature". The two Catholic missionaries worked hard to expose this Masonic "religion" of Naturalism to be no more than a thin veil for atheistic idolatry, thus winning them powerful enemies, who dared not oppose them with more lies *too openly*, due to their fame and status as beloved patriots. However, the sons of the Serpent never lost an opportunity to smudge the duo's reputation with lies and to falsely frame them up with false evidence, most of which they had maliciously arranged, like they did with Melissa's performance, thought David.

By the end of the third month of broadcasting, the Leftwing Press that remained was squealing loudly in protest against the politically incorrect exposition of traditional Catholic dogma. They loudly called for the end of 'sectarian opinion', i.e., especially when it was *Catholic*, accusing the duo of being no more than entertaining preachers. This smear job banked on popular agreement amongst a Protestant majority, but to their surprise, it was only their usual hired whiners that were complaining, and the people knew these were just spokesmen for the usual liberal opinion king-makers behind the scenes. David believed that real Catholics were usually right-wing, Christian Patriots and that patriotic Protestants were at best like the Samaritan in Jesus' parable who was praised for his unhesitating, concrete love of neighbor. David saw these "Samaritans" as potential converts because even though their beliefs were not based on true catechesis, their acts showed sincere Christian sentiments. If they could break the good-ole-boy habit and think out of the box, they could make the leap of Faith needed to convert. Jesus' parable placed the Samaritan doctrinally in company with the "untouchables", like tax collectors and prostitutes. Jesus engaged all of the above for the purpose of conversion, despite the scandal that it might have caused.

David had always made a point of openly declaring that their program had an unabashedly Catholic apologetic aim, a transparency he noted that the Freemason's deceptive liberal apparatus could not claim and could not justify by their facts. Michael consistently played a role based on his serious research of the belief systems of the world's various creeds, so that on the air he could authoritatively describe them. Followers of these creeds could participate vicariously in a realistic, rational dialogue based on accurate facts letting the *truth* arrived at, settle the differences. This method of rational truth-seeking examination was governed by a courteous, objectively neutral, fair moderator. David believed that reason is man's God-given tool and that spineless agreements were motivationally defective, a consensus based on human respect. Truth gives birth to peace and unity, while people-pleasing lies breed false hope and division. Other than divine revelation, he was convinced reason was the only means of establishing the truth.

By the end of the fourth month, their ratings were so high they exceeded every other broadcast on the air. This *really* angered and alarmed the enemy, who were absolutely deaf to anyone who opposed them. After the Chinese invasion had ended, in-country traitors may have run into hiding, but only for a while did they cower for fear of their lives; their evil intent had not been crushed, only temporarily thwarted, because their incredible *malice* reasserted itself, in undermining the known Truth. David reasoned that the war crushed the physical menace but not the diabolical spirit fueling their enemy. Also, Christ, the living Truth, had not yet been *publicly crowned* King of the U.S.A., and His mother had not been crowned Queen of all hearts, so who was the greater enemy, those who created this moral vacuum by the apathy of the Christian majority or the diabolical left filling that spiritual void. Because of this failure to enshrine Divine Truth as the public law of the land, a seedbed for Masonic evil remained; it was a 'war' to the finish, even though the Victor was foreknown to be the forces of good: It is, indeed, *One Nation but only Under God*". God's work is not yet done, due to the apathy of His ministers.

During their months on the air, the enemy's "talking heads" dished up to all those who wished to be led rather than think independently, the bogus 'scientific explanation' that the Warning had been a *merely natural* phenomenon, accompanied by equally natural psychological effects. David calmly protested this fairy tale on his talk show, arguing that the revelation of everyone's conscience, their individual memories and private sins at one moment world-wide *never* could have resulted from 'natural' material forces alone, only from the human opinion of pseudo-scientists.

David exposed the media's slant as a dodgy manipulation of public opinion based on the premise that their bold cover-up was preferable to the frightening personal truths revealed by *The Warning*. David saw that only by squelching people's consciences could they impose their ultimate claim that 'God was dead'. Destroy the ear and claim there is no Voice. These manufacturers of "acceptable" opinion, were professional unbelievers; they had to maintain that certain facts did not exist. Therefore, "The Warning" was just a "*warning story*" pedaled by "religious extremists".

The Media even produced false (bribed) witnesses claiming they experienced nothing like the purposed Warning. David saw that there were certain people who wanted to believe the Warning was the effect of some "opium" accidentally inhaled. He countered with irony, a filmed impersonation of a puppet portraying the antics of an outrageous "religious extremist," pulling his hair out and screaming in mock grief at his public exposure. This comedy 'went viral', eliciting peals of laughter throughout the land, not only online but on at least one television network news program.

In addition to publicly disputing with the left, David and Michael discussed various "private revelations" in a series of special broadcasts, where Michael played the interviewer and David answered, based on extensive research. The dynamic duo grew in awareness each day that a truly fierce spiritual war for souls was raging. They came to believe that the "battle of the spirits" referred to in Ephesians 6:12, was ongoing. The public aspect of this battle was often waged with an unbelieving media, but this 'dragon' had to disguise itself by speaking like a lamb. David knew the Media was slowly being reclaimed but only by force of its audience demanding that it speak truth, versus lies and establishment propaganda. The two knew they needed to take advantage of the urgent curiosity of people regarding spiritual things because this could not be entirely suppressed by a manipulative Media without damaging its ever-more-tenuous credibility, the foundation of its very existence.

David argued on-line in a series of podcast interviews that a free press was a *public trust* which did not tolerate the right of a few "Communist maniacs" disturbing the many by malevolent disinformation, which led to profound public disorder. Destruction of a society without good reason or purpose is anarchy, which is a crime. David detailed the manipulation of public opinion by the Media, past and present: not only managing the facts but often *manufacturing* them in order to steer the uneducated like a hapless herd of buffalo over a bluff, like the Indians did. David's audience was made to understand that a deliberately delivered and managed distortion of the truth on important issues was analogous to driving dumb animals over a precipice to their death.

David argued that publishers should probably be licensed because it was a public trust *conditionally* placed in the care of those parties who pledged and sincerely tried to accurately represent the facts and interpret them honestly, without bias. He stated that publishing licenses should be withdrawn or suspended, if they seriously violated these rules of good conduct.

It was more than curiosity David and Michael were seeing in audience feedback. A soul, in witnessing its past actions bared before Divine Judgement, will have a regard for the greatest issue of life, its own *eternal salvation*. As David saw it, God exercised great Mercy in making the culpably blind and stubborn deniers see the light by way of a worldwide Warning and the Miracle that followed. Yet, in the end, nothing stopped the majority from returning to their comfortable ignorance of the truth concerning the state of their souls. Therefore, mankind was fully responsible for the extreme danger in which it remained, that is, in the presence of *God's holy wrath*.

It had been six long months since David and Michael had constructed the two cabins for their families and received extensive catechetical instruction from Fr. Keogh. They were getting very homesick and also discouraged by the declining hunger of the common man for the Truth, since the effect of the Warning was fast forgotten by consciences whose motivation had always been founded on their selfish interests, rather than on the desire to know the truth only God knew and the good that truth points to.

"It's their decision," said David to Michael one day. "We are just witnesses to what Christ said and the Holy Spirit preserved by His Church. It would be presumptuous of us to think we can do more than lead the proverbial horse to water. We cannot determine who will drink or how many will drink." David said this as they sat by the edge of a stream, discussing possibilities and strategies. They were waiting for the time that had been set for their open-air speaking engagement that afternoon. They had already decided it would be their last. After abandoning the full-time work required of them in broadcasting, this was their second month of a relatively successful speaking tour. An element in the crowd today struck them as unruly and volatile.

"I smell a whiff of diabolical shit," David proclaimed, tossing a leaf into the current. "Let's go."

"I'm a little worried too, man," said Michael, standing up and looking David's way for confidence. "We've come this far without harm, I admit, but we're getting short."

"Do you believe we are in God's hands or not?" asked David, glancing at his friend.

"Yesss,... buut."

"No buts, man. Don't you get it yet? If you go into whatever battle with me, I don't want a 'yes-but' guy next to me."

"But, that's how I see it, man."

"I see it this way," said David, facing him sternly. "I will do my best for the Master of the show until the last act, and if He sees things are going south, He will yank me or let me suffer abuse, just like He did our beloved Apostle Paul. But it is ***He*** who is in charge! And I am okay with that. All He does or allows is for the best, Michael. I serve *Him*, my very own Self-Interest. And if you believe that, you will be able to tackle whatever He allows, even though you feel personally threatened."

"Okay; I'm with you, as usual," said Michael. "Consider me your very own 300- pound defensive linebacker, ready to tackle *anything.* To change the subject, what's this rapture talk anyway? I'm getting it from two sides. The Protestants say, 'Yeah, brother! And the Catholics say, 'Never! It's a heresy.'"

"Plenty of confusion," David agreed. "Some Protestants misunderstand the Rapture, thinking it the preface of one thousand years of paradise for the elect. This is probably based on a misinterpretation of Chapter 20 of the Apocalypse. The Church, as far as I know, has never made an official statement concerning the Rapture, one way or the other, limiting its references to the Final Resurrection of all bodies at the Last Judgment and the End of Time. I would say the Rapture is for the elect only. Many see it as a panacea, an escape from hell on earth for all believers like themselves, and they may be closer to the truth than those who do not believe it is referred to in Scripture at all. These confuse its references in Matthew 24 as referring to the Last Judgement, but as we found in our studies before in the cave, that cannot be, for Matthew in Chapter 24 affirms that a remnant will be left on earth. I think the Rapture language in Scripture definitely refers to the elect, who are those God wishes to be spared witnessing His Holy wrath in the Chastisement, whereas He will allow the fire of the Comet and nuclear war to destroy two thirds of mankind, according to Catholic prophecy, and not even the elect can fully understand that. I personally think those raptured might return to earth after the Great Chastisement in order to rebuild a Catholic world with Christ's help, as we pray in the Our Father: "*thy kingdom come, on earth, as it is in Heaven*'. Peace and justice will reign on this earth after the Chastisement. This Peace will end when the Antichrist comes as a person. The Raptured, because of their Catholic witness, would implement the prophesied Great Peace by their leadership in educating those they lead into a world where there is '*one shepherd and one flock*', with *one* doctrine defining the one Church of Christ. Adherence to God's one Church will finally unite all mankind."

"That's for me!" said Michael, jumping up. "Truth and union!"

"Jesus said, 'Ask and you shall receive.'[30] You have demonstrated the desire to receive, which usually precedes *asking*, Michael. So, ask."

"Done!" said Michael. "Where did those demons go that we ran off at the church," he asked.

"If God hasn't sent them back to Hell already, He will after the Chastisement, along with all evil people who served them," said David. "But after only *twenty-five years*, Our Lady said at La Salette, mankind's sins will once again invite Satan back to earth. And that is the time for the Antichrist to appear as a possessed individual. It may be an evil reign perpetrated in similar fashion as the present COVID-19 scamdemic, but my guess is that Satan will use terrorism, that is, a bolder, in-your-face tactic. Satan likes to lull people to sleep, so he does not persist in his attack once people are on to him. He lets them have peace, which breeds their complacency, thinking evil is gone forever, when people are breeding evil in their souls by sin."

"What a depressing story is all I have to say!" complained Michael.

"I agree 100%," said David. An hour later the crowd had assembled,

---

[30] St. Matthew 7:7

and David climbed upon the boulder they had chosen for a podium and began his prepared talk. After thirty minutes, he cut it short, giving as an excuse he and Michael needed to begin their five hundred mile walk home, but in fact he was reacting to his dull-eyed audience. Their eyes, he imagined, could have been lumps of coal. They told him they were either not listening or bored.

It was then that a group of ten menacing ruffians came out of the crowd on que, apparently assembling to teach these Christian zealots a backwards lesson. David looked calmly at Michael, "Time to get up and help me witness to the power of the Word, young man!" his voice rising in volume and tone to that of a Pentecostal preacher on *fire*. Michael scurried to David's side.

"Are we gonna get raptured?" Michael looked at David anxiously but with a wink of humor as well.

"No, Michael, I think these dudes are the ones who are going to get raptured! READY!?"

The ugly mob, some with clubs, others with knives or brass knuckles, engulfed the two missionaries like an ameba engulfs its next meal. Then a disturbance seemed to shake and quake the glob, as one hoodlum after another was ejected, falling to the ground grievously injured by a *smashing* blow. Finally, the two Christians stood alone, bloodied but uninjured.

The two men stepped upon their granite podium again, now with some evidence on their side that: "*God helps those who help themselves*," shouted Michael, full of fiery exuberance. This was greeted with cheers that lasted thirty seconds.

"Our trust is shown when we count on God's help, especially when things look hopeless or grim," shouted David, taking Michael's place. The crowd roared and applauded with good humor, shouting congratulations because they considered themselves ill-represented by the pugilistic hoodlums and quite pleased at the physical humiliation they so richly deserved. In their eyes, it truly was a demonstration of God taking the side of the innocent but ill-treated by punishing the wicked.

"Remember, faith is only possible in regard to what is *not seen or known* yet, like the outcome of our fight. Good day and God bless," said David, hopping off the rock -- which Michael promptly mounted again.

"God wants to see *acts* that demonstrate the Faith He gave us," thundered Michael, smiling and holding up his two bloody fists, shouting, "Self-defense is okay!" Loud cheers followed.

Michael's point inspired David to hop back on the rock for one last comment. "Michael is right!" he shouted. "We have to *use* Faith to do good works, otherwise it becomes *dead* faith. For example, it was your dead faith that allowed you to sit there and tolerate an attack for no good cause by six hoodlums upon two innocent men, even though you can cheer our victory *after* the fight is won by the good guys. Does that mean if we had lost, you would be cheering them?"

David could hear Michael's comment behind him: "Ouch!"

"Faith is the only means by which we move into the unknown, the future. If you do not want to be a 'frozen vegetable', act on the true Faith we have been talking about, as you slept. One more thing, we do *not* advocate violence to solve disputes even though *others* do." David cast a glance at one of the attackers still lying on the ground. A quarter of the audience chuckled. "Reason works better; the *exception* is self-defense." David descended the rock.

They began the walk home, letting Paintbrush haul their gear. In less than a month, they arrived home. Angela's round cheeks were wet with tears of happiness and Fr. Keogh was beaming with pride. News of their exploits had become well known.

* * *

In the early morning, Angela awoke to find David gone. Worried, she walked around looking for him, finally pushing the twins in their large-wheeled carriage that David had found for her to use on the rough ground, first to Michael's but her search ended at Fr. Keogh's cabin door. She could hear David and the priest talking. It seemed that David was talking in a weepy voice. She stood listening outside the door, full of concern, but she could only make out a few words or phrases. She decided she should not be eavesdropping. She would trust Fr. Keogh to take good care of her man.

Then, David quelled the self-pity in his voice and speaking more calmly said, "Father, I repeat, I feel so useless and weak. I have so much knowledge and faith, but it does not seem that I impart much of that to many people, and the few I do impart it to seem to be moved only sluggishly. I speak impromptu; I am not an organized orator. I have too much to share. It squirts out haphazardly and awkwardly. Father, it seems an impossible task for me to cogently deliver my thoughts." There was a silent pause. "Have I failed?"

"No, you have not," said the priest, firmly. "What people see, appreciate and take to heart is what God is doing to them interiorly through the person He inspires to be His witness. They see clearly that God has inspired you to be His witness. They see your personal, heartfelt love for Christ and His Church palpably reaching out to them. This is personal but also powerfully convincing evidence of God's presence in an intelligent, courageous and studious soul, *obviously* on fire with the spirit of Truth. That human witness turns souls around, because it presents to them someone they could be like themselves: passionately on fire. At that moment they are inspired to live a life of grace and hope; a life they envision being filled with love, something everyone desires because this *love* gives meaning and direction to lives. Don't you see, David?! It is not what you convey to others in 'organized' or eloquent knowledge, facts or arguments that will *move* them; it's your Faith in God which they see in *you*, a true believer, full of conviction and passion that moves them. Because of your courage in witnessing to them, David, you demonstrate your willingness to risk something vital for them. Here we must not underestimate the power of curiosity in discovering the mystery of what moves you so adamantly."

"You mean when they see me risk believing, they are encouraged to take that risk as well?" asked David.

"Yes, removing or reducing that fear of risk, frees them to try and grasp what you are saying with the desire to embrace it themselves. In other words, your motivation and enthusiasm are infectious because your real *love and devotion are evident;* they're on display. They see that your soul is mysteriously moved by the supernatural principles of God that Jesus taught. You get no credit, but your desire is fulfilled: *Jesus is reflected in you*, David: a true, if imperfect, image of Him, but at the same time you are to those whom you teach just a human being like themselves; that is why they can hope to become like you, possessing this same Holy

Spirit you speak of which compels you to speak passionately before those who will listen. You resemble Jesus, the One you give witness to by not merely human actions but supernatural intentions."

David took a while to respond. "Thank you, Father. I guess I needed to hear that it is okay to be imperfect. It is like you raised me from the dead. You definitely have the gift of healing wounded souls, Father."

"God does the work; we are His instruments. It is amazing how insignificant our part is in comparison to His, David. I leave you with this admonition from St. Padre Pio, even though you have probably heard it before: '*Don't tire yourself with things that cause anxieties, concerns and worries. Only one thing is necessary, to lift up your spirit and to love God.*'"[31]

"In other words," said David, "we are supposed to be seeking God, not seeking comfort for ourselves, as reflected in our worries and anxieties."

"That would be it," said Fr. Keogh, happy to have helped this young Christian man see more clearly and have more confidence in his ability to pass on the Word.

David opened the door to leave but turned back, "One other thing, Father. Did we do wrong in beating those guys up? Jesus wouldn't have done it that way."

"You are not God. Jesus certainly avoided His enemies, sometimes miraculously, but He also confronted them with severe tongue lashings and one recorded instance of violent zeal with moneychangers at the Temple, for His Father's house. But Scripture leaves out much of what He said and did."

"Maybe we should have trusted God to help us," said David.

"You did trust Him, and He gave you an extraordinary power to defend yourselves, from what I hear. If and when God calls someone to passively suffer injury or martyrdom, it will either be: 1) unavoidable; 2) something in which the martyr sees clearly the effectiveness of his witness to Christ resulting in conversions; or 3) there could be a serious moral obligation involved. A woman who is being raped but refusing to cooperate at the cost of her life would be an example of the latter. She

---

[31] https://www.padrepiodapietrelcina.com/en/quotes-of-padre-pio-padre-pios-words-of-faith/

refused a mortal sin against chastity at the cost of dying a martyr. A person giving up his life, rather than denying the Faith is an example of both. Mortal sin is a much greater evil than death; it takes away the eternal life of the soul, while death only takes away the mortal life of the body."

After breakfast that morning, Angela brought their adopted son, Jeremy, before David. "He has been very bad since you left," said Angela, obviously very hurt by Jeremy's behavior. "He will *not* obey me. He mocks me. I fully believe he took advantage of the fact that you were not here to stop his misbehavior." As if to deny this, the boy looked at David fearlessly, laughing and goofing around.

David walked the six-year old to the chopping block in the front yard. "You have done wrong, Jeremy, and I want you to remember what kind of reward you will always receive in the end for being bad on purpose." David laid the boy over the large stump and beat his butt so hard with the palm of his hand that Jeremy's terrified screams of terror and pain could be heard at Michael's place. When the boy's attitude-driven 'poor me' attempts to avoid the pain of a just punishment gave way to uncontrolled screams of pain, fear and desperation, David stopped. Angela came out, upset. The boy headed for her arms, but David waved a finger that said, "No!"

He took the boy by the arm roughly and told him to stop crying, with a voice of authority. The boy stopped, ending his last plea of self-pity. Then David asked, "Are you sorry, Jeremy?"

"Ya, yesss," the boy stammered through his fading sobs.

"Then go tell Angela that," David said firmly, while softening his tone of voice a little. David made sure the boy's intended apology was clear, frank, detailed and thorough by having him repeat it until it had passed those marks.

Later, alone with Angela, David said to her, "He will be better now. But if the attitude returns even a little, *nip it in the bud* by threatening to tell me. Otherwise, continue to educate him in the reason *why* his behavior is or was wrong, and be lenient in your correction and discipline of him, in as much as he is trying to improve and shows contrition. Children are not good or evil at birth, by way of their human nature; that is an error of Freemasonry's Enlightenment thinkers, like

Rousseau. If we buy into such errors, we fail those under our authority who disobey or do wrong, which, of course, is everyone. We encourage further bad behavior by allowing children to assume there will be no evil consequences for their evil beliefs or acts because authority will not punish them for the same. Most children cannot learn except through some form of discipline before the age of reason, which occurs around seven years. Pain of some kind always speaks to their self-interest after less extreme methods have failed. Reason supplies sufficient motive for good behavior when the right way is explained. Reason can supply the motivation to do what is good, but this cannot be expected before they develop this ability. We train children to sin, if we do not administer discipline in their tender years when pain, delivered with the motive of love can be a life-changing experience for good. Children so disciplined are encouraged to develop intellectually as an alternative to physical discipline. Virtuous habits are learned earlier. Parental error on this score are the spoiled brats we see everywhere."

David glanced at Angela before continuing. He could see something was brewing. "Too lenient parents may point to God's Mercy as the example excusing their laxity, but God's Mercy does not cancel His Justice; rather, it softens the punishment already due for some injustice. The Church teaches that all of us have fallen from the grace of our original, God-given perfection. We tend to sin because the very order of our human nature is subverted by the effects of Original Sin. The spirit of truth in our soul tends to be overruled by our sensitive appetite. The spirit is strong, but the flesh is weak. Therefore, discipline of the flesh is necessary to the spirit."

"Children are not angels," David continued. "They are blank tablets, who need to learn through their butts if they choose to reject instruction and admonishment. Children especially need to learn the right way or receive retribution for not learning the right way, because they are too young before *the age of reason* to grasp moral concepts and be responsible to them thus forming a conscience. It is very cruel to let those we care for do wrong without consequences, Angela. It permits their souls to form bad habits," David concluded.

"So, what does God say about this?"

"Get me a Bible, and I will show you. But first consider what God *does*: 1) eternity in Hell for unrepented mortal sin, acts which moderns may consider normal, healthy behavior, like masturbation; 2) Time in Purgatory until the absolute perfection is reached needed to be in the presence of God. In face of these facts, is it fair to raise a child without the rule of discipline and justice? No. God tells us in Proverbs 13:24," David read, "'He who sparest the rod, hateth his son.' And in Ecclesiastes 30:1, 'He that loveth his son, frequently chastiseth him,…'"

"I understand, Mr. David," said Angela, "but also heed the blurting out of my motherly concern. You can learn from me too. You lead, yes. I acknowledge your supremacy in knowledge and God-given authority, but I am here to help you with a woman's heart, right? You are rough. I can help you become gentle, less abrasive, *you know!*" she shouted, jumping up to throw her arms tightly around his neck, kissing him hard.

Within the next fifteen minutes, heeding his wife's godly counsel, David made a point of giving his Jeremy a big smile, a big hug and a ride on his broad shoulders. In this, he wanted to make Jeremy understand that his dad's motive for discipline was love, without removing the lesson taught through discipline. It was a gesture that Jeremy remembered for the rest of his life, kept in the depths of his good heart that grew stronger from that day forward. Never again did Jeremy feel the loneliness, anger and rebellion of an orphan, which he had chosen to act out as a something-for-Jeremy, pity-potty gambit before Angela, whose timidity and lack of fatherly leadership would have completed Jeremy's road to ruin. After David's loving discipline, Jeremy's fear of retribution for wrongdoing turned from a servile fear of punishment to reverence, which fears offending the one loved. As a grown up, Jeremy would attribute his life's conversion to both the 'tough-love' that stopped a young rebel's resistance to the rule of love, law and reason and also to the gentle affection and mercy of the only father and mother he had ever known.

"Overnight", little Jeremy became an obedient, loving, respectful son, an excellent student and a young person with the obvious desire to let all know he wanted to be helpful to others. Especially, he seemed to show a desire to assist those saddled with the obligations of authority. Eventually, he grew up to raise a beautiful family of his own, with well-disciplined children that drew many admiring comments from the adults who encountered them.

When David and Angela had some time to themselves one night, David said, sitting by the fire on his stretched mountain lion, pine-framed rocking chair, "Experience is a teacher. If Jeremy does what is right, first out of fear of a just punishment, he will know what is right; and he will be able to understand *why* it is right *after the experience* of actually doing right. Only then can he *do* what is right because he loves the good: that's righteousness."

"So to uncomplicate that, Professor," said Angela, "you're saying that the experience of actually doing what is right, teaches him what is right. I can see more clearly now why a child needs a father *and* a mother, not just one or the other," said Angela.

They curled up on the couch together, sipped hot chocolate out of the same large blue, stoneware mug and fell asleep together, warmed by a shaft of late afternoon sunlight. Later, after they had crawled under their bedcovers, David and Angela conceived their third child, a little girl they named Angelina.

Chapter 5

THE INDIVISIBLE LIGHT

Five hundred souls sat in the grass south of the two-foot-high limestone ledge outcropping for one hundred fifty yards across the "Meadow". Healthy, straight pines had established a narrow forest behind this water-weeping outcrop. It was here that David's little band of pilgrims had taken on the disguise of lepers. Fr. Keogh stepped up on the highest point and began to preach, his long, simple, black cassock falling straight to his sandaled bare feet in large folds. The image reminded David of the late 19th century Fr. De Smet preaching to the Sioux Indians in their western lands.

David sat in the shade of the pines ten yards behind the priest, a self-appointed security guard. He carefully surveyed the crowd for troublemakers, since he knew the priest had mortal enemies, and this event had been widely broadcast being advertised in the public media. His roving gaze hesitated. Standing at the crowd's fringes were two men in short sleeve, solid black shirts huddled with their heads together. They seemed to be conferring confidentially, one of them, probably of lesser rank, seemed to be taking notes. Intermittently, they eyed Fr. Keogh keenly, apparently listening with selective attention to his sermon, followed by negative comments or expletives. David decided to check them out up close, suspecting clerical spies, probably from the pool of leftists at the diocesan headquarters in Cheyenne.

After some introductory remarks, Fr. Keogh began. "Identity theft is the crime wave of this new century." He straightened his posture to improve volume and projection, since there was no microphone. "The identity thief, in pretending to be who he is not, takes upon himself the appearance of authority, prestige and reputation of the one whose identity he is stealing, yet he has none of these qualities. Let's say this identity theft is done as a cover for the perpetrators of a shady operation. Why else would they need to steal the identity of their victim, except to conceal their real identity and to cover up their crimes, some fraud they are perpetrating? They can blame their crimes on the one being impersonated if people are disturbed or they are criticized or caught. At the same time, the unsuspecting victim, let's say, the Church, is lending its credibility to their game; its good reputation serves to allay suspicion and legitimize the lies that serve the shady operation. The gullible fools tend to say, 'the Church we knew of old would never do the things these prelates (imposters) are suggesting, so we are leaving the Church'; or worse, they say, 'the Church declared this (through a rotten 'prelate'), so it must be Church teaching now that we are bound to believe and imitate.' Wrong! The authority of bishops, even popes, is not equal to the teaching Authority, or *Magisterium* of the Church, which is based on the Word of God, *Jesus*, found directly in Holy Scripture, for example. Those who follow Judas in betraying Jesus, will hang like he did."

"Let us dispense with the analogy, we are examining those religious identity thieves trying to rob us of our Faith by stealing the identity, authority and reputation of the Catholic Church by their impostures. They have been trying to change the Church's identity by heretical, Masonic *change agents* ever since they hijacked Vatican II, which was declared by good Pope Paul VI, a *pastoral* Council (not a *dogmatic* council); therefore, nothing coming out of Vatican II that alters Traditional dogma is valid; instead, it would be the smoke of Satan, the work of ecclesiastical Freemasons. Ecclesiastical Masons *hijacked* Vatican II, replacing the schema of the traditional, orthodox bishops headed by Archbishop Lefebvre with a schema that favored a Modernist direction."

"The Church is ultimately the Mother and Guardian of the true Faith. The imposters, on the other hand, are inspired by Satan, who hates Christ's Church and desires damnation, not salvation, for all souls. 'Misery loves company' as the old saying goes. Besides, having twenty centuries of existence, the Catholic Church boasts the Son of God as its founding Head and the Holy Spirit as its doctrinal guide and guarantor of infallible Truth until the end of time. But for the gullible, who believe not Truth (the Son of God) but the lies of Satan which assume the mere *appearance* of authority, demanding a false obedience. Tragically, these *former* sheep are now 'goats' because they failed to recognize the voice of their divine Shepherd, whose own enter only through the 'sheep-gate' of His Traditional Church."

"Who but the Devil's trained apes have the malicious audacity to steal the identity of God's two-thousand-year old Institution? The sins of humanity have given them this power, leaving the gate open, so wolves in sheep's clothing can enter. True believers recognize the wolves wearing sheep's clothing, whom Jesus warned us about; believers are not blind. But the Faithful might not be watchful because they naively presume others to be good like themselves. The Serpent is now baiting his hook with the last heresy. Modernism is the summation of all lies because it presumes to erase the Authority of Tradition itself; novelty always trumps what is known of old, that is, all past truth, including the person of Jesus Christ, the Word of God. The heresy of Modernism severs us from Tradition, in favor of clever lies, a transparent characteristic of the end times. Modernism is a denial of the self-evident: once true, always true. Modernism is marketed to the culpably gullible as being warranted by the *unquestionable* authority of the *current* 'magisterium' of the church, proposing doctrines and practices that are *not traditionally of Christ's Catholic Church*. Those who argue to the contrary on the basis of Tradition are ignored, answered by silence. Therefore, Modernism is a ploy to destroy the true Faith and replace it with a look-alike 'plastic' replica."

"Those who believe the Modernist lies will also be ready to dump the intent of our two hundred-year-old U.S. Constitution for the latest 'heresy' of those who wish to destroy this Great Nation, along with its Christian heritage." Father switched gears nicely, thought David. Cheers preceded a swelling wave of applause from the audience, which David now estimated to have swollen to nine hundred. "Genuine Catholics, as well as true Patriots, should know that any truth, once determined, is not temporal but eternal; the contrary is a lie capable of destroying all of mankind's treasures. For those who believe this lie, it is *not* 'better to obey God than men', as St. Peter told the Sanhedrin in Acts 5:29, but the exact opposite. It is worthy of repeating: *Faith is not blind*; it 'sees' what is *not present* to our human senses, but that does not cause reason to stop being fully active. Faith never contradicts reason and vice versa; the two pass the baton of knowledge between themselves. Yet the enemy constantly tells us otherwise, saying that faith and reason are always separate. Faith, whether human or divine, is necessary if we are to come to know or do anything."

"Jesus said, 'you know a tree by its fruit'[32]. Faith is not a license to be a 'guppy'; just the opposite. Faith not only allows us to think and act in defense of lies and errors, but it allows us to 'test the spirits' in regard to purported messages from Heaven or Hell, as St. Paul said."[33] Fr. Keogh straightened up again. "When you add five additional decades to the traditional *fifteen-decade* Rosary Mary gave St. Dominic, who lived in the 12th century, then one must strongly suspect that audacious, in-your-face change agents are at the top of the Church, trashing traditional devotions as part of their demolition of the Church. Regardless of whether this outrage came from a manipulated pope in his old age or is just a forgery attributed to his name, we recognize the diabolical. Popes are easily kept in the dark about the wicked plans and doings of those *pretending to be* their trusted servants and ministers but who are really 'wolves in sheep's clothing' bent on misrepresenting the word, spirit and authority of the pope and his office."

"And when *they* pretend to nullify the timeless doctrine, '*There is no salvation outside the Church*,' by a false '*Ecumenism*' which recognizes all religions as salvific, the identity of the Church, *its divine origin*, its mission and its necessity for Christ's salvation, is open to question and doubt. Those using their Faith and the Reason by which they were made in 'the image and likeness of God', will not be fooled; but the weak and cowardly will be picked off by these wolves, just as weak or sickly newborn lambs are the first to be picked off by wolves because they have been abandoned by their mother and the flock. Many whose faith is weak and undernourished by neglect will follow a pied piper over the cliff, their faith dying on the rocks far below, even as the herd of

---

[32] St. Luke 6:44

[33] 1 John 4:1

swine possessed by the demons were driven over the cliff, falling onto the rocky seashore below, as related in Mathew 8: 31,32. But Jesus told us that *His* sheep are not like these swine because they will know their Shepherd, Whom the demons fear. Those of Faith will recognize a wolf in sheep's clothing as one *not* entering through the 'Sheepgate' (Christ's Traditional Church). This one only pretends to be their shepherd in order to lead them astray. These are the 'false Christs' we are warned of in Matthew 24:24. The lesson for us is that they who were born again *by God* will recognize the Voice of their true Shepherd, Jesus, i.e., His true doctrine: what He literally said: the *Word of God*."

The priest folded his hands in prayer and looked heavenward, begging God to give him strength and wisdom. "If Salvation could come from other churches, then, obviously, the Catholic Church could not be the one and only true Church created and ordained by God, and Jesus could be rightly accused of speaking equivocally, i.e., with a forked tongue, like the devil, which, of course, is impossible for God. This convicts the devil of being the author of this Ecumenism, which is preceded by indifferentism (one belief is as good as another), both pointing to syncretism, where all beliefs become one."

"The end result of radical ecumenism is to mock and destroy God's one Church, finally destroying the very notion of truth and a believable, lovable God we can trust. This is also the aim of Satan's Communism: the murderer of millions spiritually, of whole societies and individual souls by way of error." Fr. Keogh paused to drink some bottled water; he was attempting to keep hydrated, David thought approvingly, looking out for his physical needs, at least.

"God does not equivocate; He instituted only one Church. So, if the heresies of indifferentism and false ecumenism, both of which deny the doctrine that '*there is no salvation outside the One, Holy, Catholic & Apostolic Church*', seem to come from the Church itself, then Pope Paul VI spoke truly when he said in 1972 on the Feast of Saints Peter and Paul, '*from some fissure the smoke of Satan has entered the Church*'."[34] Expressions of dismay and alarm rose from the crowd at these words.

[34] https://www.catholicworldreport.com/2018/11/15/the-smoke-of-satan-provides-clear-concise-analysis-of-the-episcopal-crisis/

"'*Smoke*'", said Fr. Keogh, "is the term traditionally used in reference to *Freemasonry*, which is documented to have made statements to the effect that they want to destroy the Catholic Church. Freemasonry also instigated the Protestant Revolt, the French Revolution and the Communist Revolution. You might say that Freemasonry is the organized *antichrist* of history. Reportedly set in motion by Herod Agrippa the Third in the second century A.D, this diabolical organization, initially called 'The Force', is reputed to have been behind the Roman persecutions, the sacrifice of infant Christians, as well as the source of many heresies. They had to take cover as a guild of masons in the 8th century, under the name 'Freemasons'. All error and heresy are designed by Satan to destroy *his greatest enemy*, the Roman Catholic Church and to replace its Head, Jesus, as the messiah (Antichrist) of human history. The good news is that God said He would be with His Church until the end of time[35]; but this does not mean His mystical body, the Church, would not be crucified like its head and master, but that Jesus would be with it nevertheless." Fr. Keogh called for a short break.

David was close enough to the two in clerical dress that he decided to take the break as an opportunity to approach them. He did not see laughter and joy in their manner but scoffing and a self-righteous anger bordering on rage. However, he had not accurately understood Fr. Keogh's meaning of a "short" break, as he abruptly began his sermon again.

"The Great Apostasy of the end times is advanced by the heresy of Modernism, called the summation and greatest of all heresies. The gullible, led by their sensual minds, believe semi-transparent fraudsters, imbibing their every error and absurdity as if it were angel-food cake, because they have discarded the Faith and Reason God gave them. Sin is a kind of insanity evolving from self-love; for narcissism is the epitome and source of all insanity. As a religion and as a disease of our fallen race, we call this spiritual disease, *Humanism*."

He seems to be wandering again, thought David, but we will see. Fr. Keogh resumed, "God is His own reason for being, but we are not; therefore, the Truth of God, Jesus Christ, is the principle of our

---

[35] St. Matthew 28:20

enlightened Reason as Christians. We generally consider the Natural Law as our *created* reason. In the case of either principle, the Natural Law or Christianity, we can trust reason to inform and orient our thinking rightly because both principles come from God, the first as Creator, the other as the revealed Son of God. I repeat, man is *not* his own principle of reason, rather, this is Satan's talking point. Humanism may assume that Reason assigns man a liberty of thought and conscience, that it rules our nature as queen, but they presume, in contradiction, that reason is flawed, artificial, man-made; only pure nature shriven of reason (decapitated) is to be trusted. No *fallen* human nature here: if the child under parental care wants it, give it to him. Nature knows best; Tradition is biased. However, we know that the Natural Law of Reason is instilled in every individual by the Creator, thereby residing in the heart of every human being as a responsible guide."

The priest continued attacking the wolves of error that had been killing his beloved sheep, and David saw how it was that he 'killed' those deceivers with Faith and Reason, while being crucified himself by the dragons of error he fought, for they were a cruel lie to the Creator, to the Truth, a 'river' sweeping souls into Hell.

"Modernism's new-trumps-old ruse is hard to expose because it is so bold, so absurd. Aristotle called those who denied the self-evident fundamentals of reason as 'cabbage heads'. And anyone who falls for Modernism's *what is new always trumps what is old* is already morally sick in sinning against the very reason God gave them. As such, they are defenseless against lies, however absurd. The blame-shifting agents of slime blame the erosion of Faith on those traditionalists who resisted them, i.e. those who did not fall for their 'slight-of-hand'. They accuse these Faithful few of frustrating the *renewal* of the Church by their 'holy spirit of confusion and of darkness'. They know that the bigger the lie, the more likely their devotees will defend it and give it credit. It's hogwash!!" shouted Fr. Keogh, visibly frustrated and audibly angry.

He has reached the edge of his endurance, thought David. "The true destroyers of the Church," Fr. Keogh continued in a weepy voice, "are obviously those disrupting its order and tranquility of true authority. Was not Jesus framed-up as a blasphemer by the same kind of hypocritical identity thieves, a mob of thieves who at that time had carved out of their interpretation of Scripture positions of responsibility in the church of Israel? Modernists claim that, ultimately, God Himself and His own Words, the doctrine of His Church, are *changeable* in being variously understood by individual interpretation (I. Kant believed reality *was* its perception[36]), this was *in deference to* man and the temptations of his times, their bestselling angle for their liberated humanity, a five hundred year project. In their version, God will bend the rules for unrepentant sinners who are pressed by circumstances. They say that leniency is God's all-merciful nature; therefore, His Church must do likewise: admitting practicing adulterers and homosexuals to Holy Communion, as non-pope Francis proclaimed, for example, in *Laudato Si'*[37]. These Freemasonic change-agents, who have captured the offices of 99% of the bishops of their false church, at least by blackmail or intimidation, are truly the prophesied *wolves in sheep's clothing*! As part of their disguise, they may give lip-service to Catholic doctrine, but in practical fact they are ripping it to pieces, tearing it from its foundation of Authority by contradictions to *what has always been taught,* which is the identity of the Church. We see this in considering that just as any one of you is known by what you habitually think and do, so too, dear people, the Word of God will *always* faithfully preserve in one doctrine the teaching of the One Holy Catholic Church, even if the Faithful few have to go into the 'catacombs'." The priest paused to let the urgent murmuring of his audience subside. He had controlled the passion of his righteous anger to speak truthfully, thought David; his alarm had been unwarranted.

"Be forewarned dear children. You have the responsibility to be alert, distinguishing the 'wolf in sheep's clothing' from the true Shepherd because *His sheep* will be separated in the Final Judgement from the *goats* by an unbridgeable, eternal chasm, recognizing God's truth from the Devil's lies. Study your Faith, so that you will recognize these *wolves* and not follow them. They are the modern-day Pharisees Jesus identified for us two thousand years ago, of whom He warned: beware of these hypocrites! Do not *ignore* your only Teacher and His salvation, falling

36 https://courses.lumenlearning.com/sanjacinto-philosophy/chapter/immanuel-kant-experience-and-reality/

37 https://en.wikipedia.org/wiki/Laudato_si%27

into the *culpable* ignorance leading to the loss of your soul." Fr. Keogh paused again, wiping perspiration from his forehead and calling for a ten-minute intermission.

David could now see that this 'martyr' was going to over-exert himself again if he continued. Surely, this brilliant man knew when to stop, he thought. But when people could leave, but did not, this preacher and lover of souls saw a green light.

David had been observing the two clerics from ten feet behind them. He took the opportunity of Father's intermission to step up and say, "Hello." Then he snapped their picture with his camera phone. "Haven't I seen you two at the diocesan offices in the Capitol?" He blurted this out loud enough for others to take notice in order to embarrass them. Once again, he thought, I am guilty of *fishing without a license.* He figured he was so commissioned as Fr. Keogh's self-appointed security chief. He now introduced himself as being just that, coming in nose to nose, in order to make them uncomfortably apprehensive. He could hear them suck in air as he explained how *he* had to deal with the hit squad that made the *fatal* mistake of trying to "mess with" Fr. Keogh at the big conference where the priest had also freely spoken his mind. Their eyes widened to harvest moon size, frozen with fear; he swiftly grabbed their notebook, phones and tape recorder, dropping them on the ground, stomping them to pieces with the heel of his boot. Those sickening sounds told the two that their mission had just *ended.* Like frightened children, they only wanted the safety of home! David's next 'suggestion' was for them to do just that, run in a hurry, as he folded his huge, bare forearms across his chest, accompanied by an unflinching stare, which read, "*Leave, immediately!!*" His priest didn't need any more trouble, David thought. Hopefully, he had put trouble on the run, as he keenly followed their increasingly speedy retreat.

"In the Old Testament," Fr. Keogh had mounted his rocky podium again, "'fornication' was the term God used when accusing His people of adulterating His doctrines and religious practices with those of pagans. *Syncretism,* the melding of all religions into one, and *Indifferentism,* the belief that religions are not qualitatively different, are defined twin heresies asserting that God's *one* salvific religion is just one of many and no more than equal to the others. But this contradicts the Bible's concern with spiritual fornication: the adulteration of God's One, Holy Religion with the impure weeds of demonic doctrines. True religion involves a covenant or solemn agreement between God and His chosen people, similar to that of Marriage. Therefore, no *baptized Catholic* who dies without practicing that Faith can save his soul. Syncretism adulterates the one true Religion by sharing its soul or spiritually procreative act (which in our analogy is *Salvation)* with any and all lovers. This adultery tries to make all religions into one by the infidelity of a false Ecumenism, so that a common denominator supposedly unites all religions into one dumbed-down creed." Approving mirth rippled through the crowd. They liked and approved of this priest's direct, somewhat 'earthy' speech which seemed to lessen the distance between them, David thought.

"So, let's say that trying to combine all religions into one, the majority agree that adultery is wrong," said Fr. Keogh, trying to explain, "but fornication is not wrong. Does this hokey democracy have the authority of God to make moral law? Surely not!! A 'religion' like that comes from Hell, sowing the seeds of error among the wheat of righteous doctrine like the 'enemy' did in Jesus' parable. Some say there are many religions because of men's naturally different beliefs about higher things. This puts the horse before the cart, making man the author of religion, instead of God. It reeks of diabolical arrogance. God, not man, dictates all the terms of Religion, its doctrine, rituals, etc."

"Indifferentism, of course, leads to Syncretism. The rationale Freemasonry preaches is that if different creeds are no better than one another (Indifferentism), why not combine them all into one religion, so we can be rid of those fractious divisions among men that cause religious disputes and wars (divisions which the enemy promotes by fanning the flames of division in order to shift blame from themselves to those who hold rigid religious beliefs). These two heresies like to say that all religious doctrines get you where you want to go, so why split hairs; why fuss over minutia. In this way, religious truth expressed as doctrine appears to be trivial and *relative*, and that is El Diablo's cup of tea." A murmur went up from the crowd. Many Mexicans were in its number, chuckling and talking to each other with their typical familiarity.

"The problem with all this subterfuge, my dear people," Fr. Keogh paused for effect and complete silence, "is that our Religion, established by God to save souls, is mocked and discredited by hypocrites, just like those who crucified, ridiculed and shamed Jesus. In fact, in crucifying His Mystical Body, the Catholic Church, they are re-crucifying Jesus. The scandalized, uneducated, unsophisticated masses are in danger of abandoning the Church and perishing. Now is the time to FIGHT!" shouted the priest, pumping a fist into the air.

"I would have you fight, but realize that in these End Times, the Devil will be given a certain latitude in order 'to separate the sheep from the goats', ending with the Chastisement and Jesus' Second Coming, which will coincide with the restoration (resurrection) of His Church followed by a Great Peace on Earth. Christians will be refined and tested. Satan will be completely defeated and cast into Hell with all his accomplices, only to return as *the* Antichrist in person. Then Jesus will vanquish Satan, as the Apocalypse describes, returning a Third Time at the end of time itself as the final Victor and Judge. You must have trust in God alone now, because the End Times test will hinge on what or who people place their faith in. Cardinal Manning, in 1861, wrote a book, *The Present Crisis of the Holy See--Tested by Prophecy*. He wrote:

> "The apostasy of the city of Rome from the Vicar of Christ, and its destruction by Antichrist: ... Malvenda, who writes expressly on the subject, states as the opinion of Ribera, Gaspar Melus, Viegas, Suarez, Bellarmine, and Bosius, that Rome shall apostatize from the faith, drive away the Vicar of Christ, and return to its ancient paganism.[38]
> Malvenda's words are: 'But Rome itself in the last times of the world will return to its ancient idolatry, power, and imperial greatness. It will cast out its Pontiff, altogether apostatize from the Christian faith, terribly persecute the Church, shed the blood of martyrs more cruelly than ever, and will recover its former state of abundant wealth, ...'"[39]

[38] Malvenda, de Antichristo, lib.iv. cap 5.

[39] Cardinal Henry Edward Manning, *The Present Crisis of the Holy See Tested by Prophecy*, Burns & Lambert, London, c 1861, pg. 88.

"Those who love the Catholic Faith are witnesses of these facts. Absurd as it may sound, dear people, the diabolical madness today has deranged man's thinking to the point that one's sexual reality is considered to be a matter of personal opinion and choice! Similarly, our choice is now supposed to determine what we *believe to be reality.* No God as Creator is needed. A sinful world produces this insanity. Yes! Supposedly reality is relative to each person's fancy. The insanity of such a philosophy of lies is now on display. God has allowed His enemies to expose themselves for what they are: sick and evil. The separation of the sheep from the goats is virtually finished. Evil is stripped naked for even the common man to see. Hardened sinners could not miss this billboard lunacy. Before He punishes man, God wants to make crystal clear the alternatives of good and evil from which a man must choose. Yes," said the priest, "you have observed that insanity afflicts many in our times. Why is that? The lost souls we speak of, believing heresies and losing sight of God and His creation, have no stable reality to anchor their mental world. Without reality, insanity is inevitable. These poor people endure a literal 'hell on earth', which we call *insanity.* But the Faithful few do not believe lies crafted by demons!" The priest intentionally raised his voice to cause the raising of eyelids in some audience listeners.

"We stand before our eternal Father," Fr. Keogh said, pointing straight up with his index finger, "where everyone is responsible for apprehending the Truth and the reality God created which, as I have said, is the basis of all Truth. The One World Religion they want to create by a manufactured consensus is chicanery. It is filthy *rot*!" the priest shouted angrily. "It is a *Lie*! So, God is therefore *merciful* in allowing Satan his time, because he unmasks himself to all, even the uneducated and ignorant, and this means a mass exodus out of his stadium of deception by those of good will."

David had lost the sense of what Fr. Keogh was saying as he had continued following the diocesan spies across the open field; they seemed to be heading for St. Joseph's church. Tiring of the game, he started to run, causing them to so the same. He laughed as they breathlessly looked over their shoulders at their pursuing nemesis. He sensed that these lower-level Pharisees were not the bishop's official agents but vermin who had emerged from some dark place, perhaps a diabolical cult like Ann

Boleyn came from when she was sent with syphilis to seduce Henry VIII by a French coven of witches, in order to destroy the Church, Henry VIII, and England. For the sake of his lust, Henry demanded from the Pope the dissolution of his marriage, which was denied, and this led to the demise of Catholicism in England. England was reputedly 98% Catholic. At least David strongly suspected the supposed clerics he chased off were operating outside the Church hierarchy, maybe employed by the shadow-church in a quasi-ecclesiastical capacity.

As David, the security guard, returned and gazed upon the small crowd and its preacher on the rock, David called to mind the itinerant preacher Jesus, teaching here, there, and everywhere to the people: rich, poor, Jew, Greek, barbarian, that is, all who would listen to Him. "And look what the people's supposed leaders did to Jesus for that," David said out loud but in a low voice, asking himself, 'was the motive of the present enemy jealousy of the individual preacher (Fr. Keogh) or the destruction of God's Church?' It was all analogous to the *crucifixion of mankind's Savior:* in this case, focused on the person of Jesus' witness, Fr. Keogh. He truly represented the Mystical Body of Christ, the Church. 'Why?' David asked himself, muttering the answer. "For threatening to take the people away from the jaws of a demonic wolf of error and for pointing out those very wolves, standing before all, dressed in the pious sheepskins of their fake authority, lips dripping with the blood of their eternal crimes of false witness.'

"I have to protect Fr. Keogh," said David to himself but without panic. However, a feeling of helplessness welled up in him. He uttered in a low voice, "But how can I? He is fearless. He follows his Master, carrying the cross of telling the Truth without fear."

As David neared the crowd, he recognized the story of the first Passover of Israel in Egypt being retold. Fr. Keogh was reading from Exodus, Chapter 12 about the Passover meal: how a lamb, the archetype of Jesus (the Lamb of God), was stretched, as if on a cross, without a bone of it to be broken; then it was to be roasted and eaten as men strengthening themselves for a journey, standing with staff in hand as they ate. The blood of this unblemished lamb was to be smeared on every doorpost in the form of a cross, so the destroying angel would pass over that household, sparing the firstborn, who was always dedicated to God at birth in Israel. And then Fr. Keogh skillfully told how the Last Supper was the celebration of Passover by the Person of Jesus who passes over all sinners who have consumed their Savior worthily (i.e., repentant of their sins). In consuming the Body and Blood, Soul and Divinity of the Lamb of God in an unbloody manner under the appearances of bread and wine, the priestly sacrifice first offered by Melchizedek, was the fulfillment of the Passover promise. This Sacrifice of Jesus on behalf of those at the banquet (Mass) removes their sins before God the Father. This Sacrifice of the Lamb of God, the second Person of the Trinity, redeemed Mankind.

"Jesus is the true Lamb of God!" intoned the priest. "He sacrificed His own Body and Blood at that first Mass with His Apostles in attendance." David saw a reverent awe on the faces of the audience, made up mostly of Catholics who had long known or suspected this truth but who had never been so struck by its profound reality, something Fr. Keogh's Faith conveyed as surely as he would soon confect the very Sacrament he referred to. Finally, Fr. Keogh read to them from the Gospel of St. John:

> *"Then Jesus said to them: Amen, amen, I say to you: Unless you eat the flesh of the Son of man, and drink his blood, you shall not have life in you. He that eateth my flesh, and drinketh my blood, hath everlasting life: and I will raise him up at the last day."*[40]

"Jesus referred to the unbloody sacrifice of Himself, the Lamb of God, celebrated at the Last Supper and thereafter in the Holy Mass by His Apostles," said Fr. Keogh.

David approached those farthest from the priest, those who appeared disenfranchised and most in need. He spied one such young man of about eighteen years, his clothes, face and hands unwashed for months, apparently. David imagined that he slept outside on the ground with the insects and wild animals. He had a bushy beard and longish, unkempt hair.

"You, you are an assistant of his?" the young man asked after David introduced himself. He motioned towards the preacher, as he spoke.

---

[40] John 6: 54-57

"This Mass that he is going to say, is it really a celebration of Jesus' Last Supper, which I think he just called a sacrifice? If so, I have a question, how can it also be the Eucharist, which means..."

"Thanksgiving," said David.

"Yes, yes, sir; how can a sacrifice also be a thanksgiving?" The youth's blue eyes were so hungry, so honestly unflinching in seeking the truth of this mystery that David spoke very earnestly and gently in attempting to answer this obviously educated young man, evidently now cast upon hard times. He was not unlike the prodigal son in Jesus' parable, David thought.

"Was not the Divine *Sacrifice* heralded by the sacrifice of a lamb at God's command also a celebration of *thanksgiving* by those whom the Angel of Death would pass over?" asked David. "The eternal *Sacrifice* of the Lamb of God made the merciful Passover possible. Jesus was sacrificed for all of us in every age, past and future. The redemptive power and mercy of the archetype stemming from the Passover meal of the Israelites, came from Jesus' later sacrifice on the Cross. As God, that Sacrifice is eternal: lasting until the end of time in the Holy Sacrifice of the Mass."

David asked the young man his name. "Martin, *are we not to give thanks for this sacrifice made by Jesus* even more so than the Jews did in the Passover?" David looked directly at the young man. "With this unbloody sacrifice, all future generations could obey the command of Jesus that Father just read in the Gospel of St. John 6:54-55." David repeated the good news of the Gospel from memory:

> *Then Jesus said to them: Amen, amen I say unto you: Except you eat the flesh of the Son of man, and drink his blood, you shall not have life in you. He that eateth my flesh, and drinketh my blood, hath everlasting life: and I will raise him up in the last day.*

"Are you thankful for the Salvation unto eternal life which Jesus' Sacrifice brings us?" David looked into the young man's eyes as he asked this question.

"I am very thankful," said the young man, bowing his head in humility. "I believe what Jesus said. Can I receive Jesus from this priest?"

"Yes. Go see the priest of God up there as soon as he is done speaking. Come," David said, "I will personally introduce you. What is your name again?"

"Martin," came the weak reply.

After Mass, Fr. Keogh received the emaciated, curly-haired, blonde beggar into the Church by Baptism. After the Sacrament of Penance (confession), Martin received his first Holy Communion. The priest made sure Martin received Jesus on his knees, on the tongue, with his hands folded in prayer, as he had instructed everyone at the end of his talk. David taught Martin all he must do interiorly and exteriorly to properly receive Almighty God, that is, with all due respect, submission and reverence. David could not understand those who dared to follow the suggestion of ecclesiastical heretics (wolves) to stand while receiving Communion, as if they were God's equal, and then insult Him further by taking the Host in their unconsecrated hand, chewing Him like a cow chews its cud; then, to top off these sacrileges, they would get up after Mass and talk out loud as if in a meeting hall rather than in a house of prayer, where *God was actually present in the Tabernacle!* David believed the Latin admonition affirming that 'faith parallels its practice', and he predicted that these small, unintentional but significant acts of irreverence would lead to a loss of faith or general apostasy in the face of threats. And so the future followers of Antichrist were born over the years in their acts of careless irreverence.

That evening Martin ate a few bites of supper and fell asleep early beside their sleeping fire. Angela covered him tenderly with a blanket, lovingly, like his own mother would have done. In the morning, they found that he had passed away, taken to Heaven by his merciful Shepherd. Fr. Keogh said a Requiem Mass for him where he lay, and they buried him there in the limestone bedrock, a strong but shallow grave. Fr. Keogh noted in his sermon that the Church taught that all punishment due to sin is washed away by the Sacrament of Baptism. "This means that Martin immediately entered Heaven," said Fr. Keogh after Mass. It was the first time David had seen tears of joy in the priest's eyes.

* * *

That evening, after burying the body and having a penitential meal of bread and water, Fr. Keogh spoke to them. The firelight flickered across the faces of the twelve who sat in the circle of firelight with him. "Just before David introduced Martin, who was surely in the last stages of starvation, though we knew it not, I had a kind of 'epiphany' in regard to one of the terms David coined over a year ago: *The Indivisible Light*. It is a symbol worthy of our Savior, Jesus Christ and His Church, even though it does not appear in the Church's dogmatic literature as far as I know; therefore, the term presently has no theological standing. However, Divine Love and the Light of Truth emanating from it, would form an Indivisible Light, as I conceive it. If there is moral evil, that Light of Truth would illuminate and correct the sinner's conscience. The sinner will experience this Light as guilt, remorse, and humility, hopefully leading to repentance. This Holy Light penetrates the emptiness of sin, since evil is merely a lack of good. But, if this Light shines upon good like Martin's soul, It *warms* his spirit, because it will be recognized and welcomed by that same God-given goodness or natural holiness in the soul. This Indivisible Light is recognized by Its reflection: good works, which are the concrete evidence of holiness, the presence of divine Love in a soul."

"I believe Martin was full of this love, witnessed by his good works. Yes, his soul was ready to receive His Redeemer. His confession alone told me that. If my memory serves me correctly, biographer Irving Stone quotes Abraham Lincoln as saying: '*Love is Eternal*'.[41] We know this is true, since all true love is from God, Who is, by definition, eternal. Holiness or goodness in a man immediately recognizes its Redeemer, Who is Infinite Good, the reason for its goodness (being). Scripture witnesses to eternal love's recognition by good souls: '*he who does not believe is already condemned*'.[42] Why is this so? Because this Indivisible Light of Christ has already penetrated all darkness, all defensive denial and is therefore *undeniable*. This is why unbelief condemns. Denying this Light is a malicious lie, a sin against the Holy Ghost, that is, a sin against the *known truth*. The reprobate, though educated in his

---

41 https://ourlostfounding.com/abraham-lincoln-marries-mary-todd-love-is-eternal/

42 St. John 3:18

error, will persevere in denying the Light of Truth, his Savior, and in this persistent lie, he rejects the very Word that created him from nothing, thus, negating himself, cutting himself off from the source and fulfillment of Life, eternal life, and that by his own choice, so that his created being is no longer recognizable to its Creator. That blackened soul is expelled by the wrath of God like a cinder from the fire of His Holy Love, which is *jealous* of all lesser loves. For such an unfortunate soul, banishment to darkness (Hell) was chosen by loving its own disordered conceits in preference to its Redeemer and Physician healing its brokenness. In short, Hell is preferable for the damned to being in the presence of Truth, because that is the place and order Justice has assigned it."

"You mean the soul is banished from the Light, by its own choice?" asked Michael, his eyes flashing white in the firelight.

"Yes, Michael," said Fr. Keogh, looking at him with love and pity at the thought of such sinners. "It is hard for many to understand the evil of unbelief, but culpable ignorance of one's God and Creator is the intentional rejection of Divine Light which penetrates the heart of every person but is possessed only by one's choice. Does that make sense?" asked the priest, turning eyes of love towards this soul searching, like a miner for the 'mother lode'.

"I think so," Michael said.

"If *love is eternal*', then God is its source, because He is eternal, therefore, true love is also eternal." Fr. Keogh was quiet for five minutes, deep in thought.

"Father, did you imply that the Church is equated with the Indivisible Light?" asked Angela, partly to interrupt his reverie, which was making her nervous.

"I think it is, at least by analogy," said the priest, glancing at her with a look of appreciation. "The Light that emanates from the Church is the Light of Christ, who is the Head of the Church and the Source of its supernatural Life. St. John says that the unbaptized John the Baptist was '*to bear witness to the light … the true light that enlightens every man who comes into the world.*' That would have to be Jesus. In John 1:18, we read that this Light has come into the world to reveal God. We, who are born of God in Baptism, receive Him in the Eucharist."

"Then we are like candles burning before Almighty God," said Angela joyfully. David smiled; that's my girl, he thought.

"How can we know if we are born of God, though?" asked Michael.

"If you receive in belief the Light, which is the truth of Christ, and you do the works of that Light, you know that you have been necessarily born of God," said Fr. Keogh. "This Light transforms you, giving birth to a new spiritual being. This is why our Baptism confers a *new* name."

"Otherwise, you could not have received Christ in His Church as you have, Michael," said Charlene.

"Exactly so, Charlene," said Fr. Keogh, smiling her way.

"Isn't Mary a symbol of the Church giving birth to a son (pope) who will flee from the diabolical Dragon that would like to devour the son in Chapter 12 of the Apocalypse?" David asked.

"Yes, and we have an analogy from Scripture: Joseph, Mary and the Christ Child, the infant Church, fleeing into Egypt when the Dragon, Herod, sought to devour the Son of Mary, Jesus, the Christ. The point is obscure, and I would say, twofold:"

"1) In the End Times, a pope and the Church will be hidden from the dragon (Satan) in the Vatican, who will cast evil waters after the children of Mary (the remnant of true believers). I interpret it this way: Francis the Freemason, a 'dragon' of Satan, has caused the true pope, Benedict XVI, to go into hiding along with the true Church (the remnant or very few who believe he is the pope). Francis orchestrates the pandemic through his bishops to destroy the Church but fails and the leaders of nations (the 'earth') stop the scamdemic framework erected by Satan's assistants (Gates and his eugenicist pals), because they serve the people morally threatened by destruction of their livelihood. As Apocalypse 12:11 says, the saints and martyrs overcame the Satanic 'river' meant to destroy the Church."

"2) The Light and Love of God comes to us only *through* Jesus' mother Mary. Jesus *gave us this* <u>*Holy Mother*</u>*, the Tabernacle of God, from His Cross when He gave her to the Apostle, John.* She is full of grace containing Christ within her spiritually, even as she did physically from the Annunciation to the Incarnation."

"I guess I don't understand why Protestants cannot accept Mary as their mother when Jesus commanded it from the Cross," said Michael.

"And I agree," said the priest. "I can only guess they didn't want to believe God's Word as much as their interpretation of God's Word, thus making themselves little gods. But remember, the Protestant heretics of old do not necessarily hold sway today. It was out of pride that Satan did not want a human intermediary before God, since he was enough! Maybe their claim to a Biblical orientation was a Protestant cover/ defense for denying it at will. Did that preface a planned rebellion and schism from the Church?"

"But even if we can see their error, we must keep in mind the parable of Jesus where the Samaritan (the equivalent of a Protestant in those days) aided the robber's victim, but those of the true religion had passed him by. Note that Jesus did not by this parable dismiss the true religion of Juda, but he shamed and accused the practitioners of Judaism for not having the spirit of God, the Spirit of divine love which *should* have been theirs as members of God's people. Sometimes the same is true today: Catholics should imitate those Protestants who do good works, rather than Catholics in name only who do not. Ultimately, Israel did not follow Jesus Christ; the Gentiles did. Are we seeing such an anomaly today? If so, and the Catholic Church is the New Israel, who are the 'Gentiles'?"

"But let me continue my former train of thought before I lose it: I can see Mary as a prototype of the *Church*, a Tabernacle which houses Jesus Christ, just as she carried Him in her womb. In the same way, every church contains God's Real Presence in its tabernacle, i.e., the Eucharistic Presence. Symbolically, the Church is the Ark which carried humanity to be saved, just as the wooden Ark carried Noah and his family. The Church of Jesus Christ resembles the people of Israel, the descendants of Jacob (Israel); for just as Jacob received the blessing Esau should have been given by hereditary custom, because Jacob was worthy and Esau was not, the new Israel, the Church is made worthy by faith in God. Since the time of Christ's crucifixion, by analogy, His Church became the Ark of the Covenant which old Israel carried through the desert. The Church contains the *Tabernacle* on its altars, which resembles the Ark and contains the Real Presence of Jesus Christ under the appearances of bread and wine. Like the Israelites, who were God's chosen people in their true belief, Catholics receive the 'blessing of

Jacob,' but in both cases, acting on Faith is key to a happy ending. God is with us, indeed, as He promised, but those who are too worldly to really believe Him and wear the badge of true religion as a status symbol are worse than those not invited to the wedding feast. They are apostates. God abandons them in the desert of their own lifeless denial of the Truth standing before them. Those who have the Faith of Peter believe the Church carries God's Presence within herself. We were reborn in this image of Christ by His Church at our Baptism and by God's grace. Mary did not inherit Adam's Original Sin (the doctrine of the *Immaculate Conception*, the title of Mary to which the U.S.A. is consecrated), so that unlike the rest of mankind, Mary is fittingly the *perfect* human Mother of God, the worthy instrument of God's Incarnation. I'm sorry if I take advantage of you, my dear friends, taking your simple questions and expanding on them to such an extent." Fr. Keogh said this in a tone of sincere apology.

"Gosh, Father," said Michael, "that's what I love to hear even if all of it does not sink in." Sincere murmurs of agreement came from all around the circle of firelight, something which Michael seemed to visibly appreciate, having first spoken for himself in behalf of all. David quietly smiled with joy that his friend recognized his Faith speaking for their small community, namely, in his ability to speak for them, one and all.

Fr. Keogh looked at David. "Maybe you could wrap this up by saying a few final words, David? I am getting pretty worn out."

David spoke in his strength. "In God, we will find our beginning and our end or purpose. He is our fulfillment, our wholeness. When we receive Jesus in Holy Communion, we can imagine that we are filled with an Indivisible Light of Love and Knowledge; so that there is no shadow of doubt or deceit in us, no sin, nor spirit of evil. In receiving Jesus we are filled with the Light of Truth Itself."

"Thank you, David," the priest said, looking one last time at those in the circle of light. He wiped the sweat from his brow and sipped water. He did not look well, thought David. "Sometimes I think the Lord is ready to take me," said the priest, chuckling awkwardly.

"It is true that I have told you nothing new," continued the priest. "'The Indivisible Light' is just a concept, another expression for what has already been revealed to us in more traditional terms. Its value is in helping us better understand or perceive. We must, therefore, consider the term '*The Indivisible Light*' subject to the judgement of the Church."

"It can be a means of better understanding the same traditional truths from a different perspective then?" asked David. Fr. Keogh nodded a tired assent.

"Faith always involves mysteries beyond our ability to comprehend," said the priest. "We can better grasp these mysteries sometimes by meditating on them from different angles, in order to more fully appreciate their beauty: like we view the different facets of a diamond. We should always begin by examining traditional sources first, like the Popes and Saints, who reveal the mind of the Church on the subject. St. Thomas, using his own unique and divinely inspired points of view, resolved disputes between great theologians by showing how their views of the matter fit together to make a holistic understanding. So, let us end by praying for the grace of understanding that we may be led by the Holy Spirit in contemplating these matters:

> *"Let me not, O Lord, be puffed up with worldly wisdom, which passes away, but grant me that love which never abates, that I may not choose to know anything among men but Jesus, and Him crucified.*[43] *I pray Thee, loving Jesus, that as Thou hast graciously given me to drink in with delight the words of Thy knowledge, so Thou wouldst mercifully grant me to attain one day to Thee, the Fountain of all Wisdom and to appear forever before Thy face. Amen.*[44]"

David and Angela decided to walk home from Meadow Heights as it had been dubbed. They had all agreed the place deserved a special name. The landscape was bathed in moonlight. The others stayed at the pines, planning to leave for home in the morning. David and Angela left quietly after tying their belongings on Paintbrush, who followed them, led by a leather tether which David held loosely. He reflected aloud: "Fr. Keogh once said the Church teaches that by our works of Faith, we can

---

43 I Corinthians 8:2

44 Venerable Bede, the Father of English History

increase in ourselves the degree of sanctifying grace and a higher place in Heaven."

"The sanctifying grace you speak of, that is also a mystery, isn't it?" Angela asked.

"Yes," David said, "and let's use an analogy to help us grasp this mystery. Look at the sky. We know the sky is full of stars, but the moonlight hides many of them, outshining them with a closer, brighter light. So let's imagine that the stars represent all the facets of a divine mystery, but some of those we cannot fully comprehend because of the moonlight, which represents worldly knowledge. We are partially blinded to those brilliant, but to us, fainter stars, facets of the mystery, because our senses are engaged by a light/knowledge closer to earth, one that shines more brightly for us, such as city lights or the moon does, obscuring stars."

"So, the moon is analogous to the lesser yet closer light which is blinding us to a greater understanding of the spiritual mysteries represented by the distant stars?" asked Angela.

"Yes." David smiled in embarrassment and admiration of her simplicity. "Lesser *lights* mean the perception of our senses which our fallen human nature causes to have priority over the light of reason."

"The moon and its light," said Angela, "must represent the world and its ways which blinds us to what lies above and beyond them."

"St. Thomas was simple and pure and prayerful; thus as such, he was able to capture the essence of mysteries, even though he was called the Dumb Ox.[45] You've captured the metaphor," said David, giving her a squeeze.

She leaned her head against his arm as they walked, as if it were her personal moving pillow. "You give me too much credit when it is really yours," she said. "I am completely happy with you as my leader." She looked at him gently, turning his face in order to meet her lips.

He smiled. "You are my diamond, sparkling in many facets: a gift of God's love."

"And you are my Sunshine, the gift of God, which makes me always happy and warm and ..."

---

45 The Dumb Ox: St. Thomas Aquinas: Free Download, Borrow, and Streaming: Internet Archive

"But you are better," said David, "more brilliant and beautiful, like a gem." They laughed, then embraced with gratitude because their hyperbole proved they were still in love.

"How does the Indivisible Light we discussed at the campfire relate to Eternal Love?" Angela asked with a smile. David's face turned serious; the expression told her she had turned on his 'search and answer' mode. Looking at him again, she saw that his intellect had been activated. She knew she would enjoy seeing him resolve the problem.

"I speculate that the Son's gift of the Indivisible Light of Truth that we assent to was ignited by the fire of the Father's Eternal Love for the Second Person of the Trinity, a Fiery Love that Tradition identifies as the Holy Spirit Itself, the Third Person of the Trinity. This fire does not burn out but consumes everything in His Love, including us, because we are the Father's adopted children."

"Until we disappear into our Maker?" Angela probed speculatively.

"Not exactly disappear," replied David, "because we are existentially distinct from God and because our individual souls are *immortal in themselves*, as God created them. Rather, we are united with God by becoming *like* Him in a love which we call, *charity*. This 'union' with God is the goal of the contemplative life, which is analogous to the union of marriage."

"But how can we be one with Him and still be ourselves?" Angela asked sweetly, like precocious children pushing buttons to see what would happen.

David thought long and hard, wrinkling his brows, and finally giving her a quick grin of satisfaction. "Because we ourselves are hidden in Christ, complete in Him at our death. St. Paul said this in Scripture.[46] Only then will we be fully revealed as to who we are, in His perfect, Creative Love, our Omega, our final, eternal end. We will be perfected by Christ, so that we can be comformable with the Trinity."

"You mean our identity is not established except in Christ?"

"Right! Our character establishes our human identity, but Christ perfects it and sanctifies it. There is the answer to the riddle you proposed. That is what I think St. Paul meant. Now listen, help me

---

[46] Colossians 3:3

with this one," said David. "Aristotle's fourth and highest cause is the final cause, which is the purpose of a thing, the *why* of a thing, its end, and this *final cause* essentially determines what a thing is. Now, if our final end as Christians is Christ, we are not fully who we are until we live in Christ's Love eternally, because that is our final end, our destiny. When our reason for being is perfectly and completely accomplished, we become, in a sense, one with Him in Whom it was necessary for us to reach our final end, achieving with His help or grace His purpose in creating us. Now," David said triumphantly, glancing at her, "enough testing. What grade do I get Ms. Inquisitoria?"

"An A+, as usual," she yawned in mock ho-hum boredom.

They fell silent as they entered the quiet darkness of the forest. In twenty minutes they came upon their little home in the clearing. "Your questions are very insightful," said David with sincere appreciation for the sharp student he had; truly, she was a blessing from Heaven, he thought. David turned to her as they broke out of the forest into the clearing where their house stood softly aglow by interior yellow lights. "You get an A+ in the question department, my cute little sassy student." Angela smiled in 'offended' appreciation. "Questions are the principle tools of exploration," said David. "They are nearly half the journey to one's goal."

"Are the twins asleep?" David asked the babysitter, peeking into their room.

"Yes," said the young girl, whom Charlene was boarding while her mother recuperated from an infection in the hospital.

Chapter 6

SACRIFICIAL LOVE

Two months later, Fr. Keogh's fifteenth ordination anniversary was fast approaching. Three weeks before the anniversary date he had put in a request to say Mass at St. Joseph's on that occasion. He had just received a note from the bishop's office granting permission for him to say Mass in a parish church on August 15, the Feast of the Assumption of Mary into Heaven, body and soul. Overjoyed, he showed the signed letter to David, who studied it and thought it suspicious, too much like the last one, except for the bishop's signature. David expressed his misgivings, but Fr. Keogh was satisfied because three priests he personally knew had volunteered to serve as deacons in the more complicated high mass liturgy used on these occasions.

David spoke to Angela and Michael about having the long-planned apologetic rally in the courtyard of St. Joseph's during Father's Mass. In this way, Fr. Keogh would be immediately available after Mass for acceptance of converts into the Church, followed by their Baptism and reception of Holy Communion.

"He could reserve Hosts from his Mass in the church for the first communicants," said Angela, "and you can provide security for Fr. Keogh after Mass."

David was satisfied that all desirable objectives would be met at one time. The bishop was getting old, and it was to be expected that his signature appeared to be a little shaky or that a secretary would have to sign for him. Still, based on the last episode, his suspicion was warranted,

David thought, and those demonic "monks" should not be in the picture any longer, according to Fr. Keogh.

The morning of August 15 was fair and beautiful, befitting the glorious feast day celebrated by the Church. The vast dome of majestic, azure blue sky overhead suggested the vault of Heaven. Fluffy, white, irregularly shaped, cotton-ball clouds marched across the faultless blue, like an exuberant parade of celebrants. Everyone with David had dressed up in their Sunday best. Especially the twins caught one's eye: one in a pinstriped white shirt and a dark vest like his dad's, his sister in a creamy white dress trimmed in Prussian blue. They were accompanied and doted upon by a very happy, attentive, loving father, continually talking to his son and daughter as if they could appreciate every affectionate over-the-top comment. David smiled at his friend. Michael was never too proud to help, he thought, never arrogant, never a stopped-ears syndrome. He always tried to understand. For the sake of this humility, David considered him blessed, but he feared to compliment him, since it could "go to his head", which he knew was enough to ruin a Christian man still in formation. Angela wore a widely bleated, ankle length skirt, in a light green floral pattern, sprinkled with pink silk roses she had found in a second-hand store. Her dress showed an exuberance of white frills; it was complimented by Charlene's solid satin, pale chartreuse dress.

According to ancient custom, they had fasted since midnight for Communion. Mass was at 8:30 AM on this Holy Day of Obligation, and the church was sure to be overflowing. They had met at 6 AM inside Father Keogh's cabin to say the Rosary, kneeling on the floor made of rough-cut knotty-pine planks. Fr. Keogh appeared in his cassock, perfectly silent and apparently enclosed within the privacy of a deep solemn, interior recollection. When he turned slowly to face them, they saw the dreadful look that spelled bad news.

The priest was sobbing quietly, something David had never seen. Stuttering at first, he finally blurted out, "They have *crucified* Pope Benedict!" Everyone gasped in shock; they were locked in stunned silence. Fr. Keogh led them in prayer for the repose of Benedict XVI's soul and for the safety of the Church, since Benedict was the last pope, according to the prophecy of St. Malachy and Pope Benedict had been surrounded by dark powers.

David had known only that Pope Benedict had fled Rome last month, just as the Red Revolution had burst upon that city and that while in exile he had managed to consecrate Russia, after publicly declaring that he was still the pope because his "resignation" had never been made according to the strict instructions of Canon Law; in addition, his supposed resignation of papal authority and power was made under threats against his life and that of the Church, which also nullified Benedict's resignation. David understood that if true, this doubled the reason his heretical "successor's" election was invalid.

A manifest (public) heretic like Francis automatically loses office, according to Tradition and the Doctors of the Church, like St. Robert Bellarmine and St. Thomas Aquinas. With an extreme leftist imposter 'pope' sitting on the chair of Peter, cooperating with the evil powers of the World, the Red Serpent's Communist Conspiracy now threatened to take over the world for Antichrist.

"God help us," David said under his breath. He thought of the Church's traditional archetype, Noah's Ark, which, like the true Church today, had been tossed about by huge waves on a vast and violent sea of dark, evil waters, seething with rage at the tiny ship of God's chosen souls, the *remnant*, which God would save, David believed, to reseed the human race and all life on earth. He imagined a giant red Sea Serpent thrashing its long tail in hateful rage in order to create that violent sea. This would be the same Red Serpent that was now snapping at the Ark of the Church, as depicted in Chapter 12 of the Apocalypse. The Holy Sacrifice of the Mass and the Papacy held back the Antichrist. Now there was only the reassurance of Christ's promise that the barque of Peter would be preserved until the end of time. David believed that the few Faithful and True under the Mother of God's watchful eye would, like the Catholics of France under St. Joan of Arc, defeat the antichrist in their time and usher in the Great Peace, repopulating the entire earth, just as Noah's family did (generating six billion souls in a period of around 4500 years). He remembered the words of Fr. Keogh: "Do the math; it's quite possible." David knew Fr. Keogh well enough to know that he was engulfed in grievous suffering at the news of the Pope's murder. Added to this was his concern for the preservation of hope and confidence in the remaining Faithful, undeceived members of the Church, an Institution which *appeared* to have sunk beneath the waves, definitively altered by Francis and his fellow Freemasonic bishops worldwide. God was testing His Faithful to the limit!

David tried to cheer Fr. Keogh a little as they all walked to the church together, recounting some of the accomplishments of the quiet, intellectual Pope Benedict XVI, now a martyr for Christ because he had finally stood up against the usurpation of the papacy and the Church by a cruel and ruthless enemy, who killed him for it. Benedict had come to recognize Francis and company for the antichristian 'Jesuit' mobsters they were, with only one good prelate, Archbishop Vigano, calling them out repeatedly from his place of hiding.

"Tell us again, Father," said David, "how Pope Benedict consecrated Russia when so many liberal, Freemasonic bishops were ordered *not* to cooperate in that Consecration by their imposter pope. We know Benedict had to escape the Vatican before he could do the consecration, but that alone does not get the job done. And we know that Heaven required that the pope and *all the bishops of the world* join the pope in consecrating Russia to the Immaculate Heart of Mary at the same time." David motioned for all to huddle around.

"Well," said Fr. Keogh, rising to the occasion, "it was masterful, I thought, how our beloved Benedict accomplished it. He just commanded every bishop in the world to join him in the consecration of Russia at the appointed time, under pain of their immediate loss of office as a bishop of the Church since that office was by appointment of the Pope. In other words, all of those cooperating in the Consecration remained bishops of the Church and those who refused were no longer bishops; therefore, *all* the bishops of the world made the consecration of Russia."

Some laughed or chuckled, but everyone was relieved to see the priest come out of his depression to rally around a heroic martyr of their times. After the considerable walk, David accompanied Fr. Keogh into St. Joseph's Church. David and Michael watched from the pews as the priest commiserated with his three priest friends from the diocesan headquarters concerning the news of the pope's murder. 'He is like a hen surrounded by foxes', David thought, studying the three dispassionate faces that barely hid their disdain for the fate of Benedict and for this simpleton priest bewailing him. These Pharisees, thought David, did not understand that religion was not about men and their schemes but about God. He eyed them with a suspicious hatred for their kind. What he could see for sure was that these three priests only feigned deference and respect for Fr. Keogh. Their disgust for him was visible. They obviously despised what they mistakenly saw as his naiveté, because they themselves had surrendered the integrity of their souls to kiss butt in order to get ahead. David knew he had to get to the church as soon as Mass was over. He didn't trust Fr. Keogh alone with these so-called friends.

"What's up, man?" asked Michael, looking at his friend minutes later, still staring daggers.

David looked at Michael, then nodded toward the trio who would serve mass with Fr. Keogh. "I'm almost afraid to leave him with those foxes. They stink," whispered David, scowling.

"They look pretty arrogant," Michael whispered back. "Maybe they will learn humility from the only person I know who demonstrates that virtue in everything he does. But I agree, Fr. Keogh looks like a type of *sacrificial lamb*. But what can happen to him before a church full of people who love and respect him?" Michael whispered.

"David! You are scheduled to speak in three minutes!!" Angela whispered close to his ear, while yanking his shirt sleeve. All three hurriedly exited the nave and ran for the podium which was setup at the far end of the 'courtyard', a fifty-by-seventy-five-yard field of closely cropped, golf-course green grass, enclosed by a surrounding hedge of shrubs, head high, with neatly trimmed currant, blueberry, raspberry and blackberries bushes interspersed. With the pastor's permission, David had asked someone to tell the people when assembled to harvest the ripe berries and take home what they could use, since the fruit would fully ripe on the vine in less than a week.

David took the portable podium in two hands exactly on time. Fr. Keogh had affirmed David's idea that while Mass was being said all those who could not yet fully participate in Mass could be evangelized by the two couples but principally by David, so that many might be received into the Church who were willing to profess the Apostle's Creed, since they had all been previously catechized in their own parish. It was a rare occasion that Fr. Keogh could do this. Now the courtyard was full of those who had responded to weeks of advertising an invitation to learn more about the Church and to fulfill in one day the remaining catechetical test for adult Baptism, which would be available after the Mass.

David faced the crowd. He made the sign of the cross, joined by fifty percent of his audience. He explained to the rest that it meant that they prayed in the name of the Triune God, following Holy Scripture when the Apostles were commissioned to evangelize all nations in that name. "We are here to discuss true Religion: the one and only relationship between God and Man. Those of you here with the permission of your pastor to join the Church, having been prepared by the indoctrination of those he appointed will be admitted into the Church today, upon your request. I will try to show today how to identity the true Religion dictated by God, not by man nor by any circumstance or event. We will be defining the terms that must be understood and agreed upon before we can even have a rational discussion about religion or come to any satisfying conclusions." The crowd had gone totally silent, sensing that all their attention would be required to follow this speaker. "What I am about to discuss is not the catechesis you have already heard, but a philosophical background necessary to actually understand that catechesis."

David paused for five seconds, as he looked at his notes, praying briefly for the intercession of St. Thomas Aquinas for the Lord's assistance, for he admitted to himself that he was not an organized, confident public speaker.

"*Point one*: We want to speak of spiritual things, but do we even know of what a spiritual, non-material soul consists? Can we demonstrate, briefly, in some simple way, what a soul is? We can always fall back to that which is *self-evident* and considered a demonstration of scientific knowledge, which we can have certainty of, our divine Faith building upon that simple knowledge. Imagine that a cow stands before you. It moves; it eats; it makes sounds, it can hear me speaking and it has some degree of instinctual animal sense or 'instinct', determined by its species; some call 'intelligence'. The cow is slaughtered. None of those traits mentioned are now possessed by that cow's body. Why? Because the body of the cow had an animal soul, and *death is the separation of the soul from the body*. I define after Aristotle the 'soul' as being the *active principle* animating a body. Soul is a collective term denoting all those active principles animating a living creature, including plants, which are distinguished chiefly by *growth*, and animals by *movement*; finally, there is man whose soul is distinguished by *rationality*. Without its invisible, active soul, the body of the dead creature does not move or think. So, death proves to us that the body is alive only by its own, individual principle of activity or 'soul'; unless there is a lifeless reflex remaining, a dead body never moves itself. By itself, it only rots and turns into dust, a pile of minerals."

"Therefore, *Fact #1: All living creatures have invisible, non-material souls, the principle of activity for the operation of their visible material body.*"

"*Point two:* The common undeniable, self-evident human experience is that we know good from evil. For example, it is observed by all that love and other virtues are *good* habits leading to many good works; it is equally apparent that hatred and other vices lead to evil habits which result in a lack of peace, passionate anger, murder, including abortion, theft, rape, etc. We also observe that it is our souls and not our amoral animal bodies that know good as opposed to evil. This shows that we are composite beings, composed of both body and soul separately."

"*Fact 2: Humans are composite beings with souls that know good from evil, right from wrong.*"

"*Point three:* Every parent can say there must be a Creator; for they can reason that our little Johnny was not here one day, but the next day tests showed he was here in the womb, and he, like all other children, steadily and *inevitably* grew to be a human being like ourselves. Johnny's parents were able to see that they were only a *means* of bringing Johnny into existence but not the efficient cause, since they could not even make a chair or a pair of boots, much less a child. Their God and Creator, on the other hand, is He Who ultimately causes something to exist, because His essence (active principle) is existence itself, and so He said to Moses: '*I am who am*'. This Creator of all things causes all that comes into being to exist. Therefore, all creatures are naturally subject to Him; nor can the Creator be at all dependent. He did not, therefore, come into being. He always was and always will be; all creation came from Him alone: therefore, He must be all-knowing and all-powerful because nothing can be known that He did not create, and to create is the greatest power. Nothing exists or operates without Him. Aristotle proved His existence by arriving at the necessity of one totally powerful and independent "*Unmoved Mover.*" Those who doubt such self-evident facts are 'cabbage heads', according to Aristotle." Laughter broke out, a sure sign of the crowd's attention. It was good to hear something positive, David thought, smiling.

"So, *Fact #3: There is an eternal, Omnipotent, Omniscient, self-subsisting Creator of all things whom we call God.*"

"*Point four:* Evil exists only because of sin. St. Thomas Aquinas defines evil as 'the absence of good'[47]; so, it is nothing in itself. It has no being in itself; so, it was not created. Therefore, God is not the author or cause of evil. All good is created and all evil is nothing but a negation of the created; therefore, evil must be caused by creatures, not by irrational animals or plants which cannot act with intention or prior knowledge. They do not have the faculty to freely will this or that but are moved by their created, pre-designed nature, which in animals we call instinct. Therefore, evil must be caused by men or angels because only they have a free will to do what is evil, that is, unreasonable and unnatural. It is self-evident that mankind commits evil acts, like theft and murder. But what about beings without bodies that we call angels. Can they sin? When sinful thoughts and imaginings come into our minds uninvited, we suspect an evil (perverse) intellect that can tempt us by invading our imaginations. In this we have evidence that there is an evil being, whom we call the Devil (or devils), who is more powerful than ourselves. But we see that his power to do evil to us is limited. For example, he can tempt, but he cannot force our will to sin, i.e., to do evil, because we can freely choose evil *or* good, *despite* his influence."

"Therefore, demons must be on God's leash. The Supreme Being, since He made creatures with souls, must intend their continued existence, goodness and well-being, so He would protect these creatures from the unchecked evil of a more powerful, fallen creature by limiting the demon to a corrective or testing role, subjecting the demon's acts and temptations to God's permission. It is self-evident that God is not the

[47] https://www.azquotes.com/quote/1230802

author of evil; our reason confirms this because creation/reality is good by definition, since goodness is the quality of all that has been made for a proper end, and God has sole propriety over all He does; therefore, evil, an aberration of created nature, is not caused by God but by the sin of rational creatures. It seems logical that some angels first rebelled from God's rule, then tempted men, as the Bible relates."

"*Fact #4: God does not create evil; willful creatures do. Evil is subject to God's permission.*"

"*Point five*: Creation rules out the non-scientific and irresponsible theory of Evolution. One species cannot become another species, because more complex creatures do not come from less complex ones, apes from amoebae or humans from apes. The second law of thermodynamics says that without an outside energy source, everything would disintegrate; therefore, much less would creatures evolve or even grow or continue to exist without God's *creative*, sustaining power. Grabbing for straws, the Freemasons insist on the theory of Evolution, which is the pretense that chance mutations first caused life and then the evolution of life into different species. A Princeton professor specializing in chance theory was asked, 'What are the chances of the Evolution of species occurring through mutation?' He replied, 'The same chance that a Webster's unabridged dictionary would have of coming into existence as the result of an explosion in a printing shop'." The crowd laughed uproariously, as if a pressure valve had been opened. David paused to drink a little water tinged with lemon from his flask before he continued.

"Only a Being who can bring something from nothing can cause in the womb one day a living human being where there was nothing of the kind yesterday. So too, the same must be true of the origin of a species; for if new beings are coming into existence, they are created. A humorous cartoon story illustrates the absurdity of Evolution: The evolutionist walks into a room and sees ten chairs set in order of their complexity, from a simple stool to an ornate throne, and the evolutionist declares with great assurance, 'each one evolved from the simpler one before it, the last evolving into a throne (representing humanity in our analogy). Then, a divine 'Carpenter' with white hair and beard, leaning against the wall in his chair, replied: "*No, first I made the simplest one, and then the more complex ones, one at a time, until at last I made the throne.*"

And that is probably the way God, the Creator, made the universe, from the simplest to the most complex, namely, the human species. We also know that *Aristotle*, who discovered the first principles of almost every science, *did not believe in Evolution*. He said that each species can only develop or change up to its potential, for adaptation to a changing environment, but it could not go beyond the limits of its nature because that would mean that it would become what it is not, which is absurd. There is only one alternative to debunked evolution: each species is created by God."

David took a drink of water. "Evolution has been maintained by various hoaxes, the last being that of Dr. Leaking Faucet," (mild laughter erupted) "who took a large number of bone fragments from a site in Africa and composed a skull that resembled a primitive ape-man. But someone with the same number of bone shards might have fashioned a giraffe's skull," said David. A few ripples of knowing laughter could be heard. "The Piltdown Man and the Peking Man 'discoveries' were shown to be hoaxes as well."

"Fact #5: *Everything was created by God; species did not evolve from one another.*"

David suggested they take a fifteen minute break to pick berries. He then ran to the church to check on things and returned in time for five minutes of conversation with the other three. They all realized that they had overestimated their available time; since there was not enough time for each one to do a good job before Fr. Keogh finished saying Mass. They decided to just let David finish what he had started, and let that be good enough.

"Our 6th *point*," David said, continuing, "is that there is only *one* true Religion, which is the relationship between the one and only Supreme Being and the race of man. This Religion must be initiated, revealed and ordered by God, because man does not tell God what He will do and how, since he is naturally and infinitely subordinate. For example, God, not man, will institute and describe how He will be worshiped. It is God's place to do that."

"Therefore, *Fact #6: Religion is <u>one</u> and Divinely ordained: i.e., by God, not man. On the contrary, there are <u>many</u> human religions. If a man could rightly choose his own religion, he could make up his own liturgy, creed, etc.,* *but that would not constitute the real relationship. Man can be used by God to institute religion but man cannot dictate true religion."*

"Point #7: Man needs to be saved. We know that finite man has sinned against the infinite Creator, because he did evil in disobeying His Holy Law. How can man repair the damage to this relationship? Who will pay the damages; who will remove this offense? It is not possible for finite man to repay his offenses to an infinite God."

"Therefore, *Fact #7: Man needs God's Salvation from the guilt and the consequences of his sin in order to be saved."*

"We propose in *Point* #8 that only a God-Man, Jesus, the Christ, could redeem all mankind from sin, precisely because He was both God and Man. Because of His human estate and His miracles, Jesus Christ must be both Man and God. By His creative power as God He is, spiritually, *all* Mankind when He became Man. Therefore, He can represent all sinners and expiate for them all by suffering for the sins of all Mankind, offering this acceptable Sacrifice to His Father as full satisfaction. Father and Son, equally God and equally good, Love each other."

"So, *Fact #8: True salvific religion is Christian."*

"Point #9 will prove which one of the many Christ-based creeds that claim their origin as being from God can truly make that claim; for if there is only one Christ, the God-Man, He will have only one true Religion. And God will surely reveal which is *His* saving religion, since He does not speak with a forked tongue; nor would He leave us ignorant and confused orphans, because He loves what He created and wants to save it. Even a good and wise man does not confuse those dependent on his wisdom by contradicting himself; so much less would God do this by setting up multiple creeds and sects teaching diverse and contradictory beliefs, having different liturgies, all of which would confuse man and prevent him from adhering to the One True Religion. And here is the simplest, most concrete proof of the True Church of Jesus Christ: there is only ***One*** Church that began with Jesus and was promoted by His Apostles (an Apostolic Church) which has endured to the present day unchanged in doctrine, preserving all that was written in Scripture, which alone is a mark of Divine predilection."

David waited a moment, until it seemed to him that the whole universe was utterly silent. "And that Church, of course, is the Roman Catholic Church. No other church began with the Divine Redeemer, Jesus Christ and exists today essentially unchanged. All other creeds either began after Christ or ended before the present, which means they are *not* the one true Church of Christ. Christ made Peter the head of His Church,[48] and said it would last until the end of time[49]. The Catholic Church has not only endured the test of time, but has an unbroken line of successors to Peter, the first pope, to the present day. This Church is holy, having many hundreds of Catholic Saints, proven by miracles only God could work. This Church is universally spread over the entire world."

"In conclusion, *Fact #9: The Roman Catholic Church is proven to be the <u>One</u> and only true Christian Religion because of its four marks: one, holy, catholic and apostolic, which no other church has. Amen.*"

David was surprised and pleased that more than seventy-five percent of his audience responded in kind with 'Amen,' followed by applause. "Let's take another fifteen-minute break before we conclude," said David. He kissed Angela and ran for the church.

David stood in the back of the church. Fr. Keogh was in the midst of his sermon. "Be forewarned, dear people, Jesus *offered* Salvation to all, but all had the choice to accept or reject His offer. He requires that man love Him to be saved, and love cannot be forced; *one must freely choose in order to love*. Therefore, He did not *effectively* shed His blood for all but for 'many', as the Bible and the Mass say. This contradicts the notion that you can be saved at once, for all time, by making a verbal commitment, which is little different in character than the creed of diabolical religions, where everyone is always saved; Jesus said, 'many are called, but few are chosen'.[50] Eternal salvation is for those who live their Faith by works of faith until their end when God calls them home. So too, we can be offered the gift of eternal salvation, purchased for us at great cost, but we do not actually have the gift, if we do not accept it by living it as a citizen of Heaven. Again, if a man were given a horse but never

---

48 St. Matthew 16:18

49 St. Matthew 28:20

50 St. Matthew 22:14

rode it, it would effectively be the same as if he had never been given it. So too, we can be offered forgiveness, but if we do not acknowledge the wrong we have done and confess it with true repentance, we imply that there was nothing that needed to be forgiven or changed in us, and that lie is how we reject the offer of eternal Salvation which is offered in exchange for our repentance. John the Baptist preached that forgiveness is offered to all but *effectively* given only to 'many', that is, *the repentant*. And to those offered Salvation in exchange for repentance and who choose their sin instead, they also choose an evil reward. These are the dead branches that will be thrown into unquenchable fire. This dead wood can never become the living wood of the Cross."

"But this abomination is practiced today under the name of Ecumenism, where the dead wood, the unbelievers and heretics, are invited into the Church by its own ministers, just as Judas betrayed Jesus and His disciples from within by inviting those who hated Him to capture Jesus secretly at night in the Garden for fear of the people."

"My point is this, since God offers you the Truth of the true Faith, you are free to accept it by doing the works of Faith or join Judas and all reprobates in rejecting this gift by living a life of sin. All of us are to be tested. But acceptance of God's gifts does not require us to be perfect. In choosing Christ, we have our perfection in Him."

"A couple asked me a few weeks ago, 'Father Keogh, how can we be of God, in union with Christ, but still be our sinful human selves?' And I answered that the Life of God which we receive without our merit, by His *grace*, overcomes the imperfection of our humanity. We must only repent of our sin and embrace the Spirit of God. Abraham was justified *by grace* after his great, yet insufficient work of faith in offering to sacrifice his only son at God's command. St. Paul said that we are hidden in Christ. Our full identity then is hidden in our glorious destiny as Christians, perfected by our union with Christ Himself. The degree of this union is determined by our witness to Christ. Do we have a part in this destiny? Most assuredly we have the choice each moment of consenting to God's will for us by our cooperation or not. And, if you seem to be lost, cry out to Jesus for help, and He will send you the Holy Spirit."

"Listen to St. John who wrote for us what Jesus said to them: *'And I will ask the Father, and he shall give you another Paraclete, that he may abide with you forever, The Spirit of truth, whom the world cannot receive, because it seeth him not, nor knoweth him: but you shall know him; because he shall abide with you, and shall be in you.'*[51] We see from this that it is God, not man, who establishes His Church and gathers its Faithful members by the indwelling of the Holy Spirit, the spirit of Truth. We know," said the priest, "that this Spirit speaks to His Church, as represented by Jesus and His Apostles and to each of its members in every age with *one Truth* for different peoples, problems, times and situations. In Acts it is written: *'And there appeared to them cloven tongues, as it were of fire, and it sat upon each of them: And they were all filled with the Holy Ghost, and they began to speak with divers tongues, according as the Holy Ghost gave them to speak.'*[52] It is the Holy Ghost who speaks through those who keep the Faith."

David had to return to his own lectern. Little did he know as he left the church what evil was transpiring beneath it in the bowels of the earth: the three witches David had thrown out of church were the criminal minds brewing evil for poor Fr. Keogh who had ordered David to remove them. In the deep basement of St. Joseph's Church there was a very small, forgotten cement bunker which formerly housed the steam generator for the building; it was directly under the altar two levels above. The dank little room had been abandoned many years ago for a modern furnace. A four-foot high sliding door leading to a narrow shaft of steel spiral stairs had been cleverly hidden by a heavy, oak slide-away chest of drawers in a niche off the vestibule on the main floor. The twenty-square foot concrete room had been totally forgotten over the decades, but the building's blueprints were preserved in the diocesan archives, where they were filed in a small library. One of the three witches, all pretending to be nuns, worked there and happened to discover the existence of the room.

The witches assigned themselves titles as wicked officers of a secret court. As in any such tribunal, they brought charges against the accused, Fr. Keogh. Their posturing as officers of an ecclesiastical court was "justified" by their (illegal) "ordination" as priestesses. All this

---

51 St. John 14: 16-17

52 Acts 2:3-4

entitlement was aided and abetted by their exceedingly wicked vanity and presumption. They now gathered around a single naked sixty-watt light bulb dangling over an old, worn oak table in this dank, moldy bunker.

The horrible redhead, *Misconception*, pretended to be a *prosecuting attorney*. The pinch-faced, dark haired *Misfit* took on the role of the *"defense" attorney* and, finally, their undisputed tyrant, *Merciless*, who had vocally interrupted the accused's sermon, pretended to be the *Judge* trying Fr. Keogh. In absentia, he was accused of crimes against *their* 'church.' Misconception, the prosecutor, garbed in pure black, as all of them were, pronounced the charges: "We, the personified wretchedness of sanctity, having secretly assumed the government of a new, one-world church which will soon grant us permission to be official women priests, we do charge 'Father' Keogh with witchcraft: 1) for pretending to conjure up God by hocus pocus upon an altar; 2) by making himself a god, pretending to know the truth with certainty; 3) by pretending to forgive sins and for other presumed magical sacramental powers; 4) by playing the hypocrite in pretending to know what is right and wrong for everyone; 5) by pontificating, preaching, teaching and telling all what to believe and what to do, while doing nothing to please us or anyone but himself, leaving a burden of guilt on the pitiful souls foolish enough to believe in him, putting themselves at his mercy."

"Enough!" screamed the 'Judge', hate streaming from her horrible, murderous, bloodshot eyes, *glaring* at a framed picture of Fr. Keogh placed on the table. They had stolen this picture from the bishop's rectory, where it had hung along with pictures of the other priests who had been ordained in the diocese.

"Defense?!" screamed *Merciless*.

"Completely guilty, your Honor," squeaked Misfit, the so-called defense attorney, quaking with incontinence. "He has no excuses, he begs for no mercy, because he deserves none, since he regularly consigns souls to Hell by his doctrine and his foul arguments. Therefore, we file no plea for mercy from your Honor Most Hideous."

"Then I pronounce him *guilty as Hell!* and condemned to a cruel death by *crucifixion* this very day," screamed Merciless, as the mock attorneys both peed their pants out of naked fear of *Her Terrible*

Wickedness, as she loved to be called. A cold sweat had distilled on her minions' pale, bloodless faces, previously scorched bare of lashes and brows in Merciless' fits of vengeful rages, a fit which she had considered an initiation ceremony. Her assistants were not innocent, but were slaves of this lesbian witch mistress in some human way. They knew the pain of her dagger's cold, ragged steel blade on their naked bodies, a blade she now flashed at them in her wrath. But slaves of Satan they all were.

Far above them, Fr. Keogh who was standing in the pulpit, seemed to be a figure aglow in the sunlight pouring through the huge stained-glass windows surrounding the sacristy depicting the greatest Saints in the Church's two thousand year history. He continued his long sermon. "Yes, Pope Paul VI warned us that the 'smoke of Satan (Freemasonry) has entered the Temple of God".[53] Judas priests (especially bishops) infiltrated the Church and tried to destroy it. Satan used Judas to try and destroy the Church of Israel by arranging the crucifixion of Jesus, but the Second Person of the Trinity would overrule the present and past attempts by Jesus' Resurrection and by the salvation of His Church, now embroiled in the End Times, even though the enemy had inserted its corrupt bishops so they had one hundred percent control, except the true pope. My dear people, we are at this *very moment* betrayed from within by clergy who destroy the priesthood by agreeing to obey false authority in shutting down the church and her Sacraments. The obedient destroy their entire religious vocation by this false compliance. On orders from Satan himself, many good priests will be murdered physically and spiritually, for we are in the last times, when Satan shall reign on earth for a short time. Unleashing Satan's reign is a just but merciful punishment from God for a sinful world that exceeds the corruption of Sodom and Gomorrah. Satan's reign is a wake-up call to return to God under the wings of His Merciful forgiveness. We must repent, reform and repair the damage our lukewarm unbelief has caused."

Fr. Keogh then turned his head to look directly at his three fellow priests with a brief but penetrating gaze, which convicted them on the spot of the wickedness strangling their hearts. "As I have said, in 1968, Pope Paul VI referred to the Freemasonic 'smoke' that had entered the

---

[53] https://returntofatima.org/2020/05/05/the-smoke-of-satan-and-an-apostate-pope/

Church. Ecclesiastical Freemasonry proposes to us fabrications, half-truths, deliberate errors and outright lies, sewn like weed-seed amongst the wheat of orthodoxy. Much of this heresy began with Vatican II, contaminating with heterodoxy God's enduring word. Practically, this doctrinal shift was effected by infiltrated clerical change-agents, Judases, some of them Communists. According to their malicious creed, there is a choice: either turn people toward salvation by doctrines of immutable truth that condemns the error and sin, especially those cited in the Decalogue, or 'turn people on' by inviting them to pursue self-satisfaction with a *tolerant* 'love' of self and others that overlooks sin and error and challenges the view of God as just. Supposedly, God's imagined tolerance is the motivation for a pastoral love that is really a treacherous lie and the doctrine of demons."

"Therefore, pastors are to fall over backwards under the pretense of *caring* in order to suggest diabolical doctrines as those of a 'renewed', modernized church. Of course, this harlot church of their own fabrication was secretly posing as God's one holy Church of Tradition in order to deceive the many. These agents of change say the Church is adapting to the times, overlooking or even approving of mortal sins against faith and morals, which is actually a recipe for eternal Hellfire, hardly 'pastoral care'. The gift of *Truth is Love*: two sides of a single coin. By maligning truth and by an evil alchemy that confuses love with moral permissiveness, the enemy constructs a guillotine for their foolish followers. *Beware!!*" the priest shouted. "Beware of this hypocrisy that we are urged to practice under the guise of brotherly love! It comes in little steps."

"Can anyone see the end of the unprincipled 'affirmation of others': what will it justify when combined with *we have to do this for your safety*. Isn't this the slogan the ongoing Covid-19 scamdemic relies on for moral justification? The end of this lie for us is when Big Brother insists that their latest cure for a headache is a sixteen-pound sledgehammer, with the reassurance that you will never have to take an aspirin again. We have been brainwashed to believe that our highest priority is to not hurt the feelings of others, even if those feelings are nothing more than a frosting of flattery on the people-pleasing cake of sentimentality. Therefore, we must beware that this sugar-sweet icing can disguise a spiritual poison."

Fr. Keogh whispered this warning confidentially, but loud enough for all to hear. "Fill in the details of my generalities yourself, my dear people. Perhaps it will begin an eye-opening, ongoing experience. Be sure to check out your own backyard."

"The Pharisees, with their hypocrisy and malice, wanted to trap Jesus in His politically incorrect truthfulness and mercy, the true affirmation of others. The forgiveness of public sinners like Mary Magdalene was the occasion for His enemies to accuse Him of spiritual ignorance and scandal. However, as God, He knew of Mary's interior repentance and treated her with lenient *affirmation* and mercy, just as He treats all repentant souls. Repentance is the key. Also scandalous, according to the Pharisees, was Jesus' healing of the infirm on the Sabbath, as if He was ignoring a violation of the Third Commandment, which forbids work on the Lord's Day. But the Church teaches that works of religiosity, mercy, necessity, and true charity have priority over this discipline; for the 'affirmation of others' can either be a work of charity or a work of pharisaical malice. Of course, with sinners forgiven and their misery relieved, there was a reduction of available revenue for the greedy Pharisees who were making money off religion by stealing from the Temple treasury, like Judas stole from the donated savings of the Apostles."

"Contrary to the doctrine invented by the hypocritical Pharisees, who wanted to divide and conquer by opposing the law of truth to the law of love, Jesus taught that truth and love are opposite sides of the same coin, because *the greatest love for another was to give them the truth that leads to their eternal salvation.* So that instructing or admonishing another regarding the moral truths that he needs to know for his correction or education, is the greatest act of love; but there is a price for such fearless charity: the rage of the Pharisees who live by an opposite code. We must, dear people, simply do what is right, despite ridicule and the false judgements of others. We are safe in admitting that we are all subject to the temptation of the sin of '*human respect*,' which is due to our common, inherited, fallen human nature. Human respect pays respect to man at the cost of disrespecting or ignoring the declared doctrines of God. The first part of the Great Commandment is to love God with our whole being and the second is to love ourselves and our neighbor as ourselves for God's sake[54], but human respect reverses that order. The Pharisees follow what pleases *man's* fallen nature, first, making God's religion second."

"The first two Spiritual Works of Mercy *commanded* by the Church are: *to admonish the sinner* and *to instruct the ignorant.* Even though the teacher of unpleasant truths may be repaid by his beneficiaries with hatred and violence, he is compensated from God with an increase of virtue and grace, which serves to purify his love, as gold is purified in a furnace. We cannot foresee the effects of our witness, but we do know that nothing we do is ever wasted with God, Who can work miracles in stony hearts. Therefore, if God inspires those who love Him to witness, it is for a useful and fruitful purpose; charity is never in vain."

Fr. Keogh hung his head, looking down at the podium, a tired and sorrowful expression etched on his face. In truth, he was not unlike his Master, Who complained that he had no place to rest his weary head. And this was not just a complaint about a place to sleep. Fr. Keogh sensed that he was about to shoulder his own cross for the journey to Calvary, recalling the words of Isaias: '*I looked about, and there was none to help: I sought, and there was none to give aid: and my own arm hath saved me, and my indignation itself hath helped me.*'[55] Thanks for bearing with me, my beloved people." Though he knew it not, many eyes, like his own, were wet upon his farewell that morning.

* * *

Out in the courtyard, David waited until he again had the attention of the hundreds reclining on the grass after the break he had called to give an opportunity for any to depart, if they wanted to avoid a commitment at that time. But he saw with some consolation that most of those present had stayed to hear his final words. He noticed a strong breeze had suddenly begun rustling the leaves of the trees, rattling the branches of the protective hedge of bushes surrounding the courtyard. Silent rain clouds had slowly enveloped them, unnoticed, dimming the

[54] St. Matthew 22:38

[55] Isaiah 63:5

light in the grounds around St. Joseph's church. David sensed that he had but a short time to hurl one last 'stone' of Truth into the diabolical head of Ignorance and Error, the formidable Giant that 'dared to defy the army of the living God'.

"I believe that every one of you and every soul ever born yearns to hear *the whole truth,* which is living in the Person of Him who made us and all things from nothing. He tells us that we were made for Him and also made to be with Him in absolute happiness for all eternity. We are, in being His creatures, one people, brothers and sisters, one human race with an invitation in hand to attend the Wedding Feast where the Holy Spirit, equal to the Eternal King, will espouse the perfect representative of our fallen race (provided by God), the sinless creature, Mary, Virgin Mother of God, *who represents all humanity as we were when created perfect in the Garden of Eden before the Fall.* We need Mary, conceived 'Immaculate" (free from original sin), because we have sinned (the Original Sin of our human race, through Adam *and* our own actual sin which ratifies Adam's sin) staining our robes, so that they have become unfit to attend the banquet of our Salvation. What the pride and unbelief of Satan (and those who think like him) find impossible to believe is that Mary is a mere creature whom God preserved as His *perfect* Mother. Christ also gave us Mary as *our Mother,* from the Cross. *She represents for sinful mankind* the wide double-doors to eternal life, God Himself. Only by passing through this celestial Gate of Mary, God's Holy Mother, may we become the adopted Christian *children of God the Father* thus obtaining a suitable 'wedding garment' needed for entering the Heavenly banquet of the *King* of Heaven and Earth, Jesus Christ."

"You will be united with Christ as an adopted son of the Father, when you believe in Him Who was raised on the Cross, having Faith that He can heal you from your sins. But if you cannot first recognize, admit and repent of your personal sins, how can you confess to having a Redeemer? And if not, how can you seek Him in His Mystical Body, the Church, which He instituted after His Resurrection from the dead, the Church built upon Peter, the 'rock' of Faith, guarded and guided by the Holy Spirit until the end of time. But if you have this divine Faith and its humble prerequisite, personal repentance, it is God the Father Who has revealed them to you and invited you to His eternal

Feast as His adopted son, whose Faith in Jesus Christ will be counted as justification before God, because Jesus, by His divine Sacrifice, has earned Justification for us. He redeemed us from the guilt of our sin and its consequence: eternal death. Abraham was justified because of his Faith in a coming Redeemer."

"*There is no Salvation outside the Catholic Church.* If you have believed my witness so far, this teaching of the Church will be understandable. This is because the Church is the Mystical Body of Christ[56] through which we are saved, crucified and resurrected." Thunder from behind the storm front rolled in overhead. "There can be only one *Divine* Church that Jesus instituted. Therefore, Salvation is exclusively from that Church. Many human professions of faith which are called churches began *after* Jesus Christ lived or ended *before* the present, either fact disqualifying them as Christ's Church." It began raining, gently ... "'Come to me', Jesus said, 'come all you who are heavy burdened.'"[57] David motioned with his arms, "Come in, out of the rain, into the arms of your Mother, the Church, where you will find Jesus waiting in the Tabernacle. I speak of the One, Holy, Catholic, Apostolic Church of all time."

David motioned everyone into the giant tent, as increasingly heavy sheets of rain drenched them. He walked to the tent meeting up with Michael who with a few others had set up under a leafy copse of maple trees the giant canvas they had rented. It appeared that virtually the whole of David's audience had come under the tent. He then announced inside that the priest would come after Mass ended to receive them into the Church after administering the Sacrament of Baptism to those who sought membership in the Church, followed by the reception of first Holy Communion. David suggested that the wait-time would be for their reflection and decision-making and that his three assistants would remain with them to answer questions and give their counsel. David thought that Divine Providence seemed to have cooperated in his proselytizing by providing the squall that drove his audience to seek shelter from a downpour. God Almighty should know what He is doing. David called out under the tent, "Upon your profession of faith, God will

---

[56] 1 Corinthians 12:12

[57] St. Matthew 11:28

bestow on each of you the *certainty* that comes with Faith." David left for the church but returned upon seeing that Fr. Keogh was still saying farewell to a long line of parishioners.

Twenty-five minutes earlier, Fr. Keogh had noticed shafts of light streaming through the stained-glass windows depicting the ecclesiastical history of Holy Tradition. That light faded with alarming speed as he finished his long sermon. The interior of the church seemed to be cast into an unnatural darkness. He felt a sudden urge to finish his life's witness to the Lord.

Fr. Keogh extended an arm toward the life sized crucifix suspended over the altar. "A crucifix must be present near the altar of every Catholic church at Mass because the Eucharistic Sacrifice goes on within His Church. Jesus is really Present here, known through the instrument of our Faith bestowed by the *power* of Christ's Divine Love."

"I will leave you, my dear people, who have endured this very long sermon, with a summation found in St. John's Gospel, chapter 3, verses 16-21:

> *"For God so loved the world, as to give his only begotten Son: that whosoever believeth in him, may not perish, but may have life everlasting. For God sent not his Son into the world, to judge the world, but that the world may be saved by him. He that believeth in him is not judged: but he that doth not believe, is judged already: because he believeth not in the name of the only begotten Son of God. And this is the judgment: 'because the light is come into the world, and men loved darkness rather than the light; for their works were evil. For every one that doth evil hateth the light, and cometh not to the light, that his works may not be reproved. But he that doth truth, cometh to the light, that his works may be made manifest, because they are done in God."*

"Jesus said, "*I would that you all be one*" but we are not so by wishing so, or by saying "have a nice day," soft giggling erupted. "Edward Cardinal Manning in the early 19th Century defined unity: '*There is no unity without truth. Truth first, unity afterwards, truth the cause, unity the effect.'*[58] Our unity as Catholics does not lie in our congregational fellowship, but in our common belief in the defined doctrines of the Church and the reception of the seven Sacraments, especially the Holy Eucharist, the Sacrament of the Altar, that we worship as the Body, Blood, Soul and Divinity of Jesus Christ, the Second Person of the Trinity become Man for our Redemption. In this Communion with our Lord, God becomes our spiritual food on the journey through the desert of this mortal life, even as the Israelites were sustained by manna as they wandered in the desert for forty years."

After Mass ended, Fr. Keogh stood in the back by the double doors, greeting individuals and informally blessing some of those he knew; others only introduced themselves with a nod. He smiled in return. To some he gave his advice for problems they briefly shared or he already knew of. To a few, he promised to help them soon. Many commented favorably on his sermon. To the last person, he was heard responding to their comment noting his lengthy sermon: "Long? Yes, but…." He patted his vest pocket, "… you're lucky I didn't get started on Apocalypse 7:13-17."

After that, the last person, Magdalene, St. Joseph's 'ancient' housekeeper hobbled up to this priest whom she silently loved so much, having been present by invitation of his parents to be one of his baptismal godparents thirty-three years ago. She spoke to him with reverent familiarity, finally whispering hoarsely, "Goodbye." Fr. Keogh read into this a real, sad farewell, as tears welled up in her eyes, rolling down her soft, wrinkled cheeks. The priest thought she might have been thinking of her own passing; but he had no knowledge of her being in ill health.

As she walked out the entrance doors, one of the three priests held a door open for her, ushering her out with a cheesy smile. Then the doors closed with a "bang." Hearing a latch fall into place, followed by the thud of bracing timbers across the doors, Magdalene stopped to listen. In less than a minute, she heard a scuffling sound inside, along with muffled shouts.

---

[58] https://www.jstor.org/stable/42974821

The three priests, their eyes gleaming with hateful vengeance, held Fr. Keogh by the arms as the three witches entered the room, emerging from the vertical stairwell with its spiral steel staircase which led to their dungeon "courtroom" two stories below. They were serious in continuing their deadly game of 'Judge, jury and executioner'.

Merciless, holding a scrap of paper, sent crawly shivers of dread through her five henchmen as she read the charges and pronounced the verdict of death in a vile, hissy, serpentine voice that could have passed for that of Satan's mistress. Suddenly, as Magdalene listened intently outside, she heard Fr. Keogh's muffled shout, as all six clerics cooperated to gag him as he struggled against them. Recognizing his terrified voice, Magdalene ran for help.

Directed by Merciless, two of the men placed the priest's wrist over their predrilled holes in one of the two-inch-thick oak entrance doors of the church. While they pinned his arm and hand over the hole, Merciless held the point of a huge, rusted twenty-penny nail to his wrist; the third priest slammed the head of the nail, driving it through the flesh above priest's palm with a small eight-pound sledge hammer. Three times Fr. Keogh involuntarily screamed as his crucifier repeated his blows until the nail was firmly fixed in the oak door. Blood had splattered everyone. The priest's screams of agony were muffled by a bandana gag.

Magdalene had begged a man to run and get the speaker, David, pointing towards the courtyard. David, standing near the entrance of the tent, saw the man running towards him, waving his arms wildly with alarm. Seeing the man's face set off all David's alarms, and he ran for the church full speed, but he was too late.

After a considerable struggle, even with the three witches helping, the priest had been nailed to the door by nails through his hands and feet. They all huddled, chests heaving, gasping for breath, jabbering like crazy magpies that had just committed a crime. Several worried out loud that he would not die before being rescued. But *Merciless* had planned ahead. She ran to the janitor's closet and brought out a sturdy five-foot, one-and-a-half-inch diameter hard-wood pole. A stout butcher knife with a newly sharpened, eight-inch blade was heavily duct-taped to the pole. When Fr. Keogh saw the spear, he knew his end was at hand. He raised his eyes and uttered his last prayer, silently, the Psalm expressing the sentiments of every Christian martyr: *"I offer to you, my Lord, all I am, for you are my rock and my strength and my Savior. In you, O Lord, I will trust; Thou wilt deliver me from iniquity."* (2 Kings 22:2-4)

Two of the wicked priests pushed the tip of the homemade spear between the two ribs marked by the witch on the priest's left side, causing him great pain. Fr. Koegh's full-length white alb had been sliced open with a box cutter to expose the bare white flesh over these ribs. Two witches pushed his left arm up, while all the others gripped the spear with both hands. On Merciless' count of three, they plunged the spear through his heart. David, outside, heard the priest's scream of agony. *Then the Satanic assassins watched him die with his last breath!*

David's loud banging on the doors, shouts and rattling of the door latch caused all but Merciless great fear. Five of them ran to a preplanned escape door on the wooded south side of the church. The sixth, flipped the lock on the double doors and ran after the others as fast as he could. David heard the priest's groans of agony subside into death as both doors swung open of their own weight, revealing Fr. Keogh's lifeless body nailed to one of them. A large sign, written in his blood, was nailed to the inside of the other door.

David stood looking at the crucifixion of his beloved priest-friend in complete emotional shock and moral agony. He could not move, but he managed to read the sign: "*Because he died on the Cross, <u>all</u> can now enter a truly universal Catholic church.*" David collapsed and fell back onto the ground. He held his chest with both hands, his eyes bulging grotesquely. Angela, who had just appeared, ran to him. She was four months pregnant and holding a twin by each hand. Angela screamed with uncontrolled hysteria. Charlene, appearing momentarily on the scene, was frozen by Angela's screams. Only Michael was able to take action, ordering every man present through the church to all its doors, with orders to collar anyone trying to exit. He plunged into the church after shouting for someone to call 911 for a doctor and the police.

David regained a dim consciousness because of Angela's many wet kisses delivered passionately between loud moaning and heart-rending sobs. He gazed at her peacefully, nodding with his eyes toward the courtyard; he managed to whisper, as she bent her ear to his pale lips,

"Bring them into the Church; get another priest." After this effort, David seemed to lose consciousness from exhaustion.

Charlene, who had followed Angela, heard this request and had someone call for the nearest priest; then she went to the catechumens, assembled them under the awning in the courtyard, and after telling them what happened, she asked for their prayers. Charlene chose some parishioners to help her. A deacon with one year from his ordination arrived. He had been told what David wanted and took over for Charlene, who remained traumatized: emotionally and physically exhausted. At the church, Angela was slowly losing consciousness as she seemed to spend her last drop of energy clinging to David. Charlene soon returned to the church and again took charge of Angela's children, who were now wailing loudly in distress even though a young lady had compassion on the scene and came to assist the helpless mother.

Ten minutes later, Angela, having regained a shaky consciousness, was led into the church, with some weak resistance on her part. Inside, Angela lay on a twin bed set up in a large coat closet off-setting the janitor's closet. Attending her were some deeply sympathetic parishioners who knew her. A man entered the room to say that a doctor had shown up and that he had quickly examined the priest and was now attending to her David. Charlene came in, whispering to Angela that the police had finally arrived, but Angela had already slipped into unconsciousness and was not responding. Ten minutes later, the doctor reported to Charlene that David was suffering from emotional shock, that his heartbeat was barely discernable and that he was going in and out of consciousness. But the doctor said that because of his generally robust state of health, he was unlikely to die and should be able to recover soon.

The deacon and a priest who had arrived, not knowing that David was unconscious, knelt and whispered to him that the Church no longer tried to convert people. At that moment, David suddenly awoke, a zealous anger blazing in his voice and eyes. As though day-dreaming, he stared past the priest and whispered hoarsely, "Bring them into Church! It is my dying wish." And then, with a great effort and in a voice of command, he said, "If not, I will ask God to *kill you both instantly* in the most horribly painful way He can think of." With this, he chuckled slightly and then peacefully closed his eyes as if instantly falling asleep.

The priest and deacon seemed to be moved by this threat into rapid action.

Angela had passed out, according to the doctor from "emotional shock and exhaustion". She and David were wrapped in double-thick blankets spread on the hardwood floor. They lay like corpses, side by side, their children sleeping about them. One of the wicked priests had been captured. He showed some self-serving remorse, blame shifting in squealing tones to the police that it was "dark individuals" at the diocesan offices who had put them up to the murder. He claimed he hardly knew Fr. Keogh except by reputation. He also ratted on their leader, Merciless, who played the judge from hell, accusing her of masterminding the whole plan in all its details from the beginning at the behest of a mysterious superior in her coven.

The priest and deacon came back to David, cowering in dread of having to complain to him that they were told by their superiors that they needed permission from the proper authorities to bring souls into the Church. Finding David unconscious, they presented their predicament to the murderous priest, not suspecting him of being the blackrobe under arrest. The Judas priest looked at them with utter disdain. But hoping to gain some leniency from the police standing there, he said, officiously, "As the bishop's special assistant, I have the faculties you require in this case. You now have official permission to bring these souls into the Church."

The detective's steely blue eyes seemed to bore holes through those of the murderous priest as he began questioning him a few minutes later: "So, you committed this crime *inside* the church and under the pretense that you were loyal friends of the victim?" The suspect demanded a lawyer. The detective roughly handcuffed him and sent him to the local jail with a guard holding each arm securely.

Michael sat on the ledge outside, his head hanging low in sorrow and dejection, fearing the loss of his friend who had suffered a terrible shock. He remembered the time David had saved him from the sharks, and how he could do nothing for that friend now who had always been there for him. Charlene rested her head on his arm, sobbing quietly in her own grief but wanting to console her husband more than herself. At Michael's request, she went to check on the two friends and their children. Looking in, Charlene saw that they seemed to remain in a deep sleep, their pulses still very weak, breathing barely perceptible. Noticing David's small Bible spilling out of his jacket pocket, she decided to retrieve it. Bringing it back, Michael took it and 'cut it' at random, as he had often seen David do. He began reading: "*Going, therefore, teach ye all nations: baptizing them in the name of the Father, and of the Son, and of the Holy Ghost. Teaching them to observe all things whatsoever I have commanded you: and behold I am with you all days, even to the consummation of the world.*" (Matthew 28:19-20)

As the hours passed, Michael and Charlene clung to each other, both crushed in spirit. They feared David's passing and Angela's too. "She might never recover psychologically from this horror, Michael, especially if she loses David, the love of her life." Charlene cried, gently pounding her forehead against his muscular arm. Michael hugged her with all the tenderness he could muster while trying to deal with his own grief. "I left their children with the wife of one of the off-duty police officers who is in the room with them all for a while. That was the couple you were talking to," said Charlene.

"Okay," said Michael weakly.

"She will be here for an hour," Charlene said.

"He was my friend," said Michael, "almost like a father or the older brother I never had." Michael suddenly buried his face in his hands, going down on one knee, "Now I know that I loved him like he loved Fr. Keogh. Let's go up to the altar and pray for them, Sweetheart, and for us too."

They slowly walked up the aisle of the empty church to kneel before the sanctuary in the first pew. Michael prayed with his eyes upturned. Charlene, genuflecting with Michael before entering the pew with him, seemed to lose strength; she could not kneel with him but crumpled in the pew, leaning against him. Charlene remembered Angela as the most dear, wise, fearless friend, the only real friend she had ever been blessed to have. Angela had been the one who had the courage and care to admonish her for her immodest dress. Her sorrow for this was only now profound and complete. She realized how much David and Angela were looked up to by so many people, yet they seemed to think so little of themselves, only of others. She and Michael looked at each other; they could see in each other how much they each yearned to see their friends.

After some time in prayer, they genuflected toward the tabernacle that housed the remaining Hosts Fr. Keogh had consecrated. They then walked briskly to the converted coat room. A policeman guarding the room, one of David's most loyal and heroic former soldiers, stopped them, but then recognizing Michael, he let them in. Michael told him they would stay with David and Angela until they recovered, all night, if necessary. Within an hour, Michael and Charlene were asleep in the room with David and Angela and the children.

In the morning, the police captain told the same guard to unlock the room. When he did so, they found the room *empty!* The guard, a good Christian man and one of David's most trusted militia, swore that *no one* left the windowless room all night; they were locked in, and he had the only key!! He pulled it out of his pocket and showed it to the captain. "They could not have left without me knowing," he said adamantly. A search was made of the church property and the two couple's cabins. The guard, Sgt. Brent James, was brought to the station for questioning; a polygraph test was administered, and it showed him to be telling the truth. The police officer in charge of the case admitted he had no leads in the disappearance of the two families.

* * *

Magdalene, the church housekeeper, came in very early that next morning; seeing the police activity at the guarded room where she knew David was, she made an excuse to get some of her cleaning equipment. She was mildly shocked upon finding the room empty. She immediately asked the captain where they had taken them, assuming it was a local hospital. He told her the puzzling story, hoping she could help his investigation. When she got to her tiny office, she cried softly to herself: 'two valiant men, taken from the battlefield of this life in one day,' she thought. What would become of those left who could not fight and teach and lead as these good Catholic men did without any apparent regard for themselves.

Magdalene had long ago researched the etymology of the name "David" because she had loved David with a special fondness from his birth, never having children of her own. "Beloved of God", she whispered to herself. "Yes, I believe he was," she said, quietly wiping away a tear from under her eye. He was true to his name, she thought, and his special friend was a holy priest whom she knew and loved. "Where have all the good men gone?" she cried to herself in a sobbing voice, now feeling more alone than she ever had in her whole life.

After signing out at the end of the day, she stopped to question the police officer on duty. She knew he had been assigned to the murder case. He said, "Lady, this church is closed until the chief clears up certain strange things, like people disappearing." With an apologetic tone, he said, "Even though we have found no trace of the two couples, we *have* apprehended all six of the murderers; and they will soon be charged, probably within the week." Magdalene thanked him for sharing this information before she left and promised confidentiality.

Realizing the closure could be indefinite, Magdalene walked slowly away from the church she had known as a parishioner since childhood; she was now 82. As she walked the half mile north to her home, she noticed that a strange glow had filled the eastern sky with rosy pinks and a rainbow of other soft pastels. As she hobbled up the mild incline of the narrow cobblestone street that her father had helped build, she stopped to rest and again study the strange lights that seemed to be rising above the eastern horizon. The Lights now filled the whole eastern sky with much more color than when she first looked at them ten minutes earlier. Why lights in the east at this time of day, she asked herself, puzzled. Lights in the east maybe, but not after 5 P.M. Getting up slowly, she staggered a little despite having her cane. Soon, she stopped to rest again, holding her head in slightly trembling hands; she was overwhelmed anew by the tragic and now mysterious events of yesterday. Then, suddenly, she understood where they must have gone! Her face lit up in a wonderful smile; she said aloud to herself: "*They were taken up!*" She calmly accepted this; the Lord was just fulfilling what He had promised, she thought. Magdalene continued up the street, lined with tiny houses built in the 1930's, all with covered front porches and tiny, picket fenced front yards, most bordered inside the fences with perennial flowers. The backyards were long and narrow, most used for growing vegetables, gardens irrigated from the nearby stream which had deposited over the years rich, silty soil, ideal for gardening.

Before Magdalene opened her front gate, she turned again to look at the eastern sky. Extraordinarily bright clouds were beginning to fill the whole sky. She was fascinated by one very peculiar, towering, luminous, billowing cloud, which seemed to be ascending as she watched. She kept thinking it was like a sunrise, but it was above where a sunrise could be. She decided to call them "the clouds of Heaven." Then, to prove to herself that these beautiful clouds were not a product of her imagination, she showed them to her next door neighbor, who was amazed at what she saw, as they both stood before the younger lady's front gate.

The clouds were sooo beautiful, she thought, looking up, but they were still far away. Magdalene, daydreaming, longed to be with Jesus, Fr. Keogh and David. At the same time, she found herself wanting to be young and happy and alive again as in her youth. Sitting on her crumbling concrete porch-step, Magdalene gazed at the sky, watching and waiting. Before going inside, she pulled from her tattered handbag the chapter and verse written in Fr. Keogh's hand which she had taken from his lifeless body when no one was looking on the day of the murder. All the commotion and confusion made that possible after he had been taken down from the door where his life had ended. Out of an old-fashioned sense of devotion for what is consecrated, she had reverently kissed his breast, quite near the pocket in which the note was found. One corner of the scrap of paper was blood-stained. She remembered again Fr. Keogh mentioning the verse to the parishioner in front of her as they filed past him after Mass. He had patted his left vest pocket, she remembered. By long habit, she missed no details. The man in front of her had complimented Fr. Keogh on his sermon, while noting how long it was. Fr. Keogh joked that they were all lucky he hadn't remembered the verse in the Apocalypse because it would have made his long sermon much longer. Before they took his body away, she stole a memento which the police *might* consider evidence, but probably would not find relevant. She had reached into his bloodied vest pocket when no one was looking. She felt a little guilty, despite believing that he would have fully approved. Later, she worried that she might be arrested if she took it to the police.

Now in her living room, she wondered if the clouds she saw outside could be the ones upon which Jesus would return at His coming just before the "Day of the Lord," which Fr. Keogh had recently told them would be the day of God's wrath, in his opinion, a day Catholic Prophecy called the "Great Chastisement". She carefully unfolded the paper and kissed the dried blood. From the torn scrap she read: "Apocalypse 7:13-17". Taking her Douay Rheims Bible from its place of honor on the coffee table, before which no guest had sat for years, she turned to the passage, softly reading out loud:

> *"And one of the ancients answered and said to me: Who are these that are clothed in white robes, and whence came they? And I said to him: My lord, thou knowest. And he said to me: These are they who are come out of great tribulation, and have washed their robes, and have made them white in the blood of the Lamb. Therefore they are before the throne of God, and serve him day and night in his temple; and he that sitteth on the throne, shall dwell over them. They shall not hunger nor thirst any more, neither shall the sun fall on them, nor any heat. For the Lamb, which is in the midst of the throne, shall rule them, and shall lead them to the fountains of the waters of life, and God shall wipe away all tears from their eyes."*

* * *

Helena was six years younger than Magdalene and had been her next-door neighbor to the south for thirty-five years. They liked each other's conversation so much that they had coffee and a pastry on Magdalene's front porch at 7 AM each morning, before Magdalene had to leave for work at 8 AM in order to clean the sanctuary before St. Joseph's 9 AM mass. Her neighbor, not knowing the church's doors had been chained and pad-locked by the police, said to her seventy-eight-year old husband during breakfast, "Gerald, if she is not home by this evening, I'm going to call Carol, the church secretary, and see if Magdalene is on leave from work or something. I'm just a little worried because I didn't see a light on over there all yesterday evening, but I did see her sitting on her front porch after work." She turned to him, "She never misses our morning coffee, Gerald. Would you go over with me now, in case something has happened. We *always* have our coffee at seven, and surely she is of the age that the good Lord could have come for her."

After knocking, ringing and calling Magdalene's cell phone, they both decided to take the key under the geranium pot on her front porch and go in. When they did not find her in the house, they left a voice message with Carol at the church and then called Magdalene's nephew, Frederick, to see if he knew whether Magdalene had mentioned plans of her leaving on some kind of trip. After saying, "Not that I know of," all three of them decided it would be best to call the police.

When the police chief arrived and listened to another disappearance story, he leaned back against Magdalene's porch rail, put his hand over his eyes, bent his head, talking to himself as one afflicted. "Lord, where is this going? People don't just disappear; they have to go *somewhere*!" Many sought David's whereabouts. Before leaving the church for the last time, Magdalene had said to the local detective, "If Judases are now murdering innocent lambs, like Fr. Keogh, then God is ready to punish the whole world." Then she had added, "Only the good listened to him. He died for the truth like Jesus did; yet there was a great treasure house of Truth he could not even articulate because it could only be expressed in the love reciprocated."

Fr. Keogh knew that the verse in his breast pocket ushered in the half hour of silence referred to in the seventh seal of the Apocalypse, the last of the seals to be broken or warnings given before the seven Trumpets announced the punishments of the Great Chastisement. But Fr. Keogh was not given by Divine Providence to personally announce the precipice that the world stood upon, because so many did not care to listen; even many of the elect were deaf, just as Jesus said it would be: "*As in the days of Noe so shall the coming of the Son of Man be ... they were eating and drinking, marrying ... until the day that Noe entered into the ark.*"[59]

'The Faithful and few' were taken up in what is called 'the Rapture', because God did not destine them to witness His wrath. Perhaps those taken up in the seventh seal were those taken up to meet Christ coming

[59] St. Matthew 24:37-38

down to earth on *'the clouds of Heaven'*; for if He had not, Scripture says, 'no flesh would be left on earth'.[60] Holy Scripture also tells us in Genesis how God preserved from death in the Flood those few good souls in the Ark whom He had selected to be saved from the waters: Noah and his family. This could be seen as an archetype of the rapture of the elect. It appears that a rapture is described in Matthew 24:30-31:

> "... *'and they shall see the Son of man coming in the clouds of heaven with great power and majesty. And he shall send his angels with a trumpet, and a great voice: and they shall gather together his elect, from the four winds, from the farthest parts of the heavens to the utmost bounds of them.*"

60 St. Matthew 24:22

Epilogue

After the Rapture, God punished the world for six days and six nights. All the unrepentant complainers against God's Justice were now those screaming loudest for His Mercy, but it was too late for them. However, *many* souls were saved in the Chastisement: those who were finally moved beyond their habitual motive of self-interest in begging forgiveness for fear of what was to come upon them but also because they had offended God. Those so hardened in their sin that even terror did not move them to repent because they had offended divine Justice, these were lost, falling into Hell along with the demons that swarmed the earth.

David, Angela, their children and their close friends entered into the state of ecstasy, an altered state of consciousness, in which one's awareness gives way to a sense of the supernatural, including euphoria and visions. Time and space faded for them as they rose, physically but also mystically, to meet Jesus and a great multitude of His Angels and Saints coming down to earth on the "Clouds of Heaven." One of those uncanonized saints was a martyr named Fr. Keogh. He was the first spirit to greet David, with great joy! Their spirits reveled with jubilation in their victory over Satan, sin and death. The elect who were raptured would have died from the intensity of their joy during this ecstasy if their lives had not been preserved by a special grace of God.

Catholic prophecy had foretold for centuries that a chastising Comet of supernatural origin, completely and immediately under God the Father's control, would cleanse the earth of evil and restore good, leaving behind a 'remnant' of the Faithful and true. The Comet's natural effects included a gravitational attraction exerted on the earth as it rushed past, which would drag massive continental fault blocks of the earth's crust along preexisting fault lines, to be suddenly released as earthquakes by the passage of the Comet and its sudden cessation of gravitational attraction. The enormous earthquakes beneath the sea would cause tsunamis capable of devastating coastal areas for up to two hundred miles inland. The greatest potential for earthquakes in North America would follow the reactivation of the largest of the ancient fault zones in existence, set off by the Comet's passing. The major U.S. fault complex, caused by continental drift, had three radiating arms, that devolved from a point of the earth's *torsion* near St. Louis, Missouri. Its northwest arm divided the USA following the Missouri River graben, then the smaller Platte River graben, across Wyoming, through the Yellowstone caldera and on to Seattle using pre-existing fault grabens, including the Snake River Plain. Such a tripartite fault zone resulted from the torsion caused by plate tectonic motion tearing a continent in two.

Poisonous gases enveloped the world but especially the Northern hemisphere, as did fire raining down like a meteor shower but composed of fiery brimstone from the Comet. A reddish dust, like volcanic ash, smothered and buried everything, raising huge boils on all flesh that it touched. Simultaneously, a nuclear World War III destroyed whole nations in seconds, especially in the southern hemisphere. Two-thirds of mankind died in the Chastisement, but many millions more perished later from its after-effects. All unrepentant people, enemies of God, and evil spirits were cast into Hell. The surviving inhabitants of earth were purified by these punishments for their sins, although far less than they would have suffered in Purgatory. The Third World War lasted only three days, as did the major effects of the fiery Comet. After six days of devastation, '*the living envied the dead.*' Worldwide starvation and disease took many more, until only 25% of mankind were left.

David, Angela, Michael, Charlene and many others worldwide, who were like them spiritually, God set back upon the earth armed with powerful graces of knowledge, courage and charity, in order to lead those left upon earth in building a 'new world' that honored its Creator and His Laws. A totally pure, Catholic Civilization rose up worldwide which constituted the Kingdom of God on earth referred to in the Our

Father prayer. David and many others were helped in this great work by angels and Saints, while Jesus Personally reigned as King overall. Homes, families, work and civilization 'rose from the ashes', while material ash from the comet fertilized the earth so much that a fantastic growth of crops and plant life resulted. Because society had returned to an agricultural economy, although automobiles still provided transport, this fruitfulness of the earth was Providential, to say the least. God preserved animals and plants of every species useful to man, just as He did for Noah. The *only* Religion was Roman Catholic, and virtually all the living had been converted to the Roman Catholic Church. A great Pope, referred to as the "Angelic Pastor" in Catholic prophecy, reformed and disciplined the Church. The Great Monarch, also appearing often in Catholic Prophesy, worked with the Angelic Pastor to subdue, convert and civilize the world. Together, they overcame all remaining opposition and ruled in justice, benevolence and peace, "*Swords were made into plowshares*"[61] in every nation.

True happiness reigned, as justice, virtue and true Religion were established. In the 'New World', material prosperity was valued far less than spiritual health. The false religious ideas and remedies of past imposters were not tolerated by the laity, the common man.

David and Angela were raptured with their three children and adopted son. They had no more children after their return to earth to lead and teach the people in Jesus' name. They were held in esteem by all, and they taught and led the people of their community by an unspoken but universal consent. The government of nations was conducted on the principles of God, not on the inventions of man, past or present. David and Angela's youthful love had matured, but it had remained strong and vibrant. Now it was directed even more beyond themselves to the love and care and spiritual nourishment of others, especially for the local community for which they felt most responsible.

Sadly, as years passed into decades and man's pride gradually returned, sin followed. In a mere twenty-five years after the Chastisement, Satan had been invited back to earth by mankind's sin according to the 1846

[61] Isaiah 2:4

prophecy of Our Lady of La Salette.[62] The powers allowed to Satan by God were now greater, in proportion to the degree of brutal ingratitude, arrogance and could-care-less-ness displayed by man, so recently schooled, rescued and redeemed by the catastrophic intervention of God. It reminded David of the rapid return of ingratitude displayed by the Israelites time after time in the years after their dramatic rescue at the Red Sea, where Pharaoh and his entire army were drowned.

David had become morally, intellectually and spiritually stronger than ever when this sinful generation overcame the gratitude of the reverent on earth. He still led those he considered the "Faithful and True", those who would follow the Truth without swerving. With certainty, he had predicted the consequences that would surely follow the current errors and the crimes being committed with increasing callousness. Eventually, an evil man of great but strange powers, the Antichrist of the Apocalypse, arose, claiming divine appointment to power and authority, because he was acclaimed the son of god. He was heralded by his mouthpiece, the False Prophet, a false pope installed by the Freemasons. The Antichrist sent terror into the heart of everyone because of his unabashed wickedness, his bold, violent crimes and his relentless, ruthless acquisition of power and control.

Angela was frightened. Michael and David talked about these times they were entering as older men. They knew the younger generation would need their help: as wise counselors, i.e., their Faith, wisdom and courage. They hoped God would raise up a Joshua.

One day, the two men sat on a huge granite boulder that marked their mutually agreed property line dividing their two log homes and the land each of them had in this verdant Wyoming mountain valley. Each of their homesteads had three thousand acres of pasture and one thousand acres of rich farmland under cultivation. Each homestead was tended by twenty-five to thirty families, some having their own employees. Their cabins, cottages and barns were sprinkled throughout the rock studded, emerald green foothills and lush pasture lands. Everything had been purchased by hard labor, endurance, hope and most of all, patience. Now they could see the Christian community they had all worked hard to

---

62 https://www.catholicplanet.com/future/lasalette-melanie.htm

build in danger of crumbling. The common enemy was man's wayward free will. Soon, monumental ignorance and pride, riding the mighty flee bag of *arrogance* entered the scene.

David, with his salted auburn beard, said to Michael, "Once again, God will show that He is the one who saves the day, out of His tremendous Love and Mercy."

"Blessed be God," said his friend, bowing his head.

"Blessed be His Holy Name," said David, pronouncing the second line of the *Divine Praises*. "The coming Chastisement will be swifter but more intense than the last, I believe, and it will end with the passing away of time and of the universe," said David. "It will see the final victory of Christ over Satan, who will be cast into the burning lake of fire, as described in the Apocalypse".

"We have waited and fought our whole lives for Heaven," Michael sighed. "And in this next battle, you say that the evil we face will be more visible and more intense?" asked Michael. David nodded in assent.

"Yes, my friend," said David, "but the heavenly help fighting with us will also be greater and equally visible. We can read of it in symbolic language in the Apocalypse where the Antichrist and False Prophet appear *in person*, opposed by Enoch and Elias, real persons who lived thousands of years in the past, now walking the earth defying evil.[63]"

"So, how do *we* deal with all this?" Michael asked, looking worried.

"The same way we have dealt with everything from the first. We *Trust in God and act upon the light He gives us.* Whether at peace or at war, we are His."

"You mean the Indivisible Light?" asked Michael.

David just smiled. "We know at least that this 'Light' is invisible now, but in the times to come, it may have a visible aspect, something we may need for our encouragement."

"So, all the cards will be on the table, you're saying?"

"Yes. God is with us, if we love Him and our fellow man for God's sake," David answered. "And we face the same eternally condemned and shamed Satan, whom God impaled as He hung upon His cross of

[63] https://romancatholiceschatology.blogspot.com/2015/12/the-future-return-of-enoch-and-elijah.html

sacrificial love. We are mere soldiers, but 'faithful and true,' serving the infinitely superior power and Majesty of our Lord. We can't lose with Him, just as we cannot win by ourselves."

"And we fight with state-of-the-art weapons," said Michael, raising his fist clutching the Rosary.

"You learn quickly," said David, chuckling.

"If I can take your sarcasm, I can take anything," said Michael fuming for fun as if hurt.

"Boot camp training is tough, as you know," said David relentlessly. "Heaven will guide us and aide us in every way, internally and externally, just as before, Michael."

"I think we should begin now gathering our forces, training them and instructing the people in general about what's coming down the pike," said Michael, characteristically practical.

"Michael, I agree with you 110%. I'm glad we spoke today. I always am. Let's do it."

Angela had walked up silently behind them. She showed off her calf-high, fringed deerskin moccasins that David had made her and the ankle length skirt she had made with their daughter. David's mentor in leatherwork was the now old and weathered Indian friend of many years, White Moon, whom they had first come to know on their honeymoon. Earlier, they had all admired the full skirted doeskin dress Angela and White Moon's wife had made. Angela's hair was also shot with silver, but her eyes, David noted, had not diminished in beauty or in the amount of love they could express, as they gazed at each other for a moment, enkindling, with nostalgia, the times passion had flashed between them like lightning.

A little later, near the deck of their generous log home of twenty years, Angela placed the beef steaks on their homemade grill, fired by wood coals. Charlene approached with drinks and helped her, the two couples's grandchildren bouncing around her heels. Their married children led a covey of those most enjoyable of all creatures, *grandchildren*, everyone a "characteristo", as Grampa David liked to say. These joyful balls of energy loved their grandparents, each claiming their turn in receiving long embraces, after which they quickly proceeded to be "too rambunctious", even as they tried to pronounce that admonition on each other, knowing it was soon to be pronounced sharply by their indulgent Grands. Finally, the meal was ready, and they all fell to the earth on their knees, as one: *Bless us O Lord and these thy gifts, which we are about to receive from Thy bounty, through Christ our Lord. Amen.*[64]

THE END

[64] https://en.wikipedia.org/wiki/Grace_(prayer) Latin Catholic prayer said before eating.

Printed in the United States
by Baker & Taylor Publisher Services